THE

EXTINCTION

TRIALS

The creature rose from nowhere, a dark-green flash, jaws wide apart, snarling, fast as lightning. All she could see were the inky fixed eyes and the scaly reptilian skin. There was no time to react – no time to do anything. The scream was lost in her throat as the boat upended, tossing Lincoln, Rune and Leif into the shallow waters.

Leif was luckiest. He landed only a few millisectars from Storm and quickly scrambled ashore. Lincoln was up to his knees in the muddy water and turned to grab at Rune.

But the creature was quicker.

It lunged, jaws gaping.

Rune let out one shriek; the muddy water flashed red. Time froze...

ABOUT THE AUTHOR

The Extinction Trials is S. M. Wilson's first teen novel.
She lives with her family on the west coast of Scotland.

susan-wilson.com
@susanwilsonbook
#ExtinctionTrials

THE

EXTINCTION

TRIALS

S. M. WILSON

USBORNE

UNCHARTED
TERRITORY

JUNGLE

MARSH

FOREST

MOUNTAINS

DESERT

PILORIA

N

NW   NE

W   E

SW   SE

S

Hadrosaurid

Apatosaurus

T-rex
nest

Pterosaur nest

Blaine's
shack

Velociraptor
nest

LOCH

Deinosuchus

Megalodon

Transporters

Landing
beach

This book is dedicated to my two sons,

Elliott Bain and Rhys Bain.

Finally, a book you can read!

First published in the UK in 2018 by Usborne Publishing Ltd., Usborne House,
83-85 Saffron Hill, London EC1N 8RT, England. www.usborne.com

Text © Susan Wilson, 2018

Cover images: face © fotoduki / Shutterstock; palm leaves © Malden / Shutterstock

This is a work of fiction. The characters, incidents, and dialogues are products of the
author's imagination and are not to be construed as real. Any resemblance to actual
events or persons, living or dead, is entirely coincidental.

A CIP catalogue record for this book is available from the British Library.

JFMAMJJ SOND/18   ISBN 9781474927345   04341/6

Printed in the UK.

PART ONE

THE BEGINNING

ONE

LINCOLN

She couldn't see him. She didn't even know he was there.

Lincoln pressed himself against the dark red walls of the cave. Maybe it was the artificial light that made her look so unwell. They'd been rushed out of their old home and moved into this one so quickly that he couldn't even remember when he'd last seen his sister in natural daylight.

She thought she was alone and that's why her defences were down. Her pale skin was almost luminous in the darkness, the blue veins evident under her skin. Her legs were tucked up underneath her on the chair, her arms pulled tightly against her chest.

He could hear the rattle. Even from here, on the other side of the room. Everything echoed in the caves – even the quietest whisper. Now that she wasn't trying to hide her illness from the family, he could see the skin blisters were swollen and painful looking. Some were red and sore, some had already burst, leaving her open to infection. Layers of skin were peeling from her hands and arms. He could see the rapid rise and fall of her chest. The shallow breaths, trying to feed oxygen around her starved body.

And no one would help. Health care wasn't a priority on Earthasia.

The dangerously overpopulated continent had a clear focus on trying to provide enough food and energy for its people. Time couldn't be allocated to anything else.

Who cared if diseases spread and people died? They couldn't provide for the current population, so losing a few more to the rapidly spreading "plague" was a welcome relief.

Only the important people had health care. Only the scientists, the leaders and the national heroes. Who else mattered? And who else cared?

Lincoln cared.

TWO

STORMCHASER

The siren blasted for the second time. Stormchaser blew her fringe off her forehead as she cut through the water. She was hoping it was only a drill and no one would care that she didn't show.

Milo was swimming right alongside her. It had almost become a ritual for them both – even though it must have been a strange sight – human and plesiosaur side by side. Swimming in the lake was Storm's therapy. It helped release the knots in her muscles from lugging hay bales all day and distracted her from her empty stomach.

The siren sounded again. This time it was different. Three short sharp bursts. The sound that told everyone under-tens shouldn't attend. This was no drill. The plesiosaur lifted its elegant head above the water and stared at her for a few seconds. In the last few years, blocks of grey housing had rapidly built up around the lake and the creature seemed to have got used to the sounds of the city. Its wide flippers slapped against the water, exposing the vastness of its grey sleek body, five times longer than any boat the loch had ever seen.

"Sorry, Milo, I've got to go." Storm bent forward and pressed her head against his. Or was Milo a her? Two years on and she still couldn't work it out. It didn't matter anyway. Her feet hit the hidden platform in the lake. She scrambled out of the water and grabbed her discarded tunic and sandals from the shingly shore. She pulled them on and walked backwards for a few steps. "Same time tomorrow." There was a flick of an enormous tail and Milo disappeared under the water.

Storm's heart quickened when she passed between the first buildings and glimpsed the number of people. The street was teeming with bodies all heading in one direction – to the city auditorium. There was no way they would all fit in there. Space was at a premium everywhere. A few years ago most families had their own home, now they had to share with another family and sleep in shifts – it was either that, or agree to move into the caves. But Storm didn't need to worry about that. She didn't have family any more. Single teenagers were housed in the Shelters – not that they offered much in the way of shelter. There was no point in having possessions there. Everything disappeared. And as for the noises in the corridors at night... Storm always made sure her door was barricaded.

She looked around. Dell was waiting for her at their designated spot. He nudged her as they were jostled along by the crowd. "Farming or energy?"

She shook her head. "I don't care." The sirens sounded at least three times a week. Most announcements were about the fact that the land wasn't producing enough food, or the stations weren't producing enough energy.

As they squeezed into the auditorium, Reban Don, the Chief Stipulator for their zone, appeared on the stage. It was unusual to see him. He normally preferred to conduct his business far away from the huddled masses, spending most of his time in the distant tree houses of parliament. His face was permanently creased in a frown. It looked painful.

"Why can't they do this some other way?" moaned Dell. "Why do we always have to come here? Why can't they just send a message to wherever we are?"

"What, and waste paper?" Another precious commodity. The textbooks in their school were around thirty years old. The paper they used for tests was uneven and scratchy. It was hard to produce paper when there were virtually no trees left.

Electricity was rationed too. Technology was only for the use of the Stipulators and the scientists. It couldn't be "wasted" on the general population.

"Citizens." Reban Don's voice boomed around the auditorium.

There was silence. People had learned quickly that the

sooner they heard the announcements, the sooner they could leave.

Reban Don glared into the crowd, his face magnified by the large viewing screen. The likelihood was that this announcement was being repeated in each of the four hundred zones across the continent. "As usual, finding space is virtually impossible. Our population and energy requirements continue to grow with no way to keep them under control. Our attempts to record how many people are living on the continent have not been" – he paused for a second – "entirely successful. Our introduction of a record of births has not been followed by all of the population. As a result, our numbers continue to grow, even though our space does not. Parliament has issued a new order to look into population control measures. The options are: compulsory registration of births to keep more accurate numbers; restricting families to only one child; measures of birth control for the whole population. We will make the final announcement in a few days."

The crowd started murmuring, heads turning to one another. "What exactly does that mean?" asked Dell. "I thought the fact no one had health care was their idea of population control."

Storm was still staring at the stage, which Reban Don was now leaving, the announcement over. "I think they'll try and implement them all if things are really bad. Or maybe, instead of one child, they'll say people can't have any for a while. The Stipulators aren't allowed to have kids."

Dell rolled his eyes. "You mean they're not *supposed* to have kids. I've seen one of them hanging around a settlement on our row – you know the guy with the really bright blond hair? The woman living there has three kids and guess what? All of them are blond."

They started to file back out with the crowd. Storm raised her eyebrows. "I bet she didn't put his name on their birth records. I bet she didn't record the births at all."

Dell shrugged his shoulders. "I don't get it. What's the big deal about Stipulators having kids?"

"You know what they say – being a Stipulator isn't a job, it's a way of life. They don't want any distractions. They have to be focused at all times on finding ways of getting more food and more energy for the good of Earthasia." Storm's stomach gave a loud grumble at the mention of food.

"So what happens if the blond guy gets found out?"

"There was a rumour a few years ago about one of the Stipulators having a family hidden away somewhere. Didn't they send him on the Trials? I don't think anyone ever saw him again."

As the crowd spilled out onto the long street, Storm tugged at Dell's arm. "Come this way, I want to head back down to the loch for a few minutes." She couldn't face going back to her tiny bare room just yet.

He frowned. "You know I hate it there."

"Oh come on, I won't be long."

The crowd around them started to thin out, most of the people heading into the entrances of the tightly packed

Blocks around them. There was virtually no land left in Ambulus City – the capital of Earthasia – that hadn't been built on. Most of the Blocks only had a hand's breadth between them and towered so high that the sun rarely reached the street below. Living here was claustrophobic. Only the dank and dingy caves were worse than the Blocks.

Food rations were gradually going down and tempers were frequently frayed. Every night, when fights broke out, the Stipulators arrived and transported the culprits off to the mines to try and salvage any useful minerals still left underground. Most of them never came back. The ancient mines were so dangerous now, going there was basically a death sentence.

The light was beginning to dim and Dell gave a shudder as they walked down the stone path towards the loch.

"Don't you ever worry about being down here, swimming in here?"

"No, why should I? I like it here, it's the only place where there's space."

"I wonder why that is?"

She waved her hand. "Don't start, Dell."

"People don't come down here because they're too scared! Who knows what could crawl out of the water? I mean, how did the plesiosaurs get in here – and how do they get out?"

She shrugged. "We're not that far from the ocean, there must be a connection. Maybe some weird kind of tunnel. Anyway, plesiosaurs don't eat people, they eat fish. They're gentle creatures." She sat down at the edge of the shingle and pulled her knees up to her chest to scan the loch.

But Dell wasn't finished – and he didn't seem to want to make himself comfortable. "But what else is in there? And where's the guarantee that it won't want to eat us? There's a reason we don't fish out on the ocean any more, Storm."

She rolled her eyes. "What else could come through? Not the megalodon or the kronosaurus. They're too big. They're the ones that attacked the fishing boats." She pointed across the loch. "And people still fish on the loch sometimes. I've seen them."

Dell's stomach growled loudly and he pressed his hand against it. "Yeah, but only the Stipulators get to eat the fish. I can't even remember what it tastes like."

"Me neither." She stood up and walked to the edge of the loch, bending down to touch some of the reeds. "Do you think we could eat these?"

Storm picked a little piece off, put it in her mouth and chewed it. "Eurgh!" She spat it back into her hand. "That's disgusting."

Dell was watching the loch surface carefully. "What do you expect – it's a reed. But if they don't find something else for us to eat soon, that might become breakfast, lunch and dinner." He gave his head a shake. "It's getting late – let's go."

She waved her hand. "I'm not in a hurry to get back to the Shelter. You go on."

"Oh yeah, sure I will." His tone was mocking. "And the

announcement for tomorrow will be that they found a skeleton next to the loch."

Storm shook her head. "I'll be fine. There's nothing in here to worry about."

Dell threw up his hands in frustration. "You're just biased because of your experience. How do you even know the plesiosaurs helped you? You were knocked out. Anything could have happened."

Her back itched. It always did when she thought about her accident on the loch – or when Dell mentioned it. He was the only person she'd told.

She walked over to him and stood right under his nose. "It happened, Dell. I'm here because of them. I'm living proof that not all dinosaurs are man-eating beasts."

"Tell that to all the creatures that live on Piloria," he shot back.

Storm held her breath for a second. "Okay, I'll give you that." One of the few things she'd learned in school was how terrifying and dangerous the dinosaurs of Piloria were. The instructors put as much emphasis on this as they did on reading and writing. She'd always been taught that Earthasia was too cold for the dinosaurs to survive. As a kid it had taken a little time for her brain to wrap around the fact that a few degrees in temperature could determine whether or not a species could survive. She only hoped what they'd told her was true.

If it wasn't, the one thing that saved them from the dinosaurs was distance.

She sighed and took a last glance at the loch. There was no sign of Milo.

She smiled to herself. A plesiosaur with a name. There was probably a law against it. She was pretty sure that some dinosaurs were as deadly and terrifying as she'd been taught. But the plesiosaurs in the loch? Not at all. She'd learned that from experience. The tiny head, tiny brain theory didn't seem true to Storm. Milo had displayed characteristics that she was sure were more than just instinctual behaviour. But discussing that with anyone except Dell, arguing against what they were told, could get her in trouble. It was best to keep her ideas to herself. The last person she'd known who had speculated that the dinosaurs were anything other than ferocious, mindless beasts had disappeared without a trace.

She flung an arm around Dell's shoulders. "Okay then, walk me back to the Shelter."

She could hear his sigh of relief at the thought of going home. It made her stomach clench.

Dell had someone to go home to. He had his father.

Storm didn't even know who her father was.

Or if he was dead or alive.

He nudged her. "We need to get some sleep. School tomorrow – I know you'll want to get your brain in gear for that," he teased.

This was why he was her friend. This was why she valued him. He knew how to distract her. How to keep things easy.

"Oh great. How about we try and get out of it?"

He smiled at her. "You get us out of it, I might even give you some of my rations."

"You're on." They bumped fists and she laughed. "I guess wishful thinking never hurt anyone."

THREE

STORMCHASER

Dell was waiting for her as she reached the front door of the school, leaning against the wall with his arms crossed. The alarm had already sounded.

She shook her head as she walked the last few steps. "Why didn't you go in, dummy? Now you'll get the same late check as me."

He shrugged his shoulders. "What can I say? Washing dishes is a pleasure. Anyway, I wasn't even sure if you were going to turn up today."

She pushed open the door and walked inside. "Neither was I."

The school building was bland and uninteresting. As space was at such a premium, it wasn't just used for school. The back end of the building housed some of the government laboratories. There were heavy doors with thick bolts between the labs and the school. But the students could still see the people in white overalls rushing around inside. The lab staff used the school dining room too. They ate lunch after the students. Storm couldn't believe how many people spilled out through the lab doors each day. How on earth did they all fit in there?

Part of the students' education revolved around whatever experiments were being carried out in the labs at the time. They were often given instructions to water various plants at certain times, or to monitor growth in certain crops. Storm didn't mind. Anything that got her outside was a bonus.

They walked down the corridor. Each room was packed with students. There were barely enough seats – and not enough desks to go around. It was just as well that, at fifteen, attendance was only compulsory one day a week.

There was too much food to grow, too much energy to produce for time to be wasted at school.

Storm gave a nod to the instructor, who checked a black mark against both of their names as they entered. "Kitchen duty," he muttered as they wound their way through the class to find a seat. He cared as little about their schooling as they did. As long as students could read, write and count, he'd done his job.

"There will be an important announcement later. Make sure you attend city hall when you hear the alarm."

"Another one?" moaned Dell. "Why can't they just do them all together?"

Storm rolled her eyes as the instructor handed out competency sheets. "For those not already allocated jobs, know that all your competency sheets will be used to assign you a role best suited to your abilities. For those already in a job" – he glanced towards Storm and Dell – "know that you can be reassessed at any point."

She shot him a sarcastic smile. He knew she'd deliberately flunked all of the competency sheets. She hated being indoors. And most of the jobs on Earthasia were indoors, in energy plants – like where Dell worked – manufacturers, food production and transport maintenance. None of these things interested her in the slightest. A select few – who scored really highly – got jobs in the parliament building. Although no one knew exactly what they did. She'd recognized one guy, who was a few years older, following one of the Stipulators around and whispering in his ear. Job satisfaction guaranteed.

She gave the instructor a fake smile. "Any messages to be delivered?" Any excuse to get back outside.

He shot her a curious stare. "Maybe later," he mumbled.

She turned over the sheet and frowned. Most of these tests were simple. Language, reading and sums. But this one was a bit different. A whole lot more interesting.

Dell gave her a nudge. "Well, whaddaya know? Something to do with the announcement last night?"

It was too much of a coincidence. The sheet started with numbers of people, then land mass, then multiplications.

Storm shook her head. "They must be trying to reinforce what they said last night. Too many people, not enough space."

The sums were complicated. But with a little time and

thought she could do them in her head. There was a personal satisfaction in knowing that she was able to complete them. But that didn't stop her picking up her marker and writing random numbers on the sheet.

"He'll bust you," Dell murmured without lifting his eyes from his sheet. "He knows you can do all this."

She put down her marker and folded her arms. "Well, he better not tell. If I get reassigned somewhere indoors I'll go nuts."

Dell finished his final calculation and put down his marker too. "Shelter not getting any better?"

He knew her. Sometimes he knew her better than she knew herself. They'd been friends for ever. Ever since he'd climbed a tree in the long-gone woods at the edge of the loch and got stuck. Storm had climbed up to help him, but they'd ended up sitting there, moving branches and pretending it was their own parliament building.

And now he wasn't her friend. He was family. The only family she'd got.

When her mother had died, it was Dell and his father who'd helped her move into the Shelter. There was no other option. Storm's mother had said her father had died before she was born. And all orphaned kids had to stay in the Shelters.

She could only take a few things. Her pale grey, soulless room was barely big enough for the slim bed. Her twisted red blanket, corn doll and black shiny stone were the only real remnants of her mother she had left. She still had some memories though – the most vivid of her mother spinning around in the forest and throwing her knives with precision at a target. A skill that had been passed down through generations of their family but come to an abrupt halt when Storm's mother died. What on earth had happened to those knives…

"I hate the place. As soon as I close the door behind me I feel as if the walls are pressing in. And the noise…" She turned and looked outside. "It's constant. There's always someone shouting, someone fighting, someone crying. I think I'll go mad in there." She gave him a smile. "Or maybe I'm mad already."

There was a loud hacking cough behind them. Dell turned round, then immediately pulled back a little. Cala, one of their schoolmates, was pale and grey. She looked even thinner than usual, if that were possible. "It's nothing," she rasped. But they could see blistered skin not quite hidden by her sleeve.

It wasn't nothing – they both knew that. Cala's brother had died last year. Her father too, a few months later. There was no help available. Years ago, Storm's mother had known a woman who could make pastes and remedies from some of the surrounding plants. But the woman had died and so had the plants. There were no cures. No remedies left. No one knew how the blistering plague was spread – lots of people had ideas, but nothing had been proved.

"We need to get out of here," Dell whispered. "I don't want to catch it."

Storm frowned. "No one knows how you catch it."

The instructor appeared before them, snatching their sheets. He glanced over Dell's before adding it to the pile in his hands, and shook his head over Storm's. "Are these your final answers?"

"Absolutely."

He frowned at her and pushed something under her nose. "Deliver this to the parliament building –" he glanced at Dell – "the two of you."

They were on their feet in an instant. Any excuse to get out of school.

Dell picked up the lumpy package. "What is it?"

The instructor waved his hand. "I don't know. Just take it to the Stipulator named on the label. It's from the lab."

Dell glanced at the package, raised his eyebrows and tucked it under his arm, nodding to Storm as they both headed for the door. "It's for the main man. What do you think's inside?"

"Who cares? At least we're getting out of here."

They pushed open the door and walked out into the brisk breeze.

The parliament building was set up across some of the few trees that still survived on Earthasia. Some ancient rule had been in place, so instead of pulling them down to give more land space, they'd just built on them. Thousand-year-old trees with bases twice the size of Storm's room at the Shelter.

It was the most impressive building around. In a world

26

where everything seemed grey, somewhere, somehow, they'd found red stone the same shade as the tree bark so the building looked like it had actually grown out of the trees. A few branches and creeping vines had wound their way around the outside of the building. Years ago, Storm's mother had told her that children used to build playhouses in the trees. This was like the grandest tree house ever built.

The parliament building creaked as they walked up the steep sloping entrance. They waited patiently to go through the security checks before the main doors opened for them. The weirdest thing about the place was the noise. As soon as the doors opened, all they could hear was shouting. There was a rabble of black cloaks in front of them – the uniform of a Stipulator. Parliament consisted of all the Chief Stipulators from around the continent. They made all the decisions for the people on Earthasia – always, with no consultation. The people only heard about these decisions when there was an "announcement". Storm wrinkled her nose. They were always led to believe that the Chief Stipulators agreed on every decision that was made – but it didn't look like that today. They all seemed to be shouting at once. The passage in front of them was completely blocked.

Storm took a step back. "What do you think they're fighting about?"

Dell looked wary. "Either something to do with last night's announcement – or whatever the next one is supposed to be."

A small wizened figure pushed his way through the cloaks.

Deep lines covered the sagging, transparent skin on his face. He had to be the oldest man Storm had ever seen. Without health care people tended to die before they reached fifty. He looked as if he'd leapfrogged that by another twenty years.

"What do you want?" His thin, reedy voice cut through the rabble.

Dell held out the package with a slightly shaking hand. "Something from the school."

The old man grabbed the package and spun round. "Wait there," he said over his shoulder. "Reban Don!"

The whole parliament building seemed to shake. Storm let out an involuntary laugh. "Where on earth did that come from?" It seemed impossible that a man so tiny could shout so loud.

But it had the desired effect. The black cloaks quietened, most of them turning towards the old man. A large figure shouldered his way through the crowd.

Almost instinctively both Dell and Storm stepped backwards. They hadn't expected him to collect his own package.

Reban Don. The Chief Stipulator for their zone, who'd made the announcement last night.

His face was grim. He took the package and tore it open, pulling out the contents and examining them on the spot.

Inside was something electrical – odd looking. But Reban Don's attention was captured by the paper label attached to it.

"This is it. The confirmation we needed. The announcement will go ahead as planned."

Reban spun away, his black cloak swirling behind him. Then he stopped dead.

It was the strangest thing. He turned back slowly, his eyes narrowing as he looked carefully at Storm. He stepped forward. "You, girl, what's your name?"

She froze. Her tongue seemed to have attached itself to the roof of her mouth. Why on earth would he want to know?

"Storm," she muttered.

"What? Speak up. And speak clearly, stupid girl."

That annoyed her. She wasn't stupid. She'd never been stupid. He didn't know anything about her.

She drew herself up and looked him straight in the eye. Fear left her. "My name," she said clearly, "is Stormchaser Knux."

Dell winced.

Reban Don bent forward and she flinched. His nose was only a few millisectars from hers. No one wanted to get this close to a Stipulator. It usually meant you were in trouble and about to be carted off to the mines. He was staring right into her eyes. "Who is your mother?"

She didn't like to admit it – but her mother's face had started to fade from her mind, and in the last five years she seemed to remember it less and less. To cover her pain, she said bluntly, "My mother is dead."

Now he blinked. He straightened up immediately. "Where do you stay?"

What a strange question. It should be obvious where she stayed. "I stay in one of the Shelters."

He flinched. He actually flinched. But there was only the briefest of pauses before his normal frown returned. He turned back to the small man and started talking, moving away.

That was it. They were dismissed.

Dell grabbed her arm and pulled her over to the door. "What was that? Why did he want to know your name?"

"I have no idea." Her mind was racing. "Maybe he knew my mother – people say I look like her, maybe that's why he was asking about her." Her footsteps quickened. Storm wanted to get away too. "But then why did he ask where I stay? Isn't that obvious if my mother is dead?"

Dell stopped walking. "Not if he doesn't know you don't have a father."

Her heart skipped a beat. She glanced over her shoulder and stumbled.

Reban Don's eyes were fixed squarely on her.

Storm tugged at Dell's arm to start him walking again. "Come on, let's get out of here."

She didn't turn round again.

But she could feel Reban Don's eyes searing into her back.

FOUR

STORMCHASER

Someone's chin was pressed up hard against Storm's back. She tried to shift but it was useless. Dell shot her a look of sympathy. A few stark figures stood along the thin platform of the auditorium. She was too far away to make out who they were, but huge cameras were beaming their faces onto the walls. Lorcan Field, one of the head scientists in the zone, and Reban Don. It was unnerving seeing him again. This was the second announcement he'd been part of in the last two days. Things must be bad. Maybe the rations were about to be cut again?

The lights dimmed, the announcement was about to start. Stormchaser tried to rack her brains – when had she last seen him before yesterday? Was it after the discovery of the new food source, cornup – the horrible grey tasteless substance they now found themselves eating on a daily basis? Or was it when the new energy restrictions were imposed on every person on the continent?

Something glistened on the screen. Something spinning. A twisted ladder.

She'd never seen anything like it. All eyes fixed on the screen in wonder.

Lorcan Field started speaking quickly, tripping over his words, making them almost impossible to interpret. The excitement was practically bubbling out of him. The picture on the screen continued to rotate. It was almost pretty. Colourful, with symbols along parts of it.

Monumental discovery…the backbone of human life…our most fundamental elements.

The words danced around her head. They meant little to Stormchaser. The science they'd been taught at school had never interested her.

Reban Don was moving forward now. He cleared his throat loudly. "Citizens, this latest discovery is what we've been waiting for. Now we've found the fundamentals of human life. We know how humans exist down to the genetic level. We can begin to understand our most basic elements. And, more importantly, we can also use this knowledge in our fight against the dinosaurs."

The display projected the familiar sight of two large continents, separated by an ocean. Reban pointed to their continent. "We all know how over-populated we are on Earthasia. We don't have enough space, food or energy to maintain our existence. Piloria is a continent we need – and have tried – to explore. As you all know, over the last nine years, through a series of Trials, we've selected one hundred of our most physically able citizens each year – Finalists – to send to Piloria. The aim of our initial expeditions was to eliminate the dinosaurs. We failed. Due to the needs of the population, our last few expeditions have had to prioritize the search for new, quick-growing food sources on Piloria." He paused for a second. "We have had some limited success."

It was clear he was building up to something.

Reban continued. "It is time to return to our ultimate goal – to eliminate the evil threat of the dinosaurs and establish human settlements on Piloria. Our new discovery could be the key to our success. We need to get to the roots of dinosaur DNA."

Stormchaser wrinkled her nose. She had no idea what he was talking about. Several of the older adults were whispering to each other.

Reban's voice grew stronger. "We need land. We need space. We need the continent that the dinosaurs inhabit. At present there is no way for humans to live safely on Piloria. The dinosaurs are savage, physically superior beasts with no intelligent behaviour – they are a blight on our world and they stand in the way of our survival. We cannot coexist. The dinosaurs target our Finalists and few of them make it back from Piloria alive. Our weapons have proved useless. We can't use chemicals. We can't do anything that would damage the land. Now, we have new knowledge. Our DNA shows every part of our make-up. Our hair colour, our eye colour – the diseases we already have and those we could develop.

We have to assume the dinosaurs have a genetic code too. One which can help us find a way to eliminate these vicious, mindless creatures."

The heat in the stuffy space was rising, but Stormchaser's body was chilled. Every tiny hair on her body stood on end. They wanted to kill the dinosaurs. They wanted to wipe them off the face of the planet.

Creatures like Milo.

Reban was trying to garner enthusiasm from the crowd. A few people started shouting questions.

Lorcan Field attempted to answer them, but his voice was almost lost amongst the swell. "We can design a virus which is targeted to specific dinosaur DNA sequences. We can design a plague to wipe out certain dinosaurs without harming humans."

The noise from the crowd grew louder as he continued. "...The best cellular material is from the young."

The babies? They wanted Milo's babies? Storm felt herself start to panic. Bodies seemed to be closing in around her. But no one else shared her reaction. No, the rest of the crowd was excited, as if this solution made sense.

The pictures on the screen changed to show Piloria. Pictures of the dinosaurs on land and pterosaurs in the air. The scientists had decided that they needed samples from both types of creature. To Storm's relief, they didn't mention the ocean-dwelling reptiles – no one wanted to get too close to them. After all, the fishing boats had stopped going out altogether once some of the sea monsters had started treating them like breakfast, lunch and dinner.

But more importantly, they didn't take up valuable space on land.

And now Reban was talking about opportunities…

Storm had heard it all before. Here it came. For the good of the people. For the good of the planet. For the good of mankind. The anthem was picked up around her as those too stupid to understand what he was proposing joined in.

"We are looking for volunteers." *Surprise, surprise.*

"Individuals who are prepared to look to the greater good of the planet." *Individuals who are prepared to die.*

"But this time our prime directive will be the collection of eggs." The murmuring around her stopped. No one had seen that one coming.

"One from the tyrannosauruses, one from the pterosaurs and one from the velociraptors." Three of the most ferocious and feared monsters alive. Three of the monsters that had caused the most casualties on any previous trip to Piloria. How on earth would it be possible to steal eggs from these dinosaurs? It was practically a death sentence.

Images appeared on the screen. But not real pictures – oh no. No one had ever got that close to a tyrannosaurus egg before. A few fragments of shell had been found in the past, but that was it. Nothing definitive.

All around her people were shaking their heads. Talking about the journey across the ocean, with no likely hope of return. Who, in their right mind, would try and steal a tyrannosaurus egg?

Then came the propaganda. The promises. Preferential health care. Promoted housing. Unlimited food supplies. Better schooling for children, and access to more power from the grid supply. All for those who were successful in securing the dinosaur DNA – and for their families.

Family didn't matter to Storm. She didn't have one.

"All who return from Piloria will be given extra food rations for a limited time. But only those who return with eggs will reap all the rewards for themselves, and their families."

Eyes were glazing over around her – people were mesmerized by the promises of all the things they'd ever dreamed of.

Storm thought back to last year's trip. The ship had been sent off with great fanfare and expected to make the journey and return in a month.

And then? Nothing, nothing at all.

The ship had finally limped home six months later, with three survivors and a whole array of inedible produce. Some of the samples they'd brought home had been poisonous – killing two other survivors on the way back. But the trip was hailed a success – and in a way it was. The grey tasteless food group cornup had been found. It was horrid, but once planted it grew in the space of one month in even the most overused soil. And to the delight of the government, it was full of energy.

There was no mention of the lost ninety-seven. It was almost as if they hadn't existed. Hadn't torn themselves away from their families and friends in order to try and create a better existence for all.

And that's exactly what would happen this time too. It all seemed such a waste.

Words appeared on the screen. Telling Entrants where to register. Telling them of the rigorous selection process. The Trials would start in six days. And the Finalists from across the entire continent would be selected here – in Ambulus City.

Stormchaser turned and let herself be carried along by the crowd, back to the bottlenecked doors, then spilling out onto the ground outside. Dell appeared next to her.

"What are you going to do?" he asked.

She leaned forward then back, arching her spine, smiling in amusement as Dell winced at the loud crack. There. Instant relief. The crick in her neck was gone. Standing in the tightly packed auditorium was never pleasant.

"Sore again?"

She shook her head. "It's always sore. Breaking something vital will do that to you."

"You should ask for a transfer. Someone with your injury shouldn't be lugging hay bales."

"And be stuck at the energy plant all day? No thanks. That would be worse than being in a classroom one day a week."

He raised his eyebrows. "You didn't answer the question."

"About what?" She was being deliberately obtuse.

"About going to the Trials? We're fifteen now. This is the first year that we're actually eligible."

She flung her hands up. "And what would be the point of that? Why on earth would I want to be part of a plan that's trying to destroy living creatures? Let's face it – I'm much more likely to die than them. The odds are distinctly in their favour."

Dell's brow wrinkled. "I don't get you. I really don't. The creatures you care about are safe. Milo is safe. No one's interested in them. Why would you want to protect some of the most ferocious monsters on the planet? They're being specific. They're targeting the ones that mean we can't settle on the land. No one wants to wake up with a T-rex breathing down their neck. What's your problem?"

A few people glanced at them on the way past. Storm kept her voice low. "What if this is just the start? They say it's only the T-rex, the pterosaur and the velociraptor now. But what if they really want to get rid of all dinosaurs?"

"We need space, Storm." Dell spoke quietly. "We're living on top of each other as it is. And do you really want to keep eating cornup for the rest of your life?"

Storm's stomach turned over. Cornup might be nutritious, but it was the most disgusting substance known to man. Even the smell made her want to be sick.

Dell's eyes widened and he moved next to her. "Do you know what I heard? Last year, at the try-outs, all the Entrants got to eat the reserved foods. I heard they had peaches. *Peaches.* There was even a rumour there were apples too. We've never even *seen* apples in the flesh. Imagine the sweet taste in your mouth? Even if you never progressed in the try-outs, wouldn't it be worth it just to eat some decent food for a few days?"

Storm's stomach gave an obligatory rumble. It certainly wasn't the worst idea she'd heard.

Dell was still trying to coax her. Just like he always did. He knew her well, he knew the right buttons to push. Just like she did with him. "Come on, Storm, think about it. We could sign up for the Trials, eat food for a few days then fail at whatever the challenge is. How hard can it be?"

Storm was turning the idea over in her mind. Any Entrant was automatically excused from their work placement *and* school for the days away. Only people who held "essential" jobs, like the scientists or Stipulators, weren't allowed to volunteer. Getting away from hay bales for a few days wouldn't exactly be a stress.

She gave a small smile. "I'm not promising anything. I'll think about it. What would we have to do at these Trials anyway?"

Dell shrugged. "Who cares? As long as they feed us." He frowned up at one of the Blocks. "I'd best get home. Just think about it. We can talk tomorrow." He waved and disappeared off through the dark streets.

Her footsteps were automatic, taking her to the only place she could get a little privacy, back to the loch. But Milo was nowhere in sight.

He'd vanished into the depths again. His appearances were becoming less frequent. It was almost as if the plesiosaurs could sense the human unrest and knew when to disappear from view.

No one cared. No one looked on the dinosaurs as anything other than a threat. Even where creatures like Milo existed, occupying lakes and lochs. Calm, peaceful creatures that were no more threat than a butterfly in the sky.

She watched, as in the distance the hump of the plesiosaur's body broke the waves.

No one cared.

Stormchaser cared.

FIVE

LINCOLN

The streets were packed, thousands of people thronging their way through at the change of shift. For the lucky ones, it was the end of the day and they could head home to bed. The unlucky ones were waking up to a night shift, then returning home to a still-warm bed, just vacated by the day worker they shared with. Space was at such a premium it had reached the stage that one person could no longer be allocated one bed.

Lincoln was lucky in a way. His family lived in the caves. No one wanted to stay in those – let alone share them. He moved swiftly through the crowd, bumping into people coming from every direction.

The exchange happened quickly. Silently. Even the street cameras could never pick up on a hidden brushing of hands amongst the crowd.

He kept walking, scrunching his hand around the paper,

keeping his shoulders back and his eyes firmly focused on the way ahead. His steps were steady, even though his heart was drumming a rapid beat against his chest. He was doing nothing to draw attention to himself.

The scrunched-up paper jagged into the palm of his hand, taunting him – a burning coal would feel more comfortable.

His legs weren't listening to the signals to stay calm. They were threatening to break into a run. He moved swiftly, heading for home. He nodded to a few people around the caves before finally lifting the makeshift door into place behind him and sliding down the cool red wall.

He uncrumpled the paper in his hand. The writing was sprawled across the page. A list.

Three days' worth of cornup rations. That's what he'd had to pay.

This better be worth it.

SIX

STORMCHASER

She hadn't seen Milo for three days. That wasn't unusual. Sometimes he disappeared for weeks at a time, leaving the loch by some unknown means and appearing along the coastline.

But sign-up for Entrants was tomorrow, followed by Camp for who knew how many days? How long could she keep up the pretence of being interested in the Trials before getting thrown out? How much food could she eat in that short space of time?

She wandered along the beach. Ambulus City had apparently started as a fishing village but had grown exponentially, reaching inland and eventually surrounding the loch. Five thousand sectars beyond the city centre, the beach was practically the only unpopulated strip of land left. Thank goodness the sands kept shifting, otherwise there'd be dwellings here too.

The sea was flat. No sign of any of the plesiosaurs. But something else caught her eye.

A flash of red to her right on the cliff face, where it jutted out into the sea. Somebody was climbing. Climbing quickly up the rugged rock. Bare hands and feet finding holds on the wall. Strong arms and legs pushing and pulling the lean body upwards. She squinted at the figure. Blond scraggy hair, sallow skin. She couldn't see the face. Not that she would know him anyway. She didn't know anyone who could climb like that.

Then he hesitated, just for a second, his hand connecting with the rock face and then losing its hold.

The body tumbled backwards through the air, like a bright red spool of thread unravelling. She held her breath, conscious of the anxiety building in her chest, willing the momentum to carry his body away from the cliffs, rather than towards the sharp rocks underneath.

He disappeared into the foam-tipped waves at the base of the cliff.

She still couldn't breathe, willing him to break the surface and reappear. Her legs carried her forward, wading through the surf. She was too far away to be of any use, but her natural instincts drove her on.

Her eyes scanned the surface of the water. It seemed an eternity before, finally, she caught a flash of red. Her breath hissed out all at once.

He was safe.

She watched. She waited. Any minute now he would turn and swim towards the shore.

Except he didn't. He swam towards the base of the cliff once again and scrambled over the rocks. What on earth was he doing?

The waves crashed over him as he stood on the rocks, staring up at the cliff face. His head tilted slightly, as if he were contemplating his course above. Was he mad?

Then he arched his back, flexed his fingers and started to climb. This time, there was no hesitation, just a show of complete determination. The sun was beginning to set behind him as she stood on the shoreline, fascinated by the sight of the gangly youth with the determined chin making his way up the cliff.

He didn't waver for a second. He scaled the wall like a spider, while she wrapped her arms around herself in the warm orange light, ignoring the waves around her ankles.

As he reached the top he hooked his arm over the edge of the cliff and hauled himself upwards. She waited for him to stand and look down at what he'd achieved.

But he didn't.

He never stopped. He just walked into the distance as if it were something he did every day.

SEVEN

LINCOLN

The bell was clanging, reverberating around the cave. No one was talking. His mother and sister were just looking. Looking at him as if it were the last time they would see him.

Last time they'd looked like this had been the day the man had appeared to tell them about the accident that meant his father would never be coming home again.

He swallowed and gave his mother a small nod. He couldn't touch her. Couldn't hug her. Arta was trying her best to look well. He couldn't touch her either. Every part of her skin was blistered, some areas red and peeling, showing signs of infection.

Arta shook her head. "There's still time to change your mind, Lincoln. This is silly. You've got nothing to prove. Who cares about the dinosaurs?"

He stayed rigid. It was the only way he could keep his

safety net in order. But his hand betrayed him and reached up and touched her cheek. There was a blue tinge around the corners of her mouth. She was getting worse.

His eyes flickered over to his mother as he dropped his hand. She could barely look at him. The last two weeks had been fraught. *I'm already losing a daughter, I don't need to lose a son too.* The words echoed around Lincoln's head.

But in amongst the anger and tension there was understanding. She knew why he was doing this. She would never ask him to do it. But the unspoken words were there.

Lincoln smiled at Arta. "It's not about the dinosaurs. It's about us. Getting us somewhere better to stay. Finding a way out of these caves."

Arta's hand touched the damp wall. "It's not so bad here, Linc. Just stay. Stay with me."

If he remained a second longer he would crumble.

She knew.

She knew she was dying. She was asking him to be by her side while she waited to die. Any second now his chest would explode.

He couldn't watch that. He couldn't let her give up. It was his job to fight for her.

He shook his head. "Just wait." He couldn't keep the harsh tone from his voice. "Wait. I'll be back. You'll see." Inside he was pleading with her to hold on, but he couldn't acknowledge that – couldn't say the secret words out loud. No one was admitting that Arta was going to die.

Tears glistened in her eyes as she nodded disbelievingly.

He picked up the bag and walked out of the door. Out into the sunshine. Out into the fresh air.

His legs were trembling, threatening not to hold his weight and let him collapse to the ground. But every stride, every step gained a little more strength, a little more momentum.

The next steps he took would determine all their futures.

EIGHT

STORMCHASER

The queue snaked around the building. "Storm, over here!"

She smiled. Dell must have got here as soon as the sun rose. He had probably been in the line before the bell had tolled. She ignored the glares of a few others and joined him with her backpack in her hands.

She looked at the long, winding queue. It wasn't quite as long as it had been last year. People were scared. They weren't listening to the propaganda so much now. They all knew exactly how many people had come back last year.

Yet there had to be more than two thousand people waiting in line and only one hundred would eventually qualify. Some people must have travelled for days to get here. They looked tired, bedraggled. But most of all they looked hungry.

There were a few in the queue who, Storm guessed, were there for the food, like her. But the Stipulators were getting wise to that. If you didn't pass the first stage, you didn't get as much as a whiff of extra rations.

The line moved forward painfully slowly. The Entrants sign hung over the glass doors of the city auditorium. It took three hours to reach it.

As soon as they stepped through the doors the heat was stifling. Reban Don was hovering in the background, casting his eyes over the potential candidates as they signed up at the tables.

"Name?" The blank-faced woman was almost looking right through her. How many times would she have to do this today?

"Stormchaser Knux."

"Age?"

"Fifteen." The woman's eyes flickered upwards, running up and down her body.

"Work placement?"

She lifted her chin. "Farm labourer." She said the words with pride. She wasn't ashamed of the job she did – in a way, she'd chosen it. The woman didn't even look up, just scribbled the note on her paper. There was nothing essential about tossing hay bales around. At least she knew they couldn't refuse her for that.

The woman waved her hands. "Stand on the scales."

"What?"

She frowned at her. "The scales. Stand on the scales."

Storm kicked off her shoes and stood on the weighing scales. It seemed bizarre.

"That's fine. Up against the wall, we'll check your height."

A man appeared beside her with a tape measure. "And your arm span, please?"

Now she was really confused.

"Hold out your arms." He demonstrated the position he wanted her to assume and ten seconds later she was done.

The woman handed her a green card with a letter on it. "Hall C." She pointed behind her and Storm followed the signs.

Her eyes swept up and down the corridor. Dell had been at the desk right next to her. There were some shouts from the registration desks, sounds of a scuffle. A few minutes later he appeared with a similar green card.

"What was all that about?"

"Didn't you hear? The woman at the end desk was too light, they sent her home. No food – nothing. She travelled for five days to get here."

"But I don't get it. What does it matter what you weigh? Or how long your arms are?"

Dell shrugged. "Who cares? They've not flung us out yet." He stepped into the hall.

"They've not fed us yet either," she muttered, following him through.

Yesterday had been hard. The rations she received hadn't even taken the edge off her hunger, or given her enough energy to carry out her job. She'd almost collapsed trying to lug the hay bales. Her supervisor had growled at her, telling her that if she couldn't keep up, she'd be assigned another job

– and that was the last thing she wanted.

The room was set out like an old exam hall. Single desks and chairs, hundreds of them, with Stipulators who she didn't recognize pacing up and down between them.

She was gestured towards a seat and Dell took the one next to her. The room was already nearly full. Had some of these people been sitting here since registration began?

She took a deep breath and closed her eyes for a second. Peaches. That's what she could picture in her head. That's why she was here. The thought of them was almost painful.

She opened her eyes again quickly. When the last seat was taken an expectant hush filled the air. People stopped murmuring and shuffling in their seats. The Stipulators walked up and down the rows putting some papers face down on the desks.

Reban Don was at the front of the room. His gaze drifted around, occasionally stopping on an individual for a few seconds. It stopped on her for the briefest pause and she shifted self-consciously in her seat before he glanced away. Should she have worried about her appearance? She never had before. She was wearing what she always wore – a simple tunic. Today's was black and, although she had a couple in different colours, she wasn't interested in standing out. Today was about getting fed. Reban Don's gaze made her more than a little nervous. Surely he didn't remember her from the other day?

He was studying a list in front of him now, making little notes. Eventually he looked up and spoke to the room.

"When the alarm sounds, you will turn the papers over and complete the exercise. Once you have finished, deposit your papers in the box at the front of the room. Only those who pass the exercise will be allowed to proceed to the next stage." He glanced towards the clock on the wall. "This exercise will be time-limited." His face broke into a sarcastic smile. "But we won't be telling you how long you have." He watched their shocked faces, waited a few moments for the muttering to die down.

"Begin."

Stormchaser hadn't moved. She didn't look at Dell. She didn't want to be distracted.

She turned over her papers and picked up the thin graphite.

Nothing was going to get between her and that food.

The papers folded out into a map. She'd never really seen a proper one before. She was used to schoolbooks with printed pictures of the two continents.

This map covered the whole of Piloria – the dinosaur continent – outlining rivers, mountain ranges and lakes. It was the first time she'd ever seen it like this. The schoolbooks usually just showed a dark green mass. This looked like a living, breathing piece of land, a place where it might actually be possible to survive and grow food.

She lifted the separate sheet of instructions. It was like the treasure hunts she'd heard legends about. People hunting for jewels, gold and coal, following treasure maps to find them.

All she had to do was follow the route set out, give the map co-ordinates of stopping points and use simple mathematics to plot journey times. Her logical brain could follow that.

But her rebellious brain didn't want to.

It didn't take a genius to work out what was happening. They were plotting routes to nesting zones. Places where they would find the dinosaur eggs and steal them.

She looked around the room. There were a number of puzzled faces. Schools didn't teach students about maps any more. These days most people didn't use them, they tended to stay in one zone all their lives – they had no need for maps.

But Stormchaser knew about them. She'd created her own. Except the ones she'd charted were for under the water – under the loch. She'd been diving. Trying to chart the caves. Trying to figure out where Milo nested.

Dell was smiling too. They'd done this before. When they were young children, the last few forests had still existed and the foresters had used maps and strange instruments to work out their course once they were deep within the trees. Dell's father had been a forester. He used to make pretend maps for them and leave things in the forest for them to find. This challenge wouldn't be a problem for Dell at all. He glanced towards her, meeting her eyes, giving a grin and rubbing his stomach.

Storm put her head back down. It only took her a few minutes to realize that following the instructions was simple enough, but not the best course of action. The plotted route had them circling lakes and forests for thousands of sectars, instead of going across or through them.

In theory, the route would take the candidates weeks.

What did it matter? It wasn't like she would be going anyway. But she couldn't help herself...

She started scribbling, applying herself in a way she never had at school. Letting her brain make the rapid calculations on sectars and timings, making notes at the side of the paper on slightly longer timings for more difficult terrain. She glanced at the clock, Reban Don was talking quietly to one of the other Stipulators. Some of the candidates looked as if they still hadn't started, the one next to her was drawing pictures of dinosaurs with his fine piece of graphite.

Even after she'd completed the task, she didn't stop. Her fingers flying over the page, her brain doing more quick-fire calculations. This time, she followed the instructions on the paper. She wrote down the exact co-ordinates and times they were looking for.

She organized both calculations side by side. Hers? Saved nearly eleven days for the total journey.

She leaned back and smiled just as a bell sounded across the room. Several candidates looked up, stricken, still frantically scribbling on their papers.

"Everyone stop now," Reban Don's voice echoed across the room. He pointed to a doorway. "File into the next room. Your results will be available within a few minutes."

She frowned, wondering how that could be possible.

But the room filled with people in blue jackets, lifting one or two papers each and walking off to the sides. They'd started marking papers before the candidates had even left the room.

Dell squeezed her arm. "How did you do?"

She hesitated. Should she tell him that she'd completely ignored the instructions and plotted her own route?

He smiled. "You went through the forest, didn't you?"

She hadn't even realized she was holding her breath. She let it out in one long, slow hiss. "You did too?"

He nodded. "Why not?"

The room was crowded, smaller than the last one. Her stomach was still churning. She stayed silent. Dell might have plotted his way through the forest, but she doubted he'd planned a route over the lochs or mountains. Best to say nothing.

Reban Don appeared at the doorway with a sheaf of papers already in his hands. "When I call your name, go to room A or B as instructed." He started shouting names and instructions, running rapidly through the papers. Every few seconds another blue-jacketed person would hand him more and more papers.

Storm's eyes were flickering as people moved across the room. Several people who'd been sitting near her, including the one sketching dinosaurs, were sent to room A. It seemed as if most people were being sent there.

"Room B: Stormchaser Knux, Lubin Crost, Dell Banst, Taryn Bes."

Dell let out a stifled yelp next to her as they moved quickly towards room B. Inside, the candidates were standing around the edges of the room. It was clear to everyone that they'd passed the test. How many of the others had plotted different routes?

Storm couldn't help but feel a little excited. It didn't matter that she'd entered for the sole reason of getting food. There was a secret pride in being in this room.

She could feel the nervous flutter in her chest. She tried to count the people in the room without murmuring the numbers on her lips. Storm and Dell seemed like the youngest. Most seemed in their twenties or thirties, with only a few older adults. How many sessions like this would there be? Were there people in rooms all over the continent doing this test right now?

She'd only reached fifty-six when Reban appeared again. He barely even looked at the candidates. "Entrants, congratulations on passing the first test." He held his hands in front of his chest, kneading them over each other again and again. What did he have to be nervous about?

"We'll be moving you all this afternoon to Camp, where you'll all become Trialists. For the next two days you'll undergo a host of physical and mental training exercises to determine who our best candidates will be. I wish you all well."

His eyes seemed to skim over Storm before he bowed his head and walked out of the room.

"That's it?" hissed Dell. "Nothing else? How about they give us some kind of clue about what we'll be asked to do?"

Stormchaser shrugged. It was the opposite of how she was feeling. "We already know we'll have to read maps. I guess we'll find out the rest later. You know how it is. The Trials are always top secret. They change from year to year. No practising. No unfair advantages." The disquiet in the room was evident, lots of whispers and wide-eyed glances.

Storm picked up her backpack as a door opened.

Dell grabbed her elbow. "Think we can beat any of these guys at the Trials?"

She took a second to steady her gaze. "I like a challenge." She smiled as they walked forward. "Let's find out."

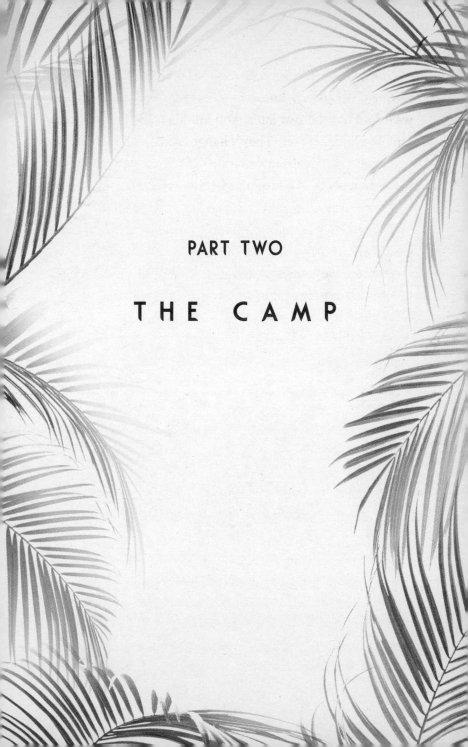

PART TWO

THE CAMP

NINE

LINCOLN

Lincoln watched as people filed off the transport wagons – solar-powered bland grey vehicles that could move around eighty people at a time. These were his fellow Trialists. There must be around five hundred people already.

He was sitting in the dust outside one of the makeshift cabins, filled with low-slung camp beds and lockable showers. He only had to get through two days here. Two days, one night and then the final selection would be made.

He was trying not to make any calculations in his head about how many more days it would take to reach Piloria, find and collect the eggs and get back. If he thought too much about the timing, he might worry that Arta wouldn't hold out long enough.

The fact he might not qualify hadn't even entered his mind.

He had an advantage. He knew exactly what the Trials

would be. He'd practised map reading, albeit with no instruction. He'd scaled the cliff wall and dived to the bottom of the ocean. He'd lifted rocks from the nearby quarry.

It didn't matter that he'd sacrificed his cornup allocation for three days in return for that crumpled piece of paper. It didn't matter that some people would think he had cheated. He *needed* to pass these Trials. He'd needed the chance to prepare.

Saving his sister's life meant everything. She'd get access to health care – something that was impossible right now. He had to believe the scientists knew more about the plague than they said. He had to believe they knew a cure.

He was scanning now. Watching the crowd. Trying to pick some potential allies out of the mob. He needed an allegiance. He needed someone to watch his back. To ensure that he made it to the sites and collected the eggs. He wasn't foolish enough to think he could do this entirely on his own.

He caught his breath as a young girl in a black tunic jumped from the transporter. He'd seen her before. Watched her diving in the lake with the plesiosaurs. He'd timed her. She could hold her breath longer than anyone he'd ever known.

He watched her walk, her stance. Her eyes moving constantly, surveying all those around her. Her feet were planted firmly on the ground, as if ready for an attack at a moment's notice. Her arms were toned and suntanned. She obviously did manual work. Under normal circumstances he'd assume that meant she couldn't use her brain. But the evidence was there – the very fact she was in front of him meant she'd passed the written exam.

Her shiny brown hair swung around as she turned to speak to her friend. Who was he? Small, slim-built with no real muscle. He didn't look old enough to be here. Minimum age was fifteen. He must be at least that old. He frowned. The friend could be a problem. If she already had an ally, she wouldn't be looking for another.

But she had potential.

That was five so far. One older man, two men who looked in their thirties, one female in her twenties and finally, the girl from the loch.

Lincoln tried to still his thoughts. He'd already made notes on the other four potential allies. The older man looked strong enough to fight off a tyrannosaurus with his bare hands – even though that was impossible. At the end of the day, as long as Lincoln could outrun him, nothing else really mattered.

But the older man seemed to be scanning the crowd too. Watching carefully. Lincoln could almost see him dismiss certain individuals with one glance. He walked over to a few and introduced himself loudly. Galen. Even the way he said hello had an air of menace about it. After a couple of sentences with one person, he'd move onto the next, leaving a waft of intimidation behind. His stocky build could be deceiving. He looked like a wall of solid muscle. But what if he also had agility? He might be a potential ally but he could also be Lincoln's biggest threat.

He watched as Galen's eyes fell on the girl and narrowed. What did he think of her? Galen took a few steps forward, then slowed, as if he'd had second thoughts. His gaze turned on Lincoln.

Every tiny hair on Lincoln's neck stood on end. He could almost feel the surge of adrenaline. Fight or flight. This guy really wasn't having a good effect on his senses.

There was a sneer on Galen's face as he walked towards Lincoln. "Taking notes, are you? Well, from the look of you, you'll need them." He laughed and shook his head. "Just as well you won't make it to Piloria. You'd be the dinosaurs' first meal." He barged past, shouldering Lincoln as if he expected him to fall to the floor. But Lincoln's feet were steady, he held his ground.

Lincoln smiled and crossed Galen off his list of potential allies. Piloria wouldn't just be about brawn. It would be about brains too. And his brain was telling him to avoid Galen at all costs.

It didn't matter. There were others. Like the girl.

Lincoln looked up at her again. She was laughing with her friend and his gut twisted. Why was that? He pushed the notebook back into his pocket. He didn't like that he was drawn to her more than the others.

Arta was his priority here. Nothing else could get in the way.

Nothing and no one.

TEN

STORMCHASER

It was the most food she'd eaten in years. Food that actually *was* food. That actually tasted of something, with an aroma that danced around her nose, taunting her, reminding her that she'd probably never eat anything like this again.

The meat and gravy slid down her throat, followed rapidly by the sweet pink fruit. It didn't matter that she didn't know what it was called. She just wanted to eat as much as she could.

"Are you having seconds?"

A leg slid around the stool next to her, then there was a bump on the table as he set his plate next to hers. She tore her eyes away from her food.

Dell had been put into a separate group for now and this boy was the only other person in the room anywhere near her age. "Where were you at registration?" The words were out before she could think. She would have noticed him.

His tall lanky frame brought an immediate thought to mind. Running. He would be good at running. Her eyes moved along his slim forearms as he leaned on the table next to her. His triceps were deceptively muscular. Strong. He would be good at climbing too. Maybe this guy was in with a chance. She might actually have just met someone who would be a Finalist.

He shrugged. "Registration was a mess. I'd be surprised if you'd noticed anyone."

She lifted her eyes and took a sharp breath. Did that mean he had noticed her?

"How did you find the test?"

He gave a flicker of a frown then shot her a smile. "Well, I obviously aced it or I wouldn't be here."

Something didn't seem quite right. She kept going. "Which route did you pick on the map test?"

He hesitated. It was only for a second. "Across the marsh."

Now Storm frowned. "The marsh? I don't remember that." She played with the food on her plate. She needed a bit of a breather. She wasn't used to eating so much. "Didn't everyone get the same test?"

He shrugged. "I guess there could have been different versions." He looked down as her brain sparked.

Scruffy blond hair tucked behind his ears, an angular jaw and bright green eyes.

Poster boy. That's what he was.

She smiled and let out her breath. He was no real competition. He'd been picked to be the poster boy. They probably wouldn't even let him off the boat at the other side.

Why would she care anyway? It wasn't like she was actually going to get on the boat herself, was it?

He was a plant. That's why she hadn't seen him at registration.

This happened every year. The expedition needed a pretty boy and girl for their propaganda posters. Smiling, handsome people who made the expedition look hopeful and could stand next to the Stipulators and pretend it wasn't as dangerous as everyone knew it was.

She watched as he leaned over his plate and started shovelling the enormous mound of food into his mouth. She raised her eyebrows. "You're certainly not wasting any time, are you?"

He shook his head as he continued to eat, his fork moving back and forth between his mouth and the plate in never-ending motion. A cheeky grin spread across his face. He gestured towards her plate. "You finished?"

She nodded. There were only a few meagre spoonfuls left. She honestly thought she would be sick if she ate any more. He didn't seem to have the same problem. He scooped up what was left and finished quickly.

He held his hand across the table. "Lincoln Kreft. Who are you?"

She hesitated. The plant was more than a little friendly. Why bother? He already knew he was getting on the boat. She slid her hand into his.

His warm skin enveloped hers, holding firmly but only

giving the slightest shake. Her first instinct was to pull away immediately. But he kept smiling and didn't let go.

It was the green eyes that made him the obvious poster boy. They were so bright. They would attract attention when his face was beamed across the continent on whatever propaganda they had planned for the expedition. If he hadn't been smiling at her so much she would have resented him.

"Your name?"

The blood rushed to her cheeks and she pulled her hand back. She wasn't used to physical contact. It felt odd. She and Dell only occasionally bumped fists. But this Lincoln had reached out and touched her as if it were the most natural thing in the world. "Stormchaser Knux."

"That's an unusual name."

"Is it?" He had a calm, easy manner – as if he spoke to strange girls all the time – and it irked her.

He shrugged. "I haven't heard it before."

"Maybe you've been hanging out with the wrong people." It was snappy. It was probably uncalled for. But she couldn't help it. Being around him seemed to put up all her natural defences.

He picked up his empty plate and swung his long leg back over the stool. "Maybe I have." Was that a trace of disappointment in his voice? She tried to ignore him, the awkwardness, shifting her weight on the stool and scanning the room in the hope that Dell would appear.

But he didn't. And she was left watching the retreating figure of Lincoln Kreft.

ELEVEN

LINCOLN

The siren blasted them awake at six a.m. The first day of the physical Trials. Lincoln wasted no time. He dressed sparsely. A thin T-shirt and shorts. He might know what the Trials involved, but he didn't know in what order they'd come.

One thing was for sure, more than a quarter of the candidates would spend most of the day being sick after the amount of food they'd put away at breakfast.

He stuck with bran and some cedar fruits. He needed slow-burning energy and a less than full stomach to complete the tasks. Tonight? He could stock up on enough food to last the next few days. He wanted to gain weight. He wanted to have some extra fuel for Piloria. Who knew what food would be available there?

The transport to the cliffs took just over an hour. There were murmurs around him as their destination became clear. Whispers about what they would be asked to do. Lincoln didn't pay attention. He was too busy focusing on the cliff as they drew closer, trying to find the best route upwards without overhangs and with possible hand- and footholds. These cliffs were vastly different from the ones he'd practised on near to home – much smoother – more difficult.

There were figures dotted along the top of the cliff and black ropes snaking down to the ground. Tether lines. The tide was far out, anyone who fell from this cliff face would be in danger of splattering on the rocks below.

He kept scanning. Some parts of the cliff were virtually smooth. Anyone positioned there would have no hope of reaching the top. He focused. There. He'd found it. His best route with two possible tether lines next to it.

The transporter convoy drew to a halt. Lincoln didn't have time for niceties. He had a purpose, a goal. He pushed his way through to the exit and walked briskly, grabbing a harness on the way past, not even stopping to listen to the instructions from the Stipulator.

Then he saw them. Storm and her friend. Already positioned at the tether lines he needed. The guy even had one of the lines in his hand. He frowned and glanced over his shoulder. How had they got there before him?

They were ready. Their harnesses in position with only the final clip to fasten. He suppressed the urge to yell as he walked up alongside.

The ground wasn't smooth here. They were all standing

on the jagged rocks. A few others came and stood next to him. He was careful not to allow anyone to get between him and Stormchaser and her friend. He moved a little, nudging her elbow. "Move up a bit," he muttered, trying to keep it light and impersonal.

But she wasn't fooled. She met him with her unusual violet gaze and clipped her tether line firmly in place, lifting her head to survey the cliff above her.

His skin prickled. This girl was no amateur. She knew exactly what she was doing.

She was focused. Just like he should be.

Reban Don's voice boomed behind them. "Trialists, the rules are simple – reach the top. Anyone whose full weight is taken by the tether rope is automatically disqualified."

Lincoln breathed deeply, grabbing the tether rope nearest to him and clipping it to his harness. He wouldn't be able to use the rope to swing across to the more favourable climbing route. His eyes quickly scanned the cliff again.

He would have to find a way to move over. No one said they had to climb in a straight line. He wouldn't do that naturally anyway. If he had to, he could always detach his tether line.

Her head was bobbing up and down and her lips murmuring. She was counting along the line, trying to see how many people had actually made it through to this stage.

He was curious too, but just didn't want it to seem obvious.

It was pointless to count right now anyway. The cliff face

was sheer. He couldn't imagine many of them would make it.

What if most of them didn't finish? How would they find the hundred people they needed for the trip?

Stormchaser was whispering to her friend, pointing out the route above them. Lincoln was still trying to guess her age. Why would someone so young want to be a Trialist? She must be at least a couple of years younger than him. Maybe she had a reason like him for being here.

"Begin!"

Reban's voice was like a bolt from the blue, making Lincoln curse under his breath. He had to get away from this girl. She was making him lose focus on the task ahead.

He rested his hands on the cool, white cliff and took a second to breathe. He could do this. He'd done it already. Not here, not with this cliff. But a cliff was just a cliff.

He flexed his fingers. A few others had already started the climb. He bent over and kicked off his boots. They would never hold on a cliff like this. It was too crumbly. Too fragile.

Underneath his boots his footwear was deceptive. He'd painted tree resin on the soles of his socks to give him a better grip. It was just as well he'd done it now – soon there would be no more trees to produce the resin. He slipped on the gloves from his pocket. They were fingerless with patches of resin around the palms. Lincoln had no intention of letting go of this cliff.

Stormchaser was already ahead of him, her arms reaching out and testing the possible handholds above, her thick boots resting precariously on tiny outward juts of the cliff.

He stretched his arms, connected with the rock and started his climb. The first hundred sectars were easy. He smiled. He could just imagine the faces back home if he scaled the first ten storeys of one of the tower blocks like this. The heat started to build in his muscles. The handholds came naturally, his arms strong enough to swing his body upwards with increasing momentum.

He was level with Storm and her friend in only a few short moves. She was kicking at the cliff wall, sending puffs of white dust falling to the ground, in an attempt to gain a better foothold. He didn't hesitate, didn't wait. His smoothest patch of wall was only another hundred sectars above.

He moved sideways, crossing over the top of her tether line. This was the path he would have logically chosen. The upward route was more natural, with nooks and crevices in the wall. His muscles were beginning to tighten, to burn, as he climbed higher.

There was a yell to his left and a flash of movement. Almost in unison a few people lost their grasp of the wall, flailing in mid-air as their tether ropes took the strain.

His fingers gripped the crumbling cliff tightly. He had no intention of being next.

The higher he climbed, the more Trialists tumbled, dangling on their ropes before being slowly lowered to the ground. The rockier base of the cliff had been easier to ascend, with more weathering and gaps that were easier to hold. The higher he climbed, the smoother the path became.

He was lucky. His height allowed him to stretch further than others; his coated soles and palms made his grip firmer.

He could see her climbing beneath him. She had slowed, letting out pants and little yelps of exasperation.

Her friend wasn't faring so well. Although his slight frame helped him ascend more easily, his lack of stretch and grip left him struggling to keep up.

She was methodical. Steady. Every move seemed considered. She sometimes stayed in one place for a few minutes at a time, looking for the most logical next step.

Lincoln moved on instinct. In another life he would have been a spider. The sideways moves were almost easier than the upwards ones. No one seemed to be ahead of him.

Only Galen was giving him cause for concern – the man who looked as if he could wrestle dinosaurs with his bare hands. At the bottom of the cliff, Lincoln would have considered him a write-off. But he was fast proving Lincoln wrong. He was moving like a man half his age, and half his weight. Upwards, without a single hesitation. Agility didn't seem to be a problem. This guy could be more of a threat than he'd thought.

Then he moved sideways. If Lincoln had blinked, he would have missed it.

Galen's foot caught momentarily in the tether line of a climber floundering a little lower down. It was a middle-aged woman with light blonde hair. He didn't hesitate.

He bent down and caught her tunic squarely between the shoulders and ripped her from the wall. Her shriek pierced the air as she tumbled for a few seconds before the strain on the tether line saved her from falling.

She looked bewildered, her hands coming out to stop her smashing into the wall. The people around her barely moved, they were too busy clinging on to save themselves. Had no one else noticed?

If Lincoln hadn't been watching, he would have assumed she'd slipped and fallen too. Galen hadn't even glanced back, just resolutely started climbing again. Ruthless. Determined. In spite of the shock he felt, Lincoln could almost relate to him. He wanted this just as much as Galen appeared to.

Another man was climbing behind Galen. He had a steady and firm pace. He didn't seem distracted by anything, or anyone else.

On any other Trial, that might have been a good idea. But just as Lincoln noticed him, Galen did too. Even from a distance the snarl on his face was evident. If Galen paused again the other guy could catch him.

But Galen did pause. He glanced at the other guy's tether line, then moved sideways towards it. The guy was too focused on the white cliff directly in front of his nose to notice. And Galen was fast. For a few seconds, Lincoln didn't even know what he'd done. It was just a flick of the wrist.

One second later Galen started climbing again, directly above the other guy. The cliff was crumbling, and untested rocks and overhangs could easily give way. The guy was gaining slowly. Galen reached a large overhang and climbed easily over it, pausing once his feet rested on it. He anchored one foot to the side to give him some grip, then used the other to kick down fiercely.

The effect was instant. The overhang gave way, a large lump of rock falling directly onto the unsuspecting climber below.

That was when Lincoln realized what Galen had done.

The guy had no chance. The rock struck the side of his head and knocked him clean off the cliff.

And he fell. And fell. And fell.

Until there was a sickening crunch below.

Lincoln pressed against the cliff, breathing in the white crumbling rock.

Galen had cut the tether line.

He'd cut the tether line and smiled.

He'd just killed one of the other Trialists.

A woman to Lincoln's left made a whimpering noise. She was pressed against the cliff too, holding on for her life. Somehow Lincoln knew she wouldn't climb any further.

Lincoln glanced across the cliff. Galen was still climbing. Powering towards his goal. Unflinching. Ruthless.

Galen was a rival. If Lincoln reported his actions, he could end up as Galen's next target. He had too much at stake. *Arta* had too much at stake. It would be sensible to stay away. But somehow Lincoln felt a burst of motivation. He might not be as ruthless, but he could match Galen's physical ability. His arms powered upwards, ignoring the burn, his legs pushing into the rock and thrusting him nearer his target. Stormchaser was still in his lower peripheral vision. She was moving steadily up the rock face, trying to match him. His pause had allowed her to gain ground. Her face was pale. Had she witnessed what had just happened?

She was directly below him now – and as his foot moved into position, her hand reached for the same jutting piece of rock. There was no avoiding her – his full weight landed on her hand. "Ouch," she yelled, but kept her hand firmly in place. She had no choice – there were no other handholds close by.

She frowned at his foot, eyes fixing on the material she was touching. Her head pulled back a little, as if she were trying to ignore the weight on her fingers and focus elsewhere.

"What is that?" she hissed. "Some kind of glue? Something to make you stick to the cliff?" She looked furious. It didn't matter that she was hanging on to a cliff by her fingertips. Face tilting upwards, she stared straight at him with flashing eyes. "Are you cheating?"

"Of course I'm not. They didn't tell us what to wear." It seemed the simplest answer. Even if it was deliberately evasive. "And at least I'm not killing anyone," he muttered under his breath.

He tried to redistribute his weight but it was impossible. His other foothold was slightly higher, meaning the bulk of his weight was on the foot below.

He tried to edge his toes away from her hand; he saw her wince. "Sorry, give me a moment."

There was a handhold above him, just out of his reach. He had to jump to try and grab hold of it. He heard Storm squeal as his leg bent to power himself upwards. He grabbed on to the outcrop of rock and, shifting his weight to the other foothold, he searched with his dangling leg for another. Seconds later his foot found resistance against a different piece of rock.

He glanced upwards. Another few minutes and he would reach the top and complete the task. But he could see Storm squirming beneath him, trying to reposition herself on the rock face, whilst nursing her injured hand. He could also see her rubbing her fingers together. Some of the resin must have come off on her skin.

No one could climb this cliff one-handed. It would be an impossible task. Lincoln's eyes scanned the cliff wall. He could only count ten figures. He'd been so focused on climbing he hadn't noticed the others falling around them, bouncing on their tether lines. How on earth were they going to find one hundred people to send to Piloria?

Storm was tentatively trying her hand on the cliff, reaching towards another rock jutting out. The change in weight put her off balance and she slipped. She reached up with her bad hand and caught her weight to steady herself. Her scream tore through his body.

This was his fault.

He hesitated on the cliff face. Galen was still climbing resolutely, destined to reach the top before anyone else. Storm would be lucky to reach the top at all.

Storm's friend was directly underneath her, climbing quickly, trying to reach her. "Storm! Storm! Hold on!" What did that skinny guy think he could do? Prop her up?

She was scrambling underneath Lincoln, trying to find a secure spot to place her foot. But Lincoln had the bird's-eye view. In her panic she wasn't thinking straight. She wasn't seeing the most logical foothold.

He took a quick glance at the rock face underneath him. He could do this. He could. He took a deep breath and released his fingers, sliding down the crumbling cliff.

It was literally only a full body length. Not enough to yank the tether line into place. The whiteness flashed before his eyes as his foot connected with a piece of rock below. He bent his leg quickly for the impact as he jolted to a halt. His arms were spread wide, to add some stability to his drop.

She was just an arm's length beneath him. Her violet eyes were wide with shock. They were the most distinctive and unusual eyes he'd ever seen. He didn't wait to explain. Just grabbed hold of her injured hand around the wrist.

"Right foot, over to your left and up a bit." It came out like a command. Something flitted across her face. The immediate instinct to say no. But her brain kicked into gear and her scrabbling foot stilled and quickly found the foothold she needed.

He kept hold of her wrist, looking upwards and immediately trying to map a route to the top. It would be difficult. If she could only hold on with one hand he would need to be immediately underneath to help steady her.

Storm's face was pressed against the white cliff. It was the first time he had really had a chance to be this close. Her skin was tan against the rock, the sun obviously leaving its mark. Her long brown hair was like a sheet around her face, shielding her violet eyes. Her hand tugged backwards, trying to loosen his grip on her wrist.

He shook his head, looking closely at her hand. The skin was red and broken in places, the swelling around her knuckles apparent already. Chances were he'd broken something and it made him feel sick.

"Don't fight me. Do what I say or you'll never reach the top."

"This is your fault." She pulled her bad hand free and waved it at him accusingly. "You did this to me."

"Do you want to reach the top or not?" He didn't have time for this. Galen was already hauling his stocky body over the cliff edge. If Lincoln waited any longer there might be others.

He pointed to the place where her hand was resting. "I'm going to give you a bump up. Put your foot there. There's another handhold just above."

She seemed surprised. It took her a few seconds to follow the path with her eyes and decide if she could manage. He didn't wait, he manoeuvred down and put his hand directly under her backside. "Now," he said, before she had a chance to object.

She moved quickly, the extra momentum pushing her further up the cliff, her right hand clenching the rock above.

Lincoln shadowed her movements, staying just behind her, directing her onwards. "Where's Dell?" she muttered as she looked down.

Her friend was fixed to the cliff; his path had taken him to the smooth section with no hand or footholds. He was marooned. Left clinging to the rock with no place to go.

"Forget about Dell. He's made it part way up. Let's get this finished."

He thought she might argue. Her chin was set but Dell was too far beneath them to try and backtrack.

He gave her another push. "Move."

It was more forceful than he meant, but the muscles in his arms were burning. He'd been clinging to this rock face for a while and the extra energy needed to boost her upwards was making the burn even fiercer.

Just as well they were near the top. If they'd been halfway up, he would have left her.

She was still grumbling as she climbed. Stormchaser was obviously the kind of girl who didn't take kindly to being helped. But he didn't care. Every time she moved the single hand that was attached to the wall upwards, he flinched. It didn't matter how securely her feet were positioned, the fact that she didn't have any other way of anchoring herself to the cliff made him cringe. The damaged hand was his fault. Even if she made it up the cliff, he'd probably just wrecked her chances for the rest of the Trials.

She released her hold a final time, reaching for the top of the cliff. The man anchoring her tether rope gave a glance along the line to ensure no one was watching, then grabbed the back of her tunic and hauled her onto the grass. Seconds later Lincoln was lying next to her, staring up at the pale blue sky and panting.

His heart was racing, his hands bruised and scraped. The extra exertion had cost him. He would need to eat even more tonight.

Her eyes were closed and she was nursing her hand on her chest. Cradling it against herself. Would broken fingers or knuckles mean automatic dismissal?

Her head flopped round to face him and she opened her violet eyes. "You broke my hand, cheater-boy." No "thank you". No relief at reaching the top. This girl was even more stubborn than he was.

He stayed calm. "I climbed the cliff – just like you did." It was difficult not to show guilt – cheating wasn't normal for Lincoln, and he was feeling uncomfortable at being responsible for Storm's injuries. He was still trying to get his head around what he'd seen Galen do too – killing another Trialist. "How do you know it's broken? Is there a medical facility you can go to?"

She sighed. "I know what a broken hand feels like. This isn't the first time. And I doubt it'll be the last." She was so matter-of-fact about the situation. She was obviously squirming with pain, but there was no shouting, no screaming, no tantrums.

Lincoln frowned. "What's your job? You do something that can break your hand?"

It was the wrong thing to say.

She was staring off across the horizon, no longer watching the last few desperate hands reaching for the cliff edge. "I lug hay bales. Big deal."

The system was archaic, antiquated and everyone knew that. Only the children who excelled in school landed somewhere good. He'd been half-lucky. He worked as an assistant in one of the labs.

She seemed defensive and he knew better than to push it. Galen had just caught his attention anyway. He was involved in a heated argument with one of the Stipulators and was gesticulating furiously, before he finally stomped off.

"What was all that about?" she asked.

He was reluctant to mention what he'd seen. He still hadn't decided who his allies should be.

She looked thoughtful. "Maybe he's worried he won't qualify?"

"But of course he'll qualify – he was first to the top." He couldn't understand her logic at all. Maybe he'd overestimated her.

"Are you really that stupid?"

"What's that supposed to mean?"

She laughed. "You don't think this is the only camp?"

"What do you mean? It always has been in the past."

"Oh come on." She waved her arm along the cliff edge. The Stipulators who had been monitoring the tether lines were easy to pick out – they were all in black. One had pulled up the cut tether line and was staring intently at the end of it. A handful of Trialists were still scrambling over the edge, and a few Stipulators were still staring down the cliff. "Look at how many people have made it. Less than ten. How on earth can they find a hundred Finalists?"

When she said the words out loud it seemed obvious.

"You think there's more than one Camp?"

"I *know* there is. I heard Reban Don on the transporter. There's at least another five. What if they all managed to climb their cliff in half the time we did?"

He could be sick. Right now, all over the grass. The realization was like a bucket of cold water had been thrown over him. "So, even if we make the top one hundred here, we still might not qualify?"

He'd gone back. He'd gone back to help her. Had his actions just cost him his place?

"Exactly."

"But there's always just been one Camp. Why would they change things now?"

She shrugged. "The stakes are different. This isn't about food. This is about something else entirely."

His brain was whirling. It was uncomfortable. Talking to her while lying on the grass. She was too close. He could see her long lashes and all the little imperfections on her skin – just like she must be seeing his.

He'd been so busy before – working, looking after his family. He should be concentrating on them right now. Instead, he was fixing on the face of a girl. A girl who was unlike any he'd encountered before. Strong, independent and unafraid. For the first time in his life he was interested in someone outside of his family. But he couldn't afford to lose focus on becoming a Finalist.

She didn't seem bothered at all by the competition, he realized, sitting up. There was something strange about her. Something off. She pushed herself up with one hand, still cradling the other across her chest.

"Why are you here?"

"What?" Her head snapped up at his sharp question.

"I mean you don't seem too worried about winning. It makes me wonder what your motivation is."

"As opposed to why you're here, poster boy?" Sarcasm dripped from her voice.

"What?"

She pushed herself onto her feet and stood in front of him. "I'm surprised you got up that cliff. Actually, I'm surprised they even brought you to this Trial in the first place. And why are you bothering to act like you care how it works for the rest of us? Don't you get an automatic pass?"

He shook his head. "Did one of the falling rocks hit you on the head? Or are you always this crazy?"

He turned away. He had no idea what she was talking about.

But she grabbed at his arm. "You. You're the poster boy. You're the one who's going to be all over their publicity shots. You don't really need to do the Trials, do you?" She waved her arm. "You're going to sail right through to the final hundred."

"Are you nuts? Why on earth would you think that?"

Then he paused. "They do that? People just get put through without doing the Trials?"

She shook her head. "Surely you remember last year. That guy, Bladen Krin. The few Finalists who did survive said when he reached Piloria he never even stepped off the boat."

He couldn't believe it. He couldn't believe he hadn't even heard any of this stuff. He should have been paying attention. He'd been focusing on his sister. Focusing on what he could do to help her.

And this was it. This was the only solution he had.

He had to be in that top hundred no matter what. Allies, friendships, they all paled in comparison. Right now, *dinosaurs* paled in comparison.

This girl was beginning to annoy him.

"So, you think I'm a poster boy? You think I've been brought here for my good looks and charm?" He started to laugh, because he'd never heard anything so ridiculous in his life. He threw up his hands. "Why? Why would they make me do the Trials?" He pointed at his face. "Wouldn't they be worried in case I damaged myself? Imagine if I'd slipped from the cliff and smashed my face on the rocks, that would have ruined everything. How would their plans have worked then?" He didn't have time for this, he really didn't. And he was uncomfortable with her drawing attention to his looks. His mother had always called him handsome. But that was different – she was his mother. A complete stranger saying he'd been picked for his looks was something else entirely.

"Why are you here anyway, Stormchaser? What is it you want? The rewards? The fame?" Even as he said it he didn't believe it. She didn't seem the fame-chasing type. But then, he really couldn't get the measure of her at all.

"The food." Her words were blunt.

"You came here for the food?" Interesting. He could have picked out the individuals in the registration queue who were only there for the food. They might have known they had no hope of qualifying, but would try anything to get a decent meal. He just hadn't considered that for Stormchaser. She was slim, but muscular, and driven, if her climb was anything to go by. The food might be a bonus, but was that really her motivation for being here?

She nodded. Her lips tight. She walked over to the cliff edge and looked down. It was the first time he'd really noticed her figure as opposed to just her muscles. With her slim frame, her shining hair and her unusual eyes, she could be the poster girl herself. But somehow he knew that suggesting that to Storm would earn him a punch on the nose.

He joined her, watching the dangling Dell being lowered back down to the rocky coastline below. The water had started to come in and was lapping round his ankles. He looked up as he waded to shore and gave Storm a wave, a frown appearing on his face once he realized who she was standing next to.

"I imagine your friend will be going home."

"I hope not." Her voice was quiet. It was the first time

he'd seen her show any kind of vulnerability. Even hanging from the cliff face she'd still been bold and furious. "He's the only family I've got."

Lincoln was confused. "He's family?" They looked nothing alike.

She swallowed as she looked down, then shivered. At the bottom of the cliff two Stipulators were covering the body.

Storm turned to him, her eyes wide. "Someone died?"

He gave a nod and pressed his lips together.

"How could that happen?"

"The tether line must have sheered on the cliff." He couldn't say anything else right now. Not until he was sure about her. If he warned her about Galen, he was trusting her – and he wasn't ready to do that.

There was another flash of vulnerability on her face. Her words were so quiet he almost missed them. "Dell's the only person who would care if I lived or died. No one else would even notice."

Lincoln gulped. He couldn't even begin to know how to respond to that. He couldn't imagine living without the bond he shared with his sister, his mother. But the moment passed as quickly as it had come.

Storm shuddered. "How many people actually finished?"

They both looked along the cliff edge and started counting. Galen was already making his way back along a path down the cliff. Two women were lying on the grass, looking as if they couldn't climb another sectar if their lives depended on it. Another three men were in varying states of exhaustion, doubled over, dripping sweat and trying to catch their breath again. "Is that it?" he asked. "Only eight of us?"

Her frown disappeared, giving way to an expression resembling pride. "That's a huge drop-out rate. They can't have only eight people going on to the next Trial. Imagine if it's the same in every Trial group – they won't have enough Finalists."

The black-clothed Stipulators were clustered together, talking. One walked towards them to usher them along the path Galen had taken. After a few minutes Lincoln realized Dell and the others had the easy way down. Being lowered on a tether line was much simpler than stumbling down an unsafe, precarious path.

They were almost at the bottom before he noticed how far the sun had lowered in the sky. His stomach rumbled. The light breakfast didn't seem like it had been such a good idea any more.

The transporters were waiting. Candidates were sitting dejectedly on the sand dunes. It was clear their trek up the cliff face had finished early. One of the Stipulators was shouting names and directing them towards the first vehicle.

Lincoln recognized a few of them; most had fallen at the very beginning.

"Do you think they're sending them back without even feeding them?" Stormchaser whispered.

He took a deep breath. "I hope not. It's been a long day. Surely they'll be allowed to go back to Camp and collect their belongings?"

"Dell!" Storm was distracted – she'd spotted Dell amongst the crowd and ran towards him, throwing her arms round his neck. "Are you okay? Are you hurt?"

"No," he muttered as Lincoln approached. "Just annoyed. I could have made it to the top."

Lincoln wasn't convinced. Even if the boy hadn't been stuck on a smooth patch of rock, he doubted Dell's skinny frame had the stamina to take him up the rock face.

Lincoln turned, hearing raised voices on his left. The heated exchange between the Stipulators was continuing, one of them was scribbling furiously on some paper. "Numbers…proportions…adequate," were the only words he could make out.

Reban Don grabbed the paper from underneath the other Stipulator's nose. His eyes scanned the page quickly. Lincoln could almost hear the calculations in his brain.

Reban cleared his throat and spoke loudly to the people scattered in front of him. "If I shout your name, head to the second transporter. All those who are left will go in the third transporter."

Stormchaser's eyes quickly shot to Dell. What would happen to those who hadn't completed the climb?

Dell turned to face her. "Well, enjoy the food without me. It was fun while it lasted, even if it was only a day."

Stormchaser looked around. "Don't be so negative. You almost made it to the top. You might not be going home yet." She sounded a little desperate.

Reban Don started shouting out the names, "Lincoln

Kreft, Galen Hux, Stormchaser Knux, Linden Brack, Frion Temb, Yuna Poran, Drenna Crax, Meren Fyndon." He looked up, "All transporter two."

Lincoln took a step forward but Storm didn't move, her feet rooted to the spot. He lifted his eyebrows and she gave the slightest shake of her head. "Not yet. I want to wait a bit. I want to see what happens." Her eyes were resting on Dell.

The rest of those whose names had been shouted were already making their way to the transporter. Six of them. Eight in total. It was hardly worthwhile doing the other Trial. With such low numbers, all of them should be selected for the expedition.

But then Reban started calling out a whole list of other names. One was the woman that Galen had pulled from the cliff. Lincoln was sure some of them had climbed more than halfway up. Maybe they all had? That was the trouble with being too focused on your task. You missed the bigger picture. The stuff that might turn out to be crucial at a later point.

Dell flinched as his name was called, but then Reban shouted, "Transporter two."

Storm's face broke into a relieved smile and she bumped fists with Dell, and hugged him. "You must have made it. They wouldn't put us in together if they were sending you home."

For the briefest of seconds, Dell let out a sigh of relief. Then his eyes darted towards Lincoln, the expression on his face quickly reverting back to distrust. "Let's go, Storm," he muttered.

They walked away towards the transporter together.

Lincoln's skin prickled and a horrible sensation swept over him. He was annoyed that they'd walked away. Ignoring him. Treating him as if he were instantly forgettable. Dell and Stormchaser were obviously more than friends; they were also a team. Caught inside their little invisible bubble that no one else could permeate. He was an outsider looking in. And it made him realize how alone he was here.

A sense of frustration grew inside him.

But it was pointless. Stormchaser wasn't a suitable ally. She was too distracted by her emotions. It was time to find another ally. But that thought burned. He knew what tomorrow's Trial was going to be – no one else did. And he was pretty sure Stormchaser would finish it long before anyone else.

He started to think about the others who had made it up the cliff today. He discounted Galen – the guy was a killer. Lincoln didn't know enough about the other five candidates. So tonight, he would have to do something about that.

He took one last look at Storm as she stepped up into the transporter, her hand still cradled to her chest.

But he wasn't the only one watching her.

Reban Don had his eyes on her too. Pointing and gesturing towards one of his colleagues. He looked furious.

Lincoln had no idea why. Was this all just a big con? Had the Stipulators already decided who they wanted to get through the Trials?

Reban's gaze swept the crowd of people still to board the

transporter, fixing on Lincoln. His scowl grew even darker. Reban's eyes had no hesitation, no sympathy.

Lincoln shuddered. It was the oddest sensation.

Suddenly, he felt like a marked man.

TWELVE

LINCOLN

The food servery was busier than he'd expected. For every person who'd left, another had taken their place. Storm's theory that there was more than one Camp must have been correct. He was kicking himself for not considering that earlier. Now, he had a whole lot of new Trialists to consider.

He dumped his tray down at a table, sliding his legs onto the bench. All the people at this table had bright blond – almost white – hair, and they seemed around the same age as him. "Hi," he murmured as he picked up his fork.

Three identical pairs of pale blue eyes looked directly at him; he almost choked. He put down his fork. "Lincoln Kreft." He held out his hand towards the nearest, who gave a little nod of his head and quickly shook hands.

"Leif Larsen. How did you fare on the cliffs?"

Lincoln blinked – nothing like getting straight to the point. But he was cautious. "Fine. You've just arrived?"

The young man sitting next to him nodded. "Trial this morning and a move to this Camp this evening."

"How many made it to the top of your cliff?"

"Fourteen. How many made it to the top of yours?"

"Eight." The words stuck in his throat. It felt like a defeat. He changed the subject quickly. "How far did you travel?"

Leif shrugged. "Who knows? Half a day maybe? We came on the silo trains." Now that was interesting. The silo trains didn't usually carry passengers, only freight, but they moved at speeds faster than any other transport system.

The guy across the table looked at Lincoln. "Rune," he said simply and nodded. The third guy looked up, his mouth still full of food. "Kronar," he mumbled before starting to eat again. A smile appeared on Rune's face. "You might have guessed we come from the North." He looked around the hall, scanning the range of faces, skin and hair colours. His eyes settled back on Lincoln, as if he couldn't quite decide which part of the continent he was from. "When did you get here?"

Lincoln hesitated. If all three of them had made it to the top of a cliff similar to his, they were possible allies. But it was difficult. Like Stormchaser and Dell, they would have allegiances to each other. They'd probably be reluctant to welcome anyone else into their group.

He gave a weary smile. "I'm from here. This is my city." His blond colouring frequently confused people. Most of the city dwellers here had dark hair and dark eyes.

Rune nodded. "So, if only eight made it up the cliff,

why are so many of you still here? When we arrived today, one of the cabins was still full. They've kept around fifty?"

Lincoln frowned. "They called back those that made it part way up. I'm not quite sure how they worked it out. The people who fell early on seem to have been sent home." His eyes caught on Dell. As usual he was at Stormchaser's side and they were laughing together. Her hand was wrapped in some tight strips. His stomach flipped. Had she broken some bones? Or was it just a strain? Would she be able to compete? "The rest of these people must be new arrivals – like you," he finished. He spooned some food into his mouth; it was getting cold quickly.

Leif looked suspicious. "There were around twenty extra people on our silo train, but none of us could remember how they'd fared in the Trial. We thought some of them hadn't completed it." Lincoln saw glances pass between the three friends. "It doesn't seem fair."

"You're from Norden? Was your first Trial there, or here?"

Rune talked through mouthfuls of food. "It was at Tarribeth City."

Tarribeth was another coastal city. Lincoln was thoughtful. Everyone knew that the Norden part of the continent was almost completely flat. From what he could remember from school there were virtually no mountains or cliffs there at all.

"How did you manage the cliffs then?"

Leif looked at his friends and smiled. "We practised."

"On what?" Lincoln was confused.

Rune spoke in a low voice, as if he didn't want those around him to hear. "We constructed our own wall. Not quite as high as a cliff, but it was good enough."

He could sense their competitive edge. They weren't here for the food. They were here to qualify and they were rapidly beginning to fascinate Lincoln. It was almost a relief. Stormchaser wasn't his only possible ally in the room.

He lowered his voice to match Rune's. "Did you know what the Trials would be then?" He tried to make the question sound innocent, even though it clearly wasn't. He'd managed to buy a Trial list, why couldn't someone else?

Rune looked horrified. "Of course we didn't." He waved his fork in the air. "It was logical. We know some of the Trials that have been set before, we decided to make sure we could fulfil them all."

It sounded plausible enough. But Lincoln wasn't sure he could believe Rune.

He'd heard rumours about previous Trials, but he didn't remember any like this. Recently they'd been about foraging for food or building a shelter. But this time their mission wasn't just to survive on the edges of Piloria. This time they had to go right into the heart of things, to plunder, to steal, to scale cliffs to reach pterosaur nests. And there was every chance they'd come face to face with some of the most dangerous creatures in the world.

Lincoln spooned more food in his mouth as he thought about that. His knowledge of dinosaurs was practically zero. Were they intelligent creatures, or just ferocious beasts?

Information like that would be crucial to his survival.

But schools didn't teach much about the other continent. Lessons concentrated on new energy sources, new food sources and, any day now, whatever population-control measures parliament decided to employ.

Health care was already neglected. Someone from his school died virtually every week.

His stomach tightened. If he didn't focus, his sister would be next.

He stared at the uneaten food on his plate. Such a waste. But he couldn't eat another mouthful.

He nodded at Rune as he stood up. "You were lucky then. You obviously picked the right Trial to practise for. Excuse me, tomorrow will be another long day. Maybe I'll see you all then?"

He gave a polite nod of his head and walked away.

Out into the cool night air. Out, away from the buzzing noise and yakking voices.

From a corner of the Camp he could see smoke rising. Someone had obviously picked some of the rushes from the beach. He could almost guarantee that tomorrow he would be able to pick that person out of the crowd by their heavy eyes and shuffling walk. What a waste.

Then he heard it. Laughter.

He didn't even need to turn round to know who it was. He flattened against one of the cabin walls. He'd come out here for some thinking space. He didn't want to get involved in another conversation.

But the laughter died down quickly, followed by some slow-moving steps and quiet murmurs. They were almost on him, just around the corner when they stopped dead.

They obviously thought they were alone. Lincoln cringed. Should he clear his throat and walk away, making it obvious he was there?

But the hissing of their voices made his mind up for him. He was too curious to move.

"What's the problem, Storm? We only came here for the food."

"I know that." Dust was floating around the corner – she must be kicking the ground. She paused and took a few steps further away. Lincoln could see her profile, outlined by the white moon in the dark sky above. She was staring back towards the food cabin, watching people around the doorway. "But how did you feel today on the cliff, Dell?"

"What do you mean? I was pissed. I was stuck. How do you think I felt?"

Lincoln smiled. Dell hadn't understood Storm's meaning. He couldn't see past the here and now.

But Storm was persistent. She walked back and pressed a hand on his chest. "But how did you feel here? Didn't you feel anything? Didn't you feel a rush of excitement, a need to win?"

Dell's brow furrowed. He just wasn't getting it at all. "Hungry," he replied. "I felt hungry."

Storm sighed and shook her head. "We started out coming here for the food, but now I think…well, I just don't know.

99

Up on the cliff, it was tough, it was painful – but it was exciting too. I felt, for once in my life, like I was really alive."

Dell lifted his hands to her shoulders. "What are you talking about, Storm? You can't possibly want to go to Piloria? It's a death sentence. Everyone knows that." There was panic in his voice.

"But what if it isn't?" The volume of her voice was increasing. "What if it means we get to hang on to that feeling? What if it's a chance?"

"It's a chance to get eaten by dinosaurs!"

She flung up her hands in obvious frustration. "What if it's a chance to experience something completely different? No grey buildings. No work regimes. No school. How do we really know what the dinosaurs are like? Maybe they're not all horrible people-eating monsters, maybe some of them are fine. How do we actually *know*? Maybe this is the only way we'll ever get to find out…" She rested her hands back on her hips and started to pace. "I don't care about the DNA stuff. I want to know more about the dinosaurs. I'm not sure I believe everything the Stipulators tell us."

"Oh no." He waggled his finger at her. "Don't you start your crusade. I'll tell you exactly how we know they *are* horrible people-eating monsters. How many people came back last time? Three. Three! Out of a hundred. How many the time before that? Why don't you go and ask Lucca Cran what she thinks about Piloria? She lost her son there three years ago, remember?"

But Storm was still shaking her head. "I know all that.

I know it. But don't you see? This is different. This isn't about searching for new food. This is about killing the dinosaurs – wiping them out. Do we even know what DNA is? We only know what they told us in the city auditorium. Is it safe to tamper with?" She stepped forward so she was face-to-face with Dell. "Should we even be doing this?" She paused. "If we go along too we can find out for ourselves what's happening, instead of having to believe everything they want us to believe."

Dell let out a yell. Any chance they had of keeping this conversation to themselves was instantly blown. "Why would they be lying? Look at us, look at where we live. There's virtually no land anywhere." He held out his arms. "We're living in caves, we're living in spaces so small we're sleeping in shifts. We can't build any higher – it's not safe. We've no food. We've no medicine. The dinosaurs have got what we need – space. If this" – he waved his hands about – "DNA thing is the way to do it, then I say, go for it!"

There was an aura about Storm, a building rage, a tremble of her jaw. People had appeared from all the surrounding cabins, moving closer to see what the row was about. "You'd happily destroy entire species? Don't you care what that means?"

Spit came flying from Dell's mouth. "I care more about people than I do dinosaurs!" Even in the dark night Lincoln could see the red fury in his face. One of Stormchaser's hands was clenched into a fist. For a moment he thought she might actually punch Dell. But while her hands quivered, her anger faded. He could hear the hiss of her breath streaming through her pursed lips. Her voice was so quiet he was sure no one else but he and Dell could hear. "Maybe you have people worth caring about."

She turned and walked away so quickly that she vanished into the dark night in a matter of seconds.

Dell looked stunned. It took him a few minutes to gather himself. People around him started to murmur, dispersing quickly now there was nothing to watch.

Lincoln stayed silent. He felt a little sorry for Dell. But there was no point in offering him any comfort – he wouldn't be here much longer anyway. And, truth be told, that suited Lincoln. If Dell and Stormchaser weren't looking out for each other any more she might be more inclined to find support elsewhere. And tomorrow's Trial would be vital. He needed all the help he could get.

Dell let out an exasperated gasp and walked towards the nearest cabin, punching the edge of the door in pure frustration. He yelped. Another injury for tomorrow.

Lincoln folded his arms and watched Dell's retreating back. He had no idea why he was so drawn to Stormchaser. Leif was a much better prospect as an ally.

And Stormchaser's comments were worrying. Why was she defending the dinosaurs? He'd never heard that before – from anyone. Dinosaurs were dangerous. Everyone knew that.

But it didn't matter how curious he was about her. His family were his only priority. Of that he was sure.

And whether Stormchaser liked it or not, he intended to snatch those dinosaur eggs as quickly as possible and get back home to save his sister.

THIRTEEN

STORMCHASER

The atmosphere the next morning was subdued. People seemed nervous about the next Trial. Maybe it was the thought of failing? Or maybe it was the thought of *not* failing?

She shifted position at the table. What if people had heard her last night saying she didn't always believe the Stipulators? She rubbed her sweating palms on her legs. Her hand still smarted. Chances were, if she'd been reported, she would soon be on her way to the mines.

In the cold hard light of day it was easier to pick out the newcomers. It seemed ridiculous to think of them that way – after all, she'd only been in the Camp herself for two days. But she'd noticed three of them talking to Lincoln last night.

He seemed to be able to do that. Just sit down next to some perfect stranger and start talking. She wasn't like him. When he'd sat next to her two nights ago her tongue had stuck to the roof of her mouth and her brain had stopped functioning properly. Snappy replies were the best she could do.

It irked her. She'd always found talking to people difficult. It was probably one of the reasons she liked the plesiosaurs so much. They didn't care that she didn't make sense and they didn't talk back. At least not in a way anyone had noticed.

She was counting in her head, trying to work out how many people, from however many Camps, had passed the first Trial and been brought here. But then again, some of them hadn't actually passed the first Trial. She had to keep remembering that.

Dell hadn't said a word to her this morning, just stalked off to the other side of the servery to sit by himself. She was trying not to care.

"What number have you got?" The low voice in her ear made her jump.

Lincoln was right behind her, a grin stretching from one side of his face to the other. Didn't he realize this wasn't a day for grinning?

"Six hundred and twelve."

He lifted his eyebrows. "How long have you been counting?"

She stirred the food in the bowl in front of her. "About an hour. I figured everyone would come to breakfast. It might be the last meal they get here."

"They?" The implication was clear. He thought she wanted it to sound like she was sure she would qualify.

But her head was all over the place. One minute she

wanted just to pack up and go home, the next, she would wait until the Trials were finished. Then there was the thing she was trying not to think about after her argument with Dell – the thing that was so big, she didn't have space in her brain for it. The fact she might qualify and actually go to Piloria.

"How many did you get?"

He shrugged. "About the same. But I didn't count on some people going up twice for breakfast." He pointed to a larger-than-average boy in a bright blue T-shirt. "That's his third visit."

She choked on her breakfast. "Really?"

"Really." The grin disappeared and his face grew serious. "Do you think they brought everyone here?"

"What do you mean?"

"You said there were other Camps. Have they all been brought here for the last Trial?"

She paused. She could almost see his brain trying to make the calculations. Was this it? Six hundred people down to one hundred. A one in six chance of making it onto the boat?

He wanted it. She could tell how badly he wanted it and it almost made her feel guilty for being unsure. Her competitive edge battled with her rational mind.

"What did you and Dell fight about?"

Dell. Her eyes shot over to the corner of the room. But the table where he'd been sitting was empty. "Nothing." The word came out automatically.

Lincoln took a bite from the fruit he was holding. "Didn't sound like nothing."

"You heard us?"

"I might have heard something. I wasn't trying to eavesdrop, but you were pretty loud." He rolled his eyes. "I think the whole Camp heard you."

Storm sighed and let her spoon drop in her bowl, sloshing half of the contents onto the table. "This seemed like a good idea at the time," she said.

"And now?"

"Now, I'm not so sure. Dell's all I've got. I hate the fact we're not talking."

Lincoln kept eating. "Are you worried about the Trial?" He looked so cool about everything.

She shook her head. "Not so much. If I can do it, I can do it. If I can't, I go home." It seemed so simple when she said the words out loud. Maybe she would luck out. Maybe the Trial would be something impossible for her to do, especially with her injured hand. She tried to flex it underneath the tight bandages but it was held fast. One of the servery staff had wrapped it up for her. She wasn't so sure it was broken now, just bruised and very sore.

"Does it hurt?" Lincoln's voice had lost its easy tone. Guilt was written all over his face.

She could be mean. She could tell him she hadn't slept last night for the pain. But she knew his action hadn't been intentional. Would any of the other candidates have helped her the way he did?

She was conscious of the leap he'd taken. He'd put himself at risk for her.

"Sometimes. Hopefully the Trial today won't require much manual dexterity."

He gave the strangest kind of smile. "I've got a feeling today might be your day."

What an odd thing to say. But there was no chance to ask him what he meant, because the alarm sounded for the transporters. It was time to head for the next Trial. She stood up and took her dishes over to the counter, searching the room to see if Dell had reappeared. But there was no sign of him, so she walked slowly behind the others, filing their way out of the servery towards the vehicles.

The journey this time was much shorter. And the view even more familiar.

A loch. *Her* loch.

She glanced sideways at Lincoln. Was this what he'd meant? Had he known this would be the next Trial? Did he know she swam in this loch?

For a second she felt uncomfortable. Just exactly how much *did* Lincoln know? About her and about the Trials?

The Stipulators were standing nearby, Reban Don in front of them. He didn't waste any time addressing the crowd. "Today's Trial is based on your abilities in the water. We want you to dive, we want you to recover some items from the bottom of the loch. You have to work in teams of five this time." He waved his hand towards another Stipulator. "Juke Altair will give you the list of items you are to retrieve. Find the items you're assigned and bring them back here."

Storm couldn't wipe the smile from her face. This was too

good to be true. Her injured hand wouldn't stop her swimming. It might still be painful, but she would manage. It wouldn't stop her diving in the loch she dived in just about every day.

She felt a nudge at her shoulder and her stomach plummeted. Dell. She hadn't even considered him. He would hate this Trial. *Hate* it. There was every chance he would refuse to take part. He didn't even like being near the water – let alone *in* it.

But it wasn't Dell. And it wasn't Lincoln. It was the stocky man who'd beaten them up the cliff – Galen. "Do you know this area?" His voice was hoarse, his presence threatening.

She wasn't quite sure how to answer. Words were sticking in her throat. The lies just wouldn't populate on her tongue. His dark eyes were staring at her and it forced the truth from her mouth. "I grew up around here."

"Then it seems you have an unfair advantage. You know this loch. You'll know where they would hide things." His eyes narrowed. "I don't like it when someone has an advantage. I like the balance to be in my favour. You can be part of my team."

"But…but, I, I already…" She felt desperate. There was something about him. Something that made her want to run off in the other direction and not look back.

He leaned forward and hissed at her, "You'll do what I say."

"She's part of my team." Lincoln's hand slid into hers. For a girl who wasn't used to physical contact it was the most welcome touch she'd ever felt. Lincoln gestured over to where his three blond companions were standing. "We're working together. It's already arranged." His voice sounded authoritative – older than his years.

Galen spat at him, "When did you arrange this?"

"Yesterday." Lincoln didn't seem to have any problem letting lies spill from his lips. She nodded quickly despite the fact she didn't even know the names of the other guys. Could they even swim? Would they be any use?

Galen grabbed her arm, his fingers pinching her skin. "I don't think so, little boy. She's with me."

Even though Lincoln was half the breadth of Galen, he was still a head taller. He stepped right up, his hand clenching hers tightly. "You're wrong. Storm gets to decide which team she's on."

She held her breath. She hadn't thought he had it in him. Something about Galen was just terrifying, but Lincoln's jaw was clenched and his teeth were gritted.

"What's the problem?" Reban Don's voice boomed next to them.

Lincoln got there first. "No problem. Storm has chosen to be on our team. Galen was just making small talk."

Reban Don looked suspicious. There was no way he believed a single word of that.

His black cloak was swirling in the breeze from the lake. He glanced at her in disgust. She got the distinct impression that he couldn't bear being around her. So, when he finally spoke to her she almost jumped out her skin. "It appears –

for reasons that I can't fathom – that people are fighting over you. We have a Trial to commence. Which team are you on?"

"Lincoln's," she said quickly, letting her breath out in a rush. "I'm on Lincoln's team."

Galen threw up his hands in disgust and stalked off. "This isn't over," he muttered over his shoulder.

Reban Don gave her a cold, hard stare. "Don't delay one of the Trials again."

It sounded like a threat.

Lincoln's hand was still holding hers and he tugged her over to the other three guys. She pulled her hand away from his and tucked it under her other arm. He'd held it just a few seconds longer than necessary.

"What was that about?"

"Galen? Or Reban?"

He shook his head. "Oh, I know what Galen is about. Be careful. If you get in his way he'll do you harm." His steps slowed. "Reban Don. He seems to have an issue with you."

All her defences rose. "I'll admit, he doesn't seem to like me – but then, he doesn't seem to like anyone much. What does it matter anyway?"

She was angry now. How should she know why Reban had reacted so strangely to her? She'd wondered before if he'd known her mother, but no – her mother had refused to have anything to do with the Stipulators. She'd had a distinct dislike of them. She'd spent most of her life ignoring them, or turning in the other direction if they appeared. At the first flash of a black cloak her mother had always herded her away.

Lincoln stared at his palm for a second before rubbing it against his tunic. "You're right. It doesn't matter. Now let's get this Trial done. Come and meet the guys."

He nodded towards them. "Leif, Kronar, Rune – this is Stormchaser. She'll be joining our team."

She could see the wary glances shooting between them. This obviously hadn't been part of their plan. Lincoln had improvised.

One held out his hand towards her. She hesitated for a second – knowing it would be rude to refuse – before giving the quickest handshake in history. "I know this area. This won't be hard." Why was she saying this? Why was she trying to convince them to let her be part of their team?

There was a couple of seconds of silence. She could see Leif and Rune looking around, first at Galen, then at Reban Don. Kronar kept his eyes firmly on the lake.

She took a final glance to try and spot Dell. He had to be here somewhere. Would he want to join her?

There. He was standing with a group of people she didn't know. Did one of them bunk next to Dell? He was talking quite agitatedly. She could hear him warning them about the plesiosaurs in the loch. Would that stop any of them from attempting the Trial?

She would have to find a way to break the news to her team more gently – to demonstrate there was nothing to be afraid of.

Rune gave a sigh. "Right, let's find out what we're doing." He walked over to where the Stipulator was handing out the list of instructions. He wrinkled his nose as he read them on his way back. "This doesn't make a whole lot of sense."

He handed the piece of paper over to Lincoln. "Red, blue, purple and green. What does this mean?"

Stormchaser looked around. There was a sea of puzzled faces, no one seemed to understand. She could see people whispering, wondering whether to go and ask Reban for some clarification.

She walked over to the edge of the water. More than six hundred people would be diving in her loch. It felt like a violation. This was her place. *Hers*.

How would the plesiosaurs respond? She knew that Milo would be confused by the sudden invasion of his territory. She could only hope that he wouldn't be here – that he'd be out in the ocean right now.

She was trying to reason how this Trial would work. She spun around. "Come here." She waded into the water.

Lincoln frowned but took a few tentative steps behind her. The others followed, allowing the water to swish around their ankles. Storm was up to her waist by now. "The loch is deceptive. The first hundred steps or so aren't deep. But there's a platform here. If you aren't aware of it, it could take you by surprise."

"What do you mean, a platform?" Leif looked confused.

Storm held out her hands. "The ground falls away, almost as if you drop off the side of a cliff. The loch is much deeper than it looks. It's why the plesiosaurs can live here."

"There are dinosaurs in this lake?" Kronar looked horrified.

"Plesiosaurs," she corrected. "Friendly ones."

Rune was quick to jump in. "None of these creatures are friendly."

"Yes, yes they are."

"But they kill people! I've heard the reports."

Storm shook her head. "No. Plesiosaurs are not like that. Yes, boats have been overturned before by other marine reptiles. People have been lost in the great ocean. But not here. Not in this loch."

Her words sounded forced. This was more personal for her than any of the others could ever imagine.

"I'm not sure I want to dive in a loch that has dinosaurs. And to retrieve what? These instructions don't even make sense." Rune waved the piece of paper in his hand.

Storm shielded her eyes with her hand and looked out across the shimmering water, scanning the pale blue. "Look, there!" she hissed, keeping her voice low to stop others hearing her. People had started to wade into the water around them. They might not understand their task, but they understood the concept of diving in the loch.

"I can't see anything." Lincoln was right next to her shoulder.

"Look again, there under the water, can you see something yellow?" She pointed with her finger. "And there, there, and there again. We must have to dive to collect one of the coloured items."

Kronar tilted his head. "But there's only yellow. What

about the other colours?" The furrow across his brow was growing deeper by the second.

"They must be further in. Off the edge of the platform. We'll probably have to go much deeper to get them." She spun round. "How long can you hold your breath for?"

Lincoln groaned and ignored the question. "Why isn't yellow on our list?"

"I'm assuming it's random. I guess we'll just need to go a bit further in." She kept wading. "Let's go, guys."

Leif and Rune hurried to join her while Lincoln stopped to talk to Kronar. It was a few minutes before Lincoln joined them, shoulder-deep in water.

"What kept you?"

His eyes darted to Leif. "There's no point us all being in the loch." He pointed up towards a nearby hill. "I told Kronar to get to a good vantage point. That way he might be able to see the colours a bit more easily and shout to us." He swished his arm around, creating waves. "The water here is remarkably clear, maybe he'll be able to see something we can't."

Leif and Rune nodded readily in agreement. Several other teams had started swimming around them, one was even nearing a yellow sunken box. Lincoln was quick to change the focus. "Let's get started."

FOURTEEN

STORMCHASER

Their feet had barely left the platform when Rune spotted the first green box beneath them. He signalled and then dived down. Storm hesitated. This was her lake. She was familiar with everything beneath the surface but she was having to learn what it meant to be part of a team. A few body lengths beneath them, Rune seemed to be struggling. He was trying to hoist the box into his arms and pushing off from the bottom with his feet. He broke the surface next to them and thrust the box towards Lincoln.

"Whoa!" Lincoln sunk beneath the surface for a few seconds then spluttered up again.

"What is it?" She put her hand underneath the box and was struck by the sheer weight of it. "What on earth…?"

Rune's face was scarlet. "I had no idea it would be so heavy." He was treading water, trying to take some of the weight in his free hand. "We're all going to need to haul this back to the shore."

Lincoln nodded and they tried to distribute the weight between them. But trying to swim in formation around a box was virtually impossible. It kept slipping from their grasp. It was a relief to finally reach the edge of the platform and wade to the shore again.

Storm placed her hands on her wet tunic top, then pulled it over her head. If all the boxes were like that, she'd be a fool to let anything else weigh her down. Lincoln and the other guys averted their eyes for a second, then finally realized she'd something on underneath. Granted, the dark-coloured vest was skimpy, but at least it kept everything covered.

Storm could almost hear the intake of breath behind her. Feel their probing eyes on her skin, looking at the ugly scar tissue around her back and sides.

But they were wise. No one spoke. No one said a thing.

They followed suit, pulling their shirts over their heads. Kronar had reached the top of the hill. He put his hands to his mouth to shout, then shook his head.

"What's wrong? Why isn't he telling us which way to swim?"

Storm tried to follow his line of vision. She was watching another team struggle out of the water with one of the yellow boxes. "Do you think the colours have anything to do with the weight?" She wasn't sure she'd be able to lift anything heavier than the one they'd just fumbled to shore.

Lincoln shook his head. "I have no idea." His eyes were

fixed on Kronar, watching as he pointed down towards one of the other teams. It took a few seconds before his face broke into a smile.

He lowered his voice. "Look, Kronar's pointing at that girl in the bright purple tunic. I'm guessing that means he can see one of the purple boxes under the water."

"Then why on earth hasn't he just shouted to tell us?" asked Rune. She saw the flicker of recognition on his scarlet face. He was finally beginning to breathe a little more easily. "I get it. If he shouts to tell us, everyone else will hear too." He glanced around. "We're the only team with anyone standing on the hill. Once they realize he can see the coloured boxes they'll all send someone up there. We'll lose the advantage."

Kronar was watching the whole area around the loch. For a second he glanced straight at them, then he gestured with one hand to the near side of the loch.

Lincoln nodded. "I guess we know where our purple box is."

Storm took a deep breath. "I think we'll all need to go again. Even if one person dives to retrieve the box, the rest of us will need to help get it back to shore."

The second box was tougher than the first. The water was still clear, but the bed of the loch was littered with debris. The purple box was so heavy it had sunk deeper into the mud and when Leif tried to retrieve it he sent clouds of muddy water rushing up towards them, obliterating their view.

When Leif finally surfaced he was desperate for air. "It was stuck in the mud," he gasped. It took some effort to drag the box through the water, leaving them breathless at the side of the loch.

Kronar signalled to them again. He gestured towards another team. One of the members wore a striking blue tunic.

"He's pointing towards the middle of the loch. How deep is it there?"

Rune looked worried and Storm could see Leif mumbling to Lincoln. "It's deep," was all she could squeak out. There was no point going into detail. There was no point telling any of them they'd have to hold their breath for over a minute to get down there and back up. They would panic.

They just had to get on with it. "Look, we don't dive till we get to the middle of the loch. We go down then we come straight back up. It's a long way to get the box back to shore. This one's going to be tough." She looked up to the hill. "Maybe we should ask Kronar to come with us. It could take all five of us."

"No." The boys spoke in unison around her. It was bad enough standing in soaking wet clothes with the temperature dropping around them and the wind picking up. But their voices made the chills on her skin feel even worse.

"What's the deal, guys? What aren't you telling me?"

Again. The quick glances. It ignited a fire of frustration inside her. Lincoln touched her arm. It felt like a sting and she yanked it back. "What? What is it?" Her voice had risen and several of the other groups looked over towards them.

As the boys closed in around her, Lincoln whispered in her ear, "Kronar can't swim."

"*What?*" This time her voice was even louder and she took a step back out of the circle, her head whipping from one face to the other. "You're joking, right?" Her eyes fixed on Kronar on the hill. He was standing with his hands on his hips, scanning the loch, still looking for the final box. His head eventually turned towards the group and he gave a little start seeing all their faces fixed on his.

Storm spun to face Lincoln. "You pulled me into this team when you knew he couldn't swim?" She was losing focus. She couldn't see past Lincoln's bright green eyes. "This could wreck everything. What if we need that extra body to pull up the last two boxes? We'll be out." The competitive edge in her was bubbling to the surface again. Was this about winning the trial, or giving her the opportunity to join the expedition?

For a second she thought she saw a tiny flare of panic in Lincoln's eyes, but it vanished in a flash. When he spoke, his voice was calm and measured. "I didn't know. I only found out when we got here. And why should it be an issue?"

"It's more than an issue." She waved her arm. "Kronar is virtually getting a free pass." She glared at Leif and Rune. "You two obviously knew. Why didn't you say anything?"

Leif was clearly annoyed. "Get a grip, Storm. This Trial is a team game. We could have been up against anything today. If it had been running, Kronar would have outpaced you within seconds, and he scaled that cliff yesterday better than any of us. Everyone has different skills. What are yours, apart from knowing this loch and being a grouch?"

She didn't even blink. "I can hold my breath for around four minutes. What about you?"

The words were out before she could think. Rune's mouth practically fell open and Lincoln's eyes widened. But Leif looked suspicious. "You can *what*?"

She folded her arms across her chest. "I can hold my breath for four minutes."

He wasn't buying it. "And why would you have to do that?"

Something clicked inside her brain. Kronar was still scouring the loch. He hadn't found the final red box yet. "I don't just have basic knowledge of this loch. I've mapped it out. I know every single part of it – including the caves where the plesiosaurs nest."

"They what?" Lincoln's mouth gaped open.

"They nest here, in caves under the water. I think there's a link from the loch to the ocean, but I've never found it."

Rune was shaking his head. "You've been in the caves where the plesiosaurs nest?"

"Yes." Their reactions were beginning to unnerve her. She'd never told anyone about this before. Not even Dell.

"But why?"

"Why not?" She wasn't about to give everything away. "What's important is that I think that's where the final box must be hidden."

Leif looked bewildered. "What makes you think that?"

"Look at Kronar. He hasn't stopped looking since he got up there. He's spotted all the other boxes quickly enough.

You've already said that the water in the loch is remarkably clear. If a red box was anywhere within his line of sight he would have spotted it by now."

Silence. They all looked out over the loch.

Lincoln spoke first. "Let's not think about it yet." He glanced around. "Most of the other teams have managed to get their second box. We need to concentrate on the blue box. If we can't do that, there's no point even considering the final one."

The rest of the team nodded. She was still mad. She was still furious at being manoeuvred into a team with a non-functioning member. But there was another reason why she was being so snarky, one she couldn't explain to them.

It was being *here*. Being at the loch where it had happened. The loch was usually a private place for her. A place where she could have time to think about how close she'd come to dying. A place where, she'd realized, she could be truly on her own. The place where she'd forged her real-life connection with the plesiosaurs – where Milo had saved her. And now it was being invaded.

All her emotions were on edge. Maybe that's why she was so rattled. Lincoln was right. She was getting ahead of herself. They might not even be able to retrieve the third box. That would be the end of the competition for them all.

It made up her mind.

"Let's do this. Let's get organized."

Rune stared at her. "Well, it makes sense for you to dive. Do you think you'll need help to get the box to the surface?"

She didn't hesitate. Her head was clearing. "I know I'll need help. I can reach the box easily, but I've only got strength in one hand. I can't manage the weight on my own."

Leif nudged her. "Then I'll dive with you. Are you two happy to tread water and help get the box to the side?"

Lincoln and Rune nodded. Rune pointed to the hill. "Look, Kronar's moved. He's pointing to the far side of the loch. Do you think he's spotted the red box?"

Storm tilted her head, trying to imagine what he was thinking. She knew in her bones that the red box would be in the cave. What could Kronar have spotted? But Lincoln realized first.

"No. I think he's stating the obvious. We don't need to try and drag the box back here. Taking it to the loch's edge over there is a shorter distance. It will be easier." He slapped his hand to his forehead. "We should have thought of it last time. Kronar could walk it around the edge of the loch while we concentrate on the fourth."

Storm had moved back into the water. After being out of it for a few minutes, it felt even colder this time. Why hadn't she thought of that? Reban had shown them where the boxes had to be left. He hadn't made any comment on how they should get there.

It annoyed her. She was used to thinking for herself. But this time around, she'd just followed the crowd. It wasn't like her at all.

The water rippled around her as the others approached. She didn't speak. She just took a deep breath, put her head down and started front-crawling across the loch.

All about her, others were swimming in a variety of directions. She glanced around quickly, trying to catch a glimpse of Dell. Finally, she saw him at the edge of the loch helping lift a pink box out of the water with the rest of his team. He seemed to be doing fine.

They passed over the top of an orange box on their way to the blue. Off to the left another team were struggling with a green box, which kept slipping from their grip and falling back to the loch floor. It took a few minutes to reach the water above the blue box. Storm felt confident. The loch floor might be deep here, but she was certain she could reach it. Leif didn't look quite so sure.

She started treading water. "Are you ready? Let's go." She took a deep breath and dived underneath the water, keeping her eyes open until she reached the loch bed. Her breath held easily, while Leif took another few seconds to reach her. He joined her, crouching on the other side of the box. A few little bubbles escaped from the side of his mouth. He gave her a quick nod and gripped on to his side of the box as they both pushed off from the sandy floor.

The weight unbalanced Storm for a few seconds. If she'd been on her own, it would have taken her straight back down, but with Leif's help she powered upwards. As soon as they approached the surface, Rune and Lincoln dived a little under the water to help take the weight.

It worked. Kronar shouted to them immediately after they surfaced and this time the journey to the edge of the loch wasn't quite so long, or quite so difficult. Maybe Kronar was more useful than she'd thought. He pulled the box from their hands as soon as they reached the edge.

"I'm sorry. I can't spot the red box anywhere. I've even walked further around the loch, but it's nowhere in sight."

"It's okay," Lincoln panted. "Storm thinks she knows where it is."

"Really?" said Kronar, surprised. "Where?"

"In caves at the bottom of the loch."

Kronar's face visibly paled. "What?"

Rune shook his head. "Never mind. Take the blue box back over to the starting point. Now, whereabouts are the caves, Storm?" It was clear he didn't want to waste any time. And he was right. From a look around, Storm could see they weren't the only team on box three.

She turned in the water to face the other side of the loch. She gave a nod of her head. "Over there. About two-thirds of the way across."

Lincoln frowned. "You said you could hold your breath for four minutes. Is that how long it takes to get to the caves and back?"

She shook her head. "No. But it probably takes about a minute and a half."

The guys exchanged worried glances and Kronar thumped the blue box down behind them. "That's crazy."

But Rune stayed focused. "I have no idea how long I can hold my breath for." He shot a look at Kronar. "You'll need to time us."

Storm nodded, it made sense. She watched as all three took a deep breath then stuck their heads under the water. She floated on her back while she waited, looking up at the darkening sky around them and counting in her head.

Leif was first to surface, spluttering with his face red and eyes bloodshot. Rune followed about ten seconds later. Lincoln was last, his face the same shade of white that Kronar's had been a few moments earlier. It didn't suit him. It ruined his poster boy good looks. It took him a few seconds to realize that he'd surfaced last.

Storm was relieved. There was something sort of reassuring about diving with Lincoln. She might barely know him, but he'd already put himself on the line for her. The other three guys seemed fine, but she didn't yet know if she could trust them – especially as she'd just made sure they were mad at her.

Teamwork. She just couldn't embrace the concept, having spent most of her life alone. Her reaction to Kronar's secret could have broken the team apart.

"Look." Rune pointed to another team struggling out of the loch. "That's their last box. We're falling behind."

Kronar stood back up, heaving the blue one into his arms. "I'll take this one back and then meet you at the other side of the loch. It will be easier to get the red box from there."

Leif gave him a small nod. "See you soon."

They started to swim across the loch. This was Storm's favourite part, her long arms slicing through the water. But it was best when she was alone. Or when Milo was by her side. She slowed and started treading water, shaking the wet strands of hair out of her eyes. "We're here. It's just beneath us."

The others stopped and started treading water next to her. They all looked down through the clear water. "I can't see anything," said Leif. "I can't see any caves."

"They're definitely there. There's lots more vegetation in the middle of the loch. We have to go through it to reach the cave entrance."

She could see the expression on Lincoln's face as he watched the long, dark green strands of kelp oscillating in the water below like an underwater forest. "It's fine," she said quickly. "I think it's nature's way of hiding the cave entrance. After all, if a plesiosaur can get through there, so can we."

He swallowed and gave a nod, but he didn't look convinced. She was beginning to worry – she'd never be able to get the box up here on her own. She needed his muscle power to help with the weight. She reached over and touched his arm. "Are you ready? Take some deep breaths before we go. If you get into trouble, just come back up to the surface."

She was trying to be reassuring, but her tone must have been wrong – which wasn't unusual for her – because there was more than a flicker of annoyance on his face. "I'm fine. Are *you* ready?"

She tucked her hair behind her ears, slowing her movements and focusing on the hill in the background.

In. Out. In. Out. This was the way she always prepared for the caves. She needed to concentrate.

She sucked in a final deep breath, gave a nod and dived underneath the rippling waves. Down, down towards the dark green forest. The strands tickled her face and nose, but she was ready for it, pushing on forward through the kelp.

The strands parted easily and the pale light from up above vanished as she swam through the cave entrance. Her eyes were still open and even in the much-reduced light she could pick out the red box easily. She punched upwards in triumph, sending a swirl through the water.

She felt the tips of Lincoln's fingers connect with her toes. He was right behind her. She didn't know whether to be happy or sad. Up till now she'd been the only person to see Milo's home.

Then it struck her. Of course she wasn't. She'd always assumed this place was hers alone, after she discovered the caves by mistake when she was training herself to dive for longer. But someone else had obviously known they were here. Her eyes adjusted to the dimming light. The box wasn't just painted red. Oh no. The paint almost glowed. Whoever had positioned this box had known exactly how dark it would be down here.

She moved towards the box, crouching on one side and waiting for Lincoln to join her. It only took him a few seconds. They had to be quick, after all. She slid her fingers under two corners of the box, feeling the dark silt underneath. Lincoln did the same and the box shifted slightly. They lifted, adjusting to the weight. This box seemed even heavier than the others, but maybe that was because they'd had to dive deeper and expend more energy.

She could feel the burn in her thighs again as she pushed off from the loch bed. Her legs kicked madly trying to steer them towards the entrance of the cave, but they were holding a dead weight. It was much harder than before. When they finally reached the entrance, Lincoln signalled to her to stop for a second. She tried to adjust her side of the box to get a better grip. Then they pushed upwards again, brushing through the fronds, but the box lurched suddenly to Lincoln's side and tumbled from her grasp. She waved her hands through the thick kelp.

Lincoln had vanished.

Panic flooded through her. She'd only ever seen plesiosaurs in this water. She'd always felt safe. But what if there was something else here?

All thoughts of the box vanished. The pressure was building in her chest, her body was crying out for air. She continued to flail through the kelp, trying to push it from her view.

There. A flash of skin. She grabbed for it. Lincoln's leg, caught fast in the stringy kelp.

His face was scarlet underwater, his eyes bulging. He was panicking, his hands tugging at the kelp wound around his ankle, tightening its grip.

She tried to help, slapping his hands away as best she could underwater but he was lashing out blindly, his eyes darting up to the surface.

She knew instantly what to do. She pushed upwards, away from Lincoln and erupted from the surface. Ignoring the shouts from Leif and Rune, she filled her lungs as quickly as she could and dived straight back down. She was trying to stay calm. Trying not to think of the seconds ticking past. She could see him underneath her, his arms still flailing madly in the water. She grabbed his shoulders, ignoring the terror on his face as she tried to push his arms to his sides. There was no time for hesitation. The panic was beginning to subside, as the last dregs of oxygen left his system. She pressed her lips tight to his.

His eyes widened, a few final seconds of awareness still there. She slid a hand across his chest and nipped the skin around the bottom of his ribs.

The effect was instantaneous. He sucked in a breath of the air she had stored in her cheeks. Then she dived down to his foot to start loosening the kelp around his ankle. As soon as he was free she gave him an almighty push, powering him upwards, and followed on behind.

His body seemed to kick into gear on the journey to the surface, hope and fear resurrecting his weakened muscles to push him onwards.

They broke the surface at the same time, where Leif and Rune were ready and waiting, still treading water. "What happened?" They grabbed Lincoln's arms to help support him.

Storm could only pant, as she tried to suck more air into her lungs. Lincoln's eyes were closed but his chest was moving up and down.

"He got stuck," she said eventually, her eyes never leaving him. "His foot got tangled in the kelp." Her lips were stinging and confusion swirled around her mind. She'd put her lips on his. It had been necessary – Lincoln could have died. She'd had to do it. But for some strange reason it hadn't felt like saving someone's life. It felt like something else. She just didn't know what.

"Why did you come back without him?" Rune's tone was accusing.

She tried to focus again. "I had to get him some air. He was panicking. I couldn't get near his foot to free it."

Lincoln's eyes flickered open, his breathing was steadying now. He shook his head, showering them all with droplets of water. Storm moved forward, pressing a hand to his chest. "Are you okay?" Now she'd touched his lips it didn't seem too odd to touch another part of him. His gaze met hers. He seemed stunned. Those green eyes of his. It was almost like he was seeing parts of her that hadn't existed before. Thank goodness she was treading water, otherwise she'd have frozen to the spot. She bit her tender lips. Trying not to think what might have happened.

"Hey! What's happening?" Kronar had reached the side of the loch. "Where's the box."

Storm pulled her gaze away and looked downwards. "We got it. We got it out of the cave. We just haven't got it to the surface. It seems heavier than the rest."

Leif spoke quickly. "Is it a straight dive down?"

She nodded. "The three of us can do it and get it over to

Kronar." It was so much easier to talk about something practical than try and make sense of the thoughts in her head.

"No." Lincoln's voice cut through. "Give me another minute. We'll all do it together."

"You don't need to. You already got the box out of the cave, give yourself a chance to recover." Guilt was flooding through her. He'd seen the kelp but he wasn't experienced at diving in the loch. She should have warned him it could tangle, but she hadn't wanted him to panic.

"Just wait." His voice was hoarse, but fierce. There was no arguing with him.

Her arms were becoming heavy treading water. Swimming was so much easier than trying to stay in one spot. "Let's get this over with. One attempt. If we don't get it, then that's it."

Her eyes were sweeping around the loch. One team had finished. The rest of the teams seemed to have stopped at three boxes, bewildered as to where the fourth could be. She'd thought there was only one red box in the cave. But maybe there were more and she just hadn't seen them.

Rune spoke. "Are we ready? Good. Then one, two, three…"

They disappeared underwater. Storm led the way through the kelp to the silt at the bottom of the loch and the red box. This time it was easier, there were four to share the load. They pushed off in unison, but instead of going straight back up, they pushed in a diagonal direction towards Kronar at the shore.

It was still tough. Her arm burned, her fingers ached at the pressure on them. As they broke the surface they could see Kronar impatiently holding his arms out and urging them onwards. He struggled to take the box from the water, grasping hold of an edge and tipping it towards him, rolling it to gather some momentum.

Rune pulled himself from the water and tried to help, while Leif pushed Lincoln out, dragging him onto the wet ground. Lincoln collapsed, rolling onto his back and breathing heavily.

Storm looked anxiously at the figures of Rune and Kronar stumbling along with the box between them. She wanted to help, she really did. But the diving, the weight of the boxes, rescuing Lincoln – suddenly everything caught up with her; her legs turned to jelly and she felt like she was about to be sick everywhere.

Leif shook his head. "Let them do it. We're good now. Hardly anyone else will have got all four boxes."

Storm pulled herself further up the bank onto some cool grass. She was trembling. Thank goodness they were finished. She couldn't do another Trial if her life depended on it. Every single bit of energy she possessed was gone.

She pushed herself up onto her elbows. "Linc? Are you okay?"

He didn't even look at her. He just fixed on the darkening clouds up above. "I don't get it."

Leif turned to look at him as Storm felt her skin prickle. It was the *way* he said it.

Leif screwed up his face. "Don't get what?"

"Don't get what it is between Storm and those creatures. Why would you even know where the plesiosaurs nest?" The unspoken accusation lingered in the air.

"It's just…I just…know. I live around here." She could feel their gazes on her. She was under scrutiny. And it was unnerving. She didn't really know these people. It didn't matter that they'd completed this challenge together. She still didn't want to share. She'd shared too much already. Too much of herself – too much personal space.

"Do you think anyone else has finished apart from that one other team?" It was a poor attempt at diversion. But she didn't care. Desperate times called for desperate measures.

Kronar and Rune were still struggling around the side of the loch with the box. Several groups were sitting on the ground, with their boxes stacked in front of them. Only one other team seemed to have four boxes, all different colours from theirs. Galen's. Of course.

He looked at Storm and laughed out loud. "Seems you weren't such an advantage after all," he shouted over.

"How did they manage that?" She pointed towards the other team. "I didn't see any other boxes in the cave. Were we the only team that had a box in there?"

Lincoln sat up and frowned. "Yellow, orange, pink and white. We didn't have any of those colours. Did you see any of those boxes?"

Leif looked puzzled. "We saw those yellow boxes at the

beginning. But I don't remember any of the other colours – then again, I wasn't looking for them."

"But surely going into the caves was the hardest task? It doesn't seem fair if the other teams didn't have to do that." Storm was standing now, hands on hips.

Lincoln pushed himself up. "Is there somewhere in the loch that's equally as hidden? Maybe you don't know this place as well as you think."

She shook her head fiercely. How dare he? "Of course I do. There's no other place that's as hard to get to." She was indignant. "Why should any other team get it easy? It's not fair."

The alarm sounded. The end of the Trial. People were still in the water, some still trying to get boxes ashore. The Stipulators appeared with a huge pile of cloths and handed them out to all the participants. Lincoln held out his hand to Leif, pulling him up, and they trudged around the edge of the loch.

By the time they reached the starting point most of the participants had returned. People were muttering to each other, all wondering what would happen next.

Storm didn't have any doubt. Reban Don fixed her with his disapproving gaze, before moving to address the crowd.

"The transporters will transfer you back to Camp where dinner is waiting for you all. Thank you for participating in the Trial. We'll announce the Finalists later when we've had a chance to analyse the results."

No one had any idea what that meant. Kronar spoke first. "What is there to analyse? You either completed the Trial or you didn't. I don't get it."

"Me neither." Lincoln looked ready to punch the nearest wall, a mask of fury covering his face. "After all this, he tells us to go back to the Camp and wait?"

Leif shrugged. "I'm quite happy to wait so long as they're feeding us."

"Me too," said Rune. "Let's go." As he turned to leave, he gave Storm a considered look and then nodded. "Glad you were on our team today. I think my sisters would like you."

They hadn't spoken about their families. "You have sisters?" she asked.

Leif laughed out loud. "Boy, does he."

Rune smiled. "I have six. I'm the only boy." He winked. "I think that makes me the favourite."

"Wow." Six sisters. She couldn't even imagine. She didn't think anyone had a family that large in Ambulus City. Big families were frowned upon.

The three Nordens started to walk towards the nearest transporter. As she watched them go, Storm realized she was starting to warm to them.

The sun was dropping and the wind was picking up. Storm scanned the crowd, trying to see if she could spot Dell. But there were too many people. It was impossible to find him in the crowd.

Lincoln appeared in front of her, blocking her view and handing her two cloths. "One for your hair and one for your body. You're trembling, Storm. You're freezing. You should get out of those wet clothes."

She looked down and folded her arms across her chest. She couldn't even remember where she'd dumped her tunic top this morning, so she wrapped one cloth around her shoulders and wound the other around her hair. She felt instant relief when her wet hair was covered.

The look behind Lincoln's eyes was gone. That glance that he'd given her in the lake after she'd saved him. It was the first time she felt as if she'd seen behind his tightly fitting mask. But the moment was lost. And she was secretly relieved.

FIFTEEN

LINCOLN

There was a strange backpack at the bottom of his bed. Lincoln looked around the room. People were still unloading from the transporters after the loch task in various states of exhaustion. Maybe someone had left it there by mistake?

But people just trudged past, no one giving his backpack a second glance. He checked the room out again. There. Another one at the other side of the room. The familiar stocky frame of Galen approached and picked it up. A smirk crossed his face before he tossed it to the floor and stretched out on his low-slung cot.

Now Lincoln was curious. The backpack was heavy. Not nearly as heavy as the boxes at the loch, but a close second. It would be tough work moving anywhere with that on your back. He unfastened the top and looked inside.

Several tunics, underwear and socks. A torch. Kindling.

Rope and a harness, along with metal clips for climbing. Balm. A kit with some kind of chemicals. A mat and bedroll. A water canteen.

The hair stood up on the back of his neck and his mouth instantly dried. Did this mean what he thought it meant?

Because this was all the equipment he would need for Piloria.

Well, that wasn't exactly true. What he'd really need for Piloria would be some kind of enormous weapon or invisible force field that would shield him from man-eating dinosaurs. But since that didn't seem like a possibility, he guessed this was as good as it got.

He stuffed the backpack under his cot. No one else seemed to have noticed it. Some people had changed out of their wet clothes and gone straight to the servery for food. Others were still washing. He pulled some of his own clothes from his bag and headed for the showers. Ten minutes later he was in the servery.

It was the most crowded he'd ever seen it and he didn't recognize anyone. He sat at the first free table and started eating quickly, listening to the voices murmuring all around him:

"They'll announce the Finalists once everyone has eaten."

"I don't think any team completed that task today, so how can they decide who the Finalists are?"

"I've changed my mind. I don't want to go to Piloria anyway. We'd probably be snapped in half by a T-rex within the first few steps."

"D'you think we can grab some seconds before they send us home?"

Lincoln was contemplating seconds. He didn't have any doubt in his head he must have qualified. His only anxiety was about the people he'd be heading to Piloria with.

There was some arguing at the other end of the servery. Tensions were high. Two days of good food and now people were contemplating going back to a life of rationing and cornup. It was funny how food could fray tempers.

Lincoln ducked as a serving tray came flying across the room, closely followed by a body landing on a table nearby. He waited to see if any Stipulators would appear. But it seemed they were all too busy. The two-man fracas started to suck other people in as fists were thrown.

Lincoln stayed calm; he finished his dinner and walked back over to the servery to deposit his tray. Several others were clamouring near the door, but he just folded his arms and stood against the wall waiting for the tensions to settle.

Galen walked past as an alarm sounded and the fighting people sprang apart. "It seems like you and I are going to the same place. Wanna take bets on how long you'll last?" He'd obviously noticed the backpack on Lincoln's bunk.

Lincoln ignored him. But despite his outward air of calm, he had to admit to himself that today's Trial – what had happened – had unnerved him.

The clear water of the loch had felt safe at first, unoppressive. Although he'd been anxious about coming face-to-face with a plesiosaur, it hadn't struck him as dangerous. Danger hadn't even entered his mind.

But the feeling of blind panic had quickly overwhelmed him. And it was something entirely new to him. Lincoln didn't do panic. He did rational, methodical thinking.

On the few occasions he'd had something to be fearful of, his brain had helped him to find a way out. Not so today.

Today his brain had turned to complete and utter mush. He hadn't been able to get past the fact he couldn't breathe. The fact his lungs were beginning to burn. When Storm had headed to the surface he'd thought she was deserting him. Memories of his sister had flashed before his eyes. He'd never see her again – he wouldn't be able to save her, and the Trials would all have been for nothing.

It hadn't even occurred to him that Storm was trying to get more oxygen. By the time she'd put her lips to his he'd barely felt conscious.

Stormchaser. She hadn't said a single word back on the transporter. She hadn't even looked at him, just closed her eyes and given a few gentle snores.

Whilst he'd felt guilty about injuring Storm's hand yesterday, he still hadn't been sure whether to consider her a rival or an ally.

But today had changed everything. Now, they were even. Now, he might even owe her.

He'd helped her complete a Trial.

She'd saved his life.

He was more curious about her than he should be. He'd

started to look for her wherever he went. He'd started to notice things that wouldn't even have occurred to him before – what upset her, why she looked so sad sometimes, and how the independence he'd admired at first was now beginning to look like self-preservation.

Someone nudged him from behind, pushing him in the direction of the door, as everyone headed outside. He followed them out to find Reban Don standing in the middle of the sandy courtyard. He was surrounded by the rest of the Stipulators.

A silence fell over the crowd. There was just the sound of people breathing. Everyone waiting. Everyone watching.

Lincoln still couldn't see Storm, but he caught sight of three blond heads – Leif, Kronar and Rune.

The edges of Reban Don's mouth flickered upwards. He liked this, Lincoln could tell. He liked being the focus of everyone's attention.

"Trialists. I thank you for your participation. Our decision has been made. We've scored you on every Trial – the test, the cliff climb, the diving and the teamwork. Remember why you did this and what you hope to achieve. Remember the rewards. Food, health care and better housing."

"Teamwork was part of the Trial, I didn't know that," someone muttered next to Lincoln.

"Our *Finalists* are…" Reban paused for effect. It worked. You could hear a single grain of sand dropping on the ground.

"Froan Jung, Tena Koll, Lopus Thran." Lincoln didn't recognize any of the names, or any of the faces. He watched the named people move over to a giant circle on the ground behind Reban. Very theatrical. But then people would be watching this broadcast in the city auditoriums all over Earthasia.

Another few names were called every ten seconds. He didn't recognize any in the second batch either. Then one familiar woman, he'd seen her at registration. By the time half the places were filled, Lincoln realized he hardly knew any of them. Knew nothing of their skills, or their potential to be allies.

Galen was next. He was smug, conceited and walked straight into the middle of the circle as the rest of Finalists parted to let him enter. He raised his hands above his head. "Bring it on!" he roared. "No dinosaur can hide from me."

There was a smattering of applause, followed by a lot of anxious glances. Reban ignored him completely and kept calling out names.

Finally, some people that he knew. Leif, Rune and Kronar. It must be his turn any second now.

But the names kept coming and his wasn't one of them. He started trying to count the number of people in the circle. Maybe he'd been wrong about the backpack. Maybe it wasn't his. Maybe it should have gone to someone who'd bunked alongside him.

"Stormchaser Knux."

His heart pounded in his chest. If Storm and the three Norden guys had made it, he *must* have qualified.

Reban stopped. He watched as Storm made her way to

the edge of the circle. There was no sign of Dell, and Storm didn't look particularly happy to be there. Maybe she would decide not to go.

But the way Reban watched her made Lincoln uncomfortable. It was too intense. Too direct. He hadn't looked at any of the others like that.

People started to murmur around him. They thought it was finished. They thought all the Finalists had been called.

Lincoln's legs started to move, striding forward towards Reban. The chance to save his sister was slipping through his fingers. His indignation was making him bold. His determination was driving him to act in a way he never would before.

He was good enough. He knew he was good enough. He had every right to be there.

He walked through the black-clothed Stipulators until he was right under Reban Don's nose. He didn't speak, just folded his arms across his chest and tilted his head in question.

The mumbling had stopped. If the silence had seemed intense as Reban Don announced the list, now it was electrifying.

The temptation to fill the silence was overwhelming. Out of the corner of his eye he could see Storm with her hand over her mouth, watching with her violet eyes wide.

Patience had never been Lincoln's strong suit – particularly when it came to his sister.

But right now it was vital. So, he stood. And stared.

Reban's lip curled upward into a sneer. His dark gaze unwavering.

"The last Finalist is Lincoln Kreft." And with a sweep of his black cape, he was gone.

SIXTEEN

STORMCHASER

The first thing she felt was pride followed by a surge of disappointment. Dell's name hadn't been called. She rushed back into the dorm room. He was stuffing things in his bag.

"The transporter is pulling up. Everyone get ready," shouted one of the Stipulators.

"Dell. Dell, I'm sorry. I'm sorry you weren't chosen."

He looked up. She couldn't read the expression on his face. "I'm not."

"But I thought—"

"You thought what? That I would want to go to Piloria because you did? That I would want to be trapped on a continent full of dinosaurs? Are you mad? I knew I wouldn't qualify, Storm, because I didn't go in the loch. My feet didn't even get wet. Did you even think I would?" He reached over and grabbed her by the tops of her arms. "We came here for the food, Storm. The food. Nothing else. I've had a few days of eating well and now I'm done. Just like you should be too."

He was tugging at her emotions, tugging at their connection. "But think of what we could learn… We could see a place that only a few hundred people have been to."

He shook his head and gave her a look that chilled her to the bone. "Look at you…the wonder in your eyes. You must be mad. I think you've lost your mind." He waved his arm. "Why would anyone do this? Have you taken a good look at some of your travelling companions? What about Galen? I don't want to share air with that guy, let alone go on a journey to the dinosaur continent with him. He'll throw you to a T-rex in a heartbeat. He's lethal. Why would you want it, Storm? What possible reason do you have to go?"

It was a good question. And it was one she couldn't fully answer even in her own head. But curiosity had got the better of her. She wanted to see the dinosaur continent. She wanted to know what it looked like, what it smelled like, what it felt like. She wanted to visit a place where you weren't surrounded by tall grey blocks everywhere you looked. She'd dreamed of casting her gaze over a land that was green instead of grey.

A land where she might actually experience moments of silence. Living in an overpopulated city meant that she was constantly surrounded by people and noise. Half your life could be spent in a queue for rations. The only quiet she found around here was at the loch – and Piloria could have a whole continent's worth of lochs.

She knew there were killer dinosaurs. But she couldn't believe every single species of dinosaur was a danger. This was a chance to find out more. Maybe even a chance to connect with other dinosaurs, like she had with Milo.

The only thing she definitely wasn't sure about was retrieving the dinosaur eggs.

Part of her wanted to do it; part of her felt, if she could retrieve the eggs from the killer dinosaurs, it could help to protect the gentler creatures, like Milo. But could she really believe the Stipulators' plans?

Dell was waiting. He was glaring at her accusingly – like he thought she was betraying him.

She couldn't stop her voice from shaking. "I don't know. I don't know why I want to go. I just do. I want to see it. I want to see if what they tell us about the dinosaurs is true."

"And if it isn't – do you think they'll actually let you come back and tell anyone?"

His words stung. She hadn't even considered that. It hadn't even entered her mind that they might not be allowed to talk about what they found.

He touched her arm. "Come home, Storm. Stop this. Stop this now." He picked his backpack up and slung it over his shoulder.

Home. She hadn't had a home since her mother's death. The Shelter wasn't a home. Dell had his father – someone who would miss him if he were gone.

Who would miss her?

Her room in the Shelter would just be assigned to the next orphaned teen.

She pulled her arm gently away from Dell's.

"I'm sorry," she whispered. "I have to go. I just have to."

She reached up and touched his cheek. It was the first time she'd ever done that. But he was her only family. What if this was the last time she saw him?

He met her gaze, only for a second, before he shook his head and started to walk away. "Be careful, Storm," he said over his shoulder. "I don't trust that guy."

Which one? Galen? Reban Don?

"Who?"

He'd reached the door. He looked back for the last time. "Lincoln. We might not be blood but we're as good as family. Just remember, he's not."

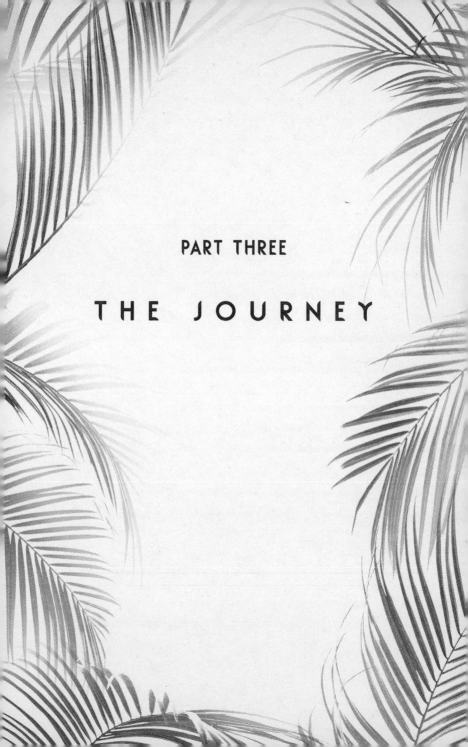

PART THREE

THE JOURNEY

SEVENTEEN

STORMCHASER

The boat didn't look anything like she'd imagined it. Dark and grey, it sat, sleek, in the water. The word *Invincible* was tattooed in black along its side.

Seven days. That was how long it would take to get to Piloria.

She must be losing her mind. Dell's words had left her reeling and questioning her own actions. There had been no other chance to talk. She hadn't been able to get to the bottom of what he'd meant about Lincoln.

Things had moved so quickly. One minute they'd been at the Camp, the next they'd been transported to the ship.

She'd been right about Lincoln being the poster boy – even if he hadn't known it. As the transporters had taken them to Camp she'd seen publicity materials in all the streets, huge pictures of Lincoln and some blonde woman, both standing with their arms folded across their chests.

It was perfectly posed, with Piloria as the backdrop.

He'd been horrified. "Where on earth did they get that? I never posed for any picture."

She'd shrugged. Nothing surprised her any more. The Stipulators seemed to do whatever they wanted.

The competitive edge that had been driving her these last few days had vanished. The voices in her head were back. Asking her what she was doing. Asking why on earth she'd want to set foot on Piloria. Why would she even contemplate stealing dinosaur eggs?

All around her she could hear in-depth discussions. Most of the other competitors seemed to think about nothing but finding the eggs and claiming the rewards. A few were talking about maybe living on the other continent eventually.

Storm watched as the others started to board. It felt strange. She loved the water. Even Lincoln nearly drowning in the Trial hadn't scared her off. But feeling the water all around your body was different to being on a boat. Swimming in a loch was a million sectars away from crossing an ocean to another continent.

"Ready?" The voice made her jump. Lincoln. He looked serious. He'd lost the easy manner he'd had in the servery when they first met.

"I'm not sure." She twisted the straps on her bag.

"Well, make up your mind. Once the boat sets sail they'll expect you to get off at the other side. Are you ready for that?"

The big question. Was she ready? Because right now she wasn't sure. "Are you?"

"Of course I am." He swung his bag up onto his shoulder as if it were as light as a feather.

He paused for a second, looking her up and down, like he was about to say something. But instead he shook his head and strode forward. "See you on board," he said and disappeared up the ramp.

It was now or never.

She sucked in a deep breath. She'd come for the food, but it wasn't the rewards that called to her now. It was the chance to see a different land and its awe-inspiring creatures. Curiosity was flooding through her veins. Excitement too. It was a mixture of unknown, completely unexpected feelings. She'd never intentionally set out to become a Finalist. But there was so much to learn. So much to bring back and share.

Could she really walk away from that?

No. Not a chance. Her black backpack didn't swing as easily as Lincoln's had as she bumped it onto her shoulder. *Piloria. Here I come.*

EIGHTEEN

LINCOLN

The sensation of being on an ocean-going ship was weird. After a few hours on board, at least half of the Finalists were vomiting over the side. Lincoln had to admit to feeling a little sick himself, but luckily not enough to part with any of the food he'd been eating.

The sway of the boat was calming, peaceful. After the first night, when he'd almost rolled out of his bunk, he'd grown used to it. It was like being rocked to sleep as a baby.

What didn't help was sharing a room with nineteen other people. Thankfully, they'd split up the men and women on the ship. Storm was in another dorm. That suited him. Being around her confused him. He wanted her as an ally. She was smart, she was quick and she could hold her breath for longer than anyone he'd ever known. And that was as far as he could think.

Decisions would have to be made – one way or another.

She might be safer with him than with any of the other Finalists.

The ship had slowed to a halt and a small boat had been lowered. It seemed the crew were used to catching their own fish. This part of the ocean apparently had the best-tasting catch and they were determined to get some.

A few of the more adventurous Finalists had joined the crew on the boat to have a swim in the ocean. There wasn't exactly much to do on the ship. Swimming was one way of keeping up their fitness levels for whatever lay ahead. Leif and Rune preferred brisk jogs around the deck against the bracing ocean winds, while Kronar hadn't come topside the whole time he'd been on board. He really didn't like water at all.

Storm sat down next to them in the mess hall. "What's the plan for today?"

"No plan, just a bit more exercise," Lincoln answered. "Who knows what the terrain will be like on Piloria. I want to hit the ground running."

"Sounds reasonable. What else?"

Rune held up his spoon. "What else is there?"

"I'm still a bit curious about what we'll find when we get there," Storm answered. "The Stipulators haven't exactly been forthcoming. Has anyone looked at the supplies in their packs? Has anyone used anything?"

"Of course I've looked, but everything we need for now is on the ship. Why use anything from our packs?" Rune was still eating.

Lincoln glanced around to check if anyone else was listening. "I don't trust the Stipulators."

He noticed Storm drop her spoon in shock. "Do you have to say that out loud?" she hissed.

"I agree," said Leif, whispering now, leaning across the table towards him. "There's so much more they could have told us by now. The information is so limited I'm beginning to think we've been sent here as a human sacrifice." He laughed under his breath. "I mean, think about it, a paper map, a compass, virtually no medicines, some crap food, clothes and a water bottle. Before I was only thinking about the Trials. But now that we're here" – he held out his hands – "there isn't exactly much else to think about."

Storm stared at him with her violet eyes. "What did you think they might tell us?"

"Something useful, like more information about the dinosaurs," Lincoln cut in. "How many in a pack? How do they hunt? How do they use their senses? Can they see us, smell us, hear us?"

"Some weapons that might actually be useful against the dinosaurs," put in Kronar.

"Isn't that the whole point?" said Storm. "We don't have anything that works against the dinosaurs."

Leif leaned back in his chair. "You tell me. You must know more than the rest of us."

"What's that supposed to mean?" Storm snapped. Lincoln could see she was getting frustrated. It wasn't news that the Stipulators couldn't be trusted. What had they expected?

And why should she know any more than them?

Leif shrugged, staring off into space, clearly not wanting to go any further. Storm picked up her plate and marched off towards the servery again.

The three Nordens shot glances at each other.

"Why are you looking like that?" asked Lincoln.

Rune shook his head. "Don't you know?"

"Know what?"

He smiled. "Have you actually *looked* at Stormchaser?"

"Of course I have. What do you mean?" He looked at her retreating back. Slim figure, muscled arms, tanned skin and a sheen of dark hair. He was lost.

The three guys smiled at each other again. "Her eyes. Have you looked at her eyes?"

They were certainly an unusual colour. "Yeah. What about them?" Lincoln was starting to feel self-conscious, shifting in his seat.

Rune sighed. "Have you ever seen eyes like that before?"

"No. Why?"

Leif shook his head and smiled. "Think again. You have. Who else has a set of eyes like that?"

Lincoln was frantically trying to make sense of this conversation.

Kronar lifted his eyebrows. "Reban Don?"

Reban Don. Yes. The same eye colour. Distinctive. Why hadn't he noticed?

Then he realized. Reban Don's eyes were hard, cold. They might be the same violet colour, but Storm's eyes had warmth behind them. That's why he hadn't made the association.

"Do you think they're related? She hasn't said anything, and he didn't act as if he knew her."

The three pairs of pale blue eyes looked at him as if he were some kind of idiot.

"What? She *hasn't* said anything." It was odd, he felt strangely protective towards her. He hadn't exactly shared his own motives for becoming a Finalist with Storm, and he was sure there was something she wasn't telling him. But he'd seen no sign at all that she had any familiarity with Reban Don.

"There's the eyes – and the way he watched her," put in Leif.

The words sparked an awareness in his brain. They were right. And he had noticed that. He'd thought it was strange the way that Reban Don had seemed to single out Storm with his gaze. Had Reban seen their developing friendship? Maybe that was why he'd been off with Lincoln too. He should have thought about it a little more.

"If he is a relation she might get special treatment. It might be worth hanging around Storm," said Rune as he started eating again. Storm was walking back across the room towards them, her food plate refilled and her eyes blazing.

"But he's a Stipulator. They don't have families." The words just came out automatically.

Kronar gave a smile and shook his head as she approached. "Supposedly. But who knows?"

Lincoln's brain started to spin. Storm had her secrets – just like he did. But something as big as this? From what he'd learned of her so far it seemed unthinkable. But how well did he really know her?

NINETEEN

STORMCHASER

The first night on the ocean had been rough. The second, completely peaceful. Some waves were definitely bigger than others but the Captain let them know if they were in for stormy weather.

So the first sign that something wasn't quite right was when the ship gave a violent lurch to the side. Plates scattered from the tables in the servery and several people slid along the benches, landing on the floor.

"What was that?" asked Kronar. "Did we hit something?"

They all stood up and crowded towards the door as the second jolt hit. This time there was a different kind of noise, a scraping along the hull.

They scrambled towards the exit, Kronar heading down into the belly of the ship and the rest heading up towards the deck.

The deck was crowded; some people standing around the

handrail were screaming. But it was the screams from the crew on the boat below that chilled their blood. The boat for the crew members and Finalists who'd opted to go swimming.

"What is it?" Someone pointed towards a massive, pale grey shape cutting across the water amid a sea of red.

"Get in the boat, get in the boat," screamed one of the crew members to the few swimmers left in the ocean, who were fast-crawling towards the boat. Everyone was panic-stricken.

Storm was still confused. "What is it?" she asked the person next to her.

"I think it's a megalodon." The ship lurched again as the grey mass banged angrily against it, before disappearing beneath the waves.

The tail of the giant shark whipped upwards, allowing the spectators no illusions about its true size. "Oh my, it's as big as a transporter," breathed one of the Finalists.

In fact, the megalodon was nearly half the size of the ship. No wonder it made such an impact as it thumped into the hull. They were stuck in the middle of the ocean with a massive beast attacking – and there was no safe haven out here.

"It's got the taste of blood," muttered the person next to her. "It won't stop now."

The screaming continued from below as people scrambled onto the boat. Several of the crew members above on the ship stood next to the hoist, ready to lift the boat from the waves.

The last person was frantically swimming for safety. Storm recognized him. It was one of the Finalists, Lopus Thran. He'd been good at the Trials. Fast on the cliff face, competent and strong in the water. She'd imagined he'd have a good chance of collecting some eggs.

She blinked. One second he was there. Next, he was gone.

There was a gasp around the boat, then shouts from below: "Lift us up. Lift us up now!"

There was a blip beneath the waves, followed by a bright red pool rising to the surface of the ocean. Storm turned her head away, putting her hands across her eyes. She couldn't bear to think about what had just happened.

That was it? One snap of the megalodon's jaws and a person just disappeared for ever?

The crew started working frantically, trying to hoist the boat from the waves. Leif ran over to help, arms cranking the wheel as fast as possible.

But it was too late – too slow. The megalodon rose from the waves, jaws wide, revealing rows of giant teeth. The boat was snapped in half in an instant. No time for thought. No time for action.

Everyone screamed. The true magnitude of the megalodon was revealed. It wasn't just big, it was enormous.

Lincoln sprinted to the side, closely followed by Galen.

They grabbed ropes, throwing them over the side of the ship towards the people still in the water below, scattered from the remnants of the boat. Others did the same. The megalodon wasn't finished feasting yet and as soon as someone scrambled to hold onto the ropes, Lincoln and Galen shouted in unison, "Pull!"

Others on the deck ran to help. Storm snapped out of her shock and moved to grab the rope behind Galen. She didn't think about the effect of the thick-hewn rope on her skin. She didn't think about her still-damaged fingers. She just pulled with all her might.

The adrenaline surged through her body. With enough hands on the rope the weight of a person was negligible. Galen stayed at the front as he grabbed a man by the arms and hauled him onto the deck. Some of the crew members next to them did the same with another survivor. "Again," Galen shouted, ignoring the quivering body lying next to him. The rope slid back down the side of the ship into the water. The strain was taken immediately as someone grabbed on to it. "Pull," shouted Galen as he started heaving the next person from the water.

Storm was pulling too. Anything to help. But after a few seconds of strain she felt an almighty thud. It knocked her clean off her feet and the rope sagged in her arms, the weight gone.

"No!" Galen gave a shout as he tugged again on the rope – and its frayed blood-soaked end landed on the deck next to him.

Storm rushed to the side. The ocean beneath her was empty, scarred with a cloud of red once again. There was no sign of life. No more survivors to be rescued.

Her whole body started to shake and her vision clouded. She pushed herself away and started to walk without thinking, heading inside. People were still screaming on deck, others rushing to help those they'd pulled from the water. But Storm was at breaking point. Black spots appeared in her vision. She had to move. She had to get away. She couldn't suck air into her lungs any more.

She pushed through the door and walked down the grey metal steps towards the bunk rooms. Kronar was right to stay inside. It was the only safe place.

Her mind was swimming, haunting memories flashing through her mind.

She needed to get away from all of this.

TWENTY

LINCOLN

It took over an hour to find her. Most people had stood shell-shocked on the deck for a while after the attack. The megalodon had circled for a long time, snapping at floating remnants of the boat on the surface of the water. Red quickly faded to pink, the colour disappearing completely within a few minutes, leaving no trace of the lives that had been lost.

The crew were quiet, moving silently, dealing with the equipment left lying around.

Lincoln walked for ever. There wasn't a bit of this ship he hadn't explored. He finally found her at the lowest point Finalists were allowed access to, sitting alone in a dark corridor.

He didn't speak, he just slid down the wall next to her and sat on the floor.

There was hardly any light in the corridor at all. But he

could see the glint of wet tears on her cheeks and hear her rapid breathing. So he kept quiet. He just reached over and captured her hand in his.

She didn't pull away. She didn't object. She just sat. Her breathing finally slowed and she leaned her head on his shoulder.

"How many?" she whispered.

"Seven. Three crew. Four Finalists."

Silence ensued. Both thinking about the people lost.

"What about Galen?"

"What about him?"

She let out a long slow breath. "I didn't expect that from him. I didn't expect he'd help anyone else."

"I think he got a fright. I heard he'd been in the water himself earlier." He paused for a second. "Do you want to go back up to the others?"

She shook her head. "Not yet. Let's just sit a while."

He could do that. There was something soothing about being down here, listening to the throb of the engine, out of the way of the other crew members and Finalists.

He was trying to push the thought of the megalodon from his mind. Trying not to picture its poor victims. He didn't want to consider what actually lay in the ocean surrounding them. The loch had been bad enough.

He had to stay focused. He had to think about Arta. Nothing else mattered. Winning the health care she needed was the only chance he had of keeping her alive.

Family came first. Always.

"Why did we come?" Her voice cut through the darkness, breaking his train of thought.

"What?"

He didn't want to answer that question – he didn't want to reveal his vulnerability to any of the other competitors, even Storm. So, he did what he always did. He turned the question around.

"Why did *you* come?"

"I don't know." She sat up and ran her fingers through her tangled hair.

His earlier conversation with the Norden boys was playing on his mind. "There's really no family back home – or anywhere else for that matter?"

She sighed. "I told you before, Dell's my only family now – at least, he was." Her words tailed off a little. "And I hope he still will be."

His skin prickled. The thought of being without family was unthinkable to Lincoln. His family were his world. The most important people in his universe. His anchor point in life.

Storm's voice was sad. Alone.

"What about your mum and dad?"

"My mum died a few years ago. My dad, who knows? I never met him, it was just me and her. She wouldn't talk about him."

Reban Don's face and violet eyes were circling around in his mind. Had *she* noticed his eyes? Had she noticed the way that he watched her?

"Where do you live?" She could only be fifteen.

"I stay in one of the Shelters."

He sat up. "You do?" He knew the Shelters existed. He'd just never met anyone who actually lived there. They were soulless places. Tiny single rooms, with barely enough room for a bed and cupboard. For teenagers with no place else to go. For teenagers with no one left to take care of them.

He couldn't imagine it. His underground home was damp and dark. But the love and warmth from his mother and sister eclipsed that. Where they *stayed* didn't actually matter, he'd learned that early on.

But Storm had none of that. No one to worry whether she came home or not. No one to talk things through with. No one to ask if she'd had a good day – or had enough to eat. No one to question her odd relationship with the plesiosaur.

No one to ask about the scars on her back.

PART FOUR

PILORIA

DAY ONE

TWENTY-ONE

STORMCHASER

The first thing that struck her was the smell. As soon as the small boat neared the coastline there was a huge assault on her senses. It was rich, evergreen and alive with the noise of insects. And yellow sand like she'd never seen before stretching on for thousands of sectars.

The sand on Earthasia was grey, the same colour as the stones. There were small patches of grass around the loch, but nothing more.

She'd never seen a forest like this before – never expected it to be only a few steps from the beach. The remnants of forest back on Earthasia were scant and scarce. The huge array of colours here seemed to pull her in. She'd never seen greens like it. From the dark green of the moss, to the intense green of the forest trees. Bright green reeds lined the wet ground near the entrance of the forest. And every so often there was a bright blast of red or orange flowers that stood out from their dark green surroundings.

It felt exciting. It felt alive.

Something swept around her, like a warm, soothing blanket enveloping her skin. Earthasia was never this warm. And even though her home was packed with people, it never felt this alive. When she'd imagined Piloria in her head it had never looked like this. She'd imagined one shade of green covering everything. She hadn't even contemplated the random bursts of colour. But then she'd never even known that places *could* look like this. It was so different from Earthasia.

But despite her excitement, she was nervous too. She ached for Dell, even though she knew he'd never have come. She didn't want to explore Piloria with virtual strangers. She couldn't trust any of them. They made her feel on edge – even Lincoln. Dell would have made this place feel different. She would have *known* someone was watching her back.

Storm stood on the sand and fingered the metal-and-glass compass in her hand. They'd all been given one, and right now it was the most precious thing she'd ever owned. There was a real beauty to it. The weight in her hand felt solid, tangible. The only part of the trip so far that did.

The small boats were unloading all around her. There was a Stipulator on each boat, still giving instructions. None of them put a foot on the ground. Several kept looking anxiously to their ship anchored further out, obviously worried about crossing that little part of ocean again after the megalodon attack. They kept glancing towards the rustling leaves of the forest too as if, at any moment, a whole army of dinosaurs could come crashing through.

The Stipulator from Storm's boat started shouting instructions. "Use your maps, follow the directions you have been given." He was busy supervising the unloading of a large wooden crate.

"What do you think that's for?" Storm said out loud.

The woman next to her shrugged. "Who cares?" She wandered off along the beach unfolding her map as she went.

Storm frowned and stared at the crate. What on earth could be in there? She paused for a second, waiting to see if any of the Stipulators would open it and reveal its contents. But they were all too preoccupied keeping their eyes towards the treeline. Perhaps whatever was in the crate was for when they returned to the beach – *if* they returned to the beach.

She pushed that from her mind and started tilting the compass in her hand, still fascinated that the needle stayed true to one direction. The map was covered in a thin film to protect it from the elements. The information it gave was limited. The forest, a mountain range, a loch that looked much bigger than her own back home, a desert wasteland. Who had charted Piloria? She knew that for the last nine years Finalists had been sent here to look for food. But who had taken the first steps and mapped it out before anyone else came? Had they been amazed by what they had seen – or just plain terrified? As far as she knew, the expeditions for food had only skirted around the edges of Piloria. The few

Finalists who'd returned to Earthasia had mentioned the terrifying dinosaurs, but further information had been scant.

The Stipulator wasn't finished. "Beyond the forest you will find a cache of weapons and some transport vehicles. They should still function."

How reassuring.

"From this point onwards you're on your own. Remember, the eggs are your priority. You may have to function in a team in order to retrieve them and any eggs obtained must be kept safe at all costs. Everyone must be back here in seven days. The *Invincible* will leave at midday. If you haven't returned, we will assume you are dead." He paused to let this sink in. "The Finalists who return with the most eggs will win the greatest rewards on Earthasia: new housing, unlimited food supplies and medical care for themselves and their family. Any other surviving Finalists will be entitled to extra food rations for a limited time. May the best candidate win."

The words were brutal. Storm had been filled with doubts since she'd set foot on the ship. Words like those made her want to dive into the ocean and swim straight back to Earthasia. But the ocean wasn't her safe loch. She'd seen proof of that.

A few people started to run straight towards the forest. Stormchaser's feet were sinking into the cool sand. Maybe she could stay here – live on the beach for the next seven days then go home again. It might be safer than stealing eggs that she'd much rather leave in their nests. But the ocean was starting to lap at her heels. While her loch was safe, who knew what kind of creature could crawl out of the ocean and snap her in half?

At least on land there was a chance of somewhere to hide – in the ocean, there was nowhere.

A shadow fell across her. The outline was unmistakeable. "Ready?"

There was no fear in his voice or on his face. Lincoln had no doubts whatsoever.

She stared down at the map that showed the three known nesting areas. She'd marked what she thought would be the optimum route on the ship. Did she want to share that?

Lincoln held his map next to hers. It wavered in the breeze but not before she could see an almost identical route in grey graphite. "Looks like we're going the same way. Makes sense to stick together."

She frowned. How had he managed that? He hadn't seemed to know much about maps when she'd quizzed him on the Trials.

She shook off the thought.

For now, teaming up seemed the logical decision.

The independent streak in her wanted to say no. But she didn't really want to face a T-rex on her own. "Let's take it one day at a time." It seemed the safest thing to say.

Lincoln looked amused. He gestured towards the forest. The crowd of Finalists were slowly disappearing amongst the thick leaves. "After you."

She inhaled deeply, letting the smells and essence of this

new land permeate her body. It was the strangest sensation. It felt so right, so in tune with every part of her. She'd never even imagined anything like this place; by rights she should have been feeling unsettled as soon as she set foot on Pilorian soil. But the truth was she was too curious to stay still.

She picked up her backpack, swinging its awkward weight up onto her shoulders and striding towards the forest. "What are you waiting for?" she shouted over her shoulder as the green enveloped her into another world.

TWENTY-TWO

LINCOLN

Lincoln was trying not to notice things. He was trying to ignore the beauty of the land around him. He was trying to ignore the constant buzz and hum of insect life. Earthasia wasn't like this. All that could be heard in Earthasia was the sound of machinery churning out power, churning out food. Building, drilling or digging.

Piloria was a completely different land.

The land of the dinosaurs.

He needed to remember that. He batted away the large green leaves that kept slapping against his cheeks. Even the ground felt different. He could have lingered by the beach all day, digging his toes into its soft yellow sand. But the forest soil beneath his feet squelched as he stepped on it. It unnerved him. The earth almost felt alive.

In the heat, sweat was already running down his back. They'd been allowed to pick from a variety of clothes. His socks and gloves with the resin soles and patches were tucked into a pocket at the side of his backpack. He'd no intention of climbing a cliff without them. He'd also been given thick boots and an array of black, blue and green tops. Could dinosaurs even see colour? He hoped not.

He watched Storm thrashing through the forest in front of him. She walked with confidence even though he'd seen a tremor in her hands. This place was new to them all.

Some had already charged ahead and around him he could hear the constant murmuring of voices. Everyone was nervous. No one had any real idea of what lay ahead.

The forest went on and on. There were insects everywhere and eventually he pulled one of the thick green leaves from a plant on the ground to try and bat them away from his face. It felt as if the million little flapping wings were inside his chest as well as outside. Nerves had never been a problem for Lincoln before – not even when he was scaling the cliff – but this was an entirely different situation.

The trees started to thin, and eventually they came to a clearing covered with dark green grass.

He squinted in the bright sunlight, his eyes trying to adjust to the surroundings. People were breathing heavily, though the air seemed thicker, purer than back home. Surely that should make things easier?

The view was astonishing. It was the kind of picture a kid might draw in school. A broad open space, the grass stretching far into the distance; beyond that the largest loch he'd ever seen and a range of mountains in the background with a strip of red earth in front of them.

There were no buildings here, not a single one, and the landscape was truly astonishing. All that was missing was the outline of a few elusive dinosaurs. There were black spots on the horizon, but they were too far away to be distinguishable.

Directly ahead of them stood a variety of rust buckets – maybe a lifetime ago they'd been transport vehicles – but a few had chunks missing from them and one was missing its whole rear end. He tried not to picture a T-rex chewing the metal. The reality was stark enough without his imagination running riot.

Galen was already sitting in the seat of one vehicle, pulling at pedals and levers. There were no instructions. The Stipulators had only mentioned that the vehicles existed. It was obvious no one had any idea how they worked.

One sprung to life behind Lincoln with a splutter and a cloud of acrid black smoke. His lungs quickly filled with dust and he stumbled away choking. Another flared into action, with Galen smiling broadly in the driving seat. It was the first time Lincoln had even seen anything resembling happiness on his face. The engine didn't sound good – it was loud and clunky. But the wheels started to turn as the sun glinted off the metallic panels on its roof. Like most things on Earthasia, the Pilorian transporters seemed to be solar powered.

Galen gestured towards another Finalist to climb on board,

and the transporter started bumping over the uneven ground. Lincoln watched in fascination. He'd never seen a transporter as small as this. It looked as if it could only hold around six people. A few other people scrambled to get on board but Galen had obviously decided that two people were more than enough and he kicked and punched them clear of the vehicle. Within a few seconds it was churning up mud and leaving an ugly trail over the bright green grass.

People started climbing into the other vehicles. Lincoln jogged over to the nearest and dumped his backpack on the front seat, Storm following. If they waited any longer the only vehicle left would be the one with the missing rear end.

There was a ruckus over by the weapons' locker. Lincoln hesitated. He should get something – anything – to protect them against the dinosaurs. But he had no clue at all what to look for. Rune's white-blond hair stood out in the crowd; he shouldered his way through and reappeared with a triumphant smile on his face and some kind of shell gun in his hand.

A shell gun. Lincoln wouldn't even know where to begin with one of those. But Rune's success made him decide to join the clamour. Turning to Storm, he hissed, "Guard the transporter," then he took off before she could respond. He elbowed his way through, away from the guns but towards the spears and broad axes. He grabbed one of each, keeping them low, and shouldered his way back out.

He'd never had cause to use a weapon before. He'd never even seen anyone else use a weapon before. Everything about this made him uncomfortable. In any case, what good would a spear or an axe be against a T-rex? It was laughable really.

He walked back over to the transporter and shoved the weapons in the back. Storm was leaning against a rock nearby, studying the map. Rune appeared around the other side of the vehicle and dumped his backpack next to the weapons. "I guess I'll be coming with you, seeing as you've found yourself some wheels."

Lincoln felt himself bristle, but he knew it made sense to have allies on Piloria. There weren't enough vehicles to go around, so surely it was better to team up with fellow Finalists he already knew?

"What about the girl wonder? Is she joining us?" Kronar called as he walked towards them with Leif. Of course. It made sense Rune's two companions would appear. Leif said nothing, just gave a knowing smile as he climbed inside. "Who wants to drive?"

There was a strange bench seat that could easily fit three people. The three Nordens made themselves at home in the back while Lincoln went over to Stormchaser.

She was still studying her map and the markings that indicated the three nests of the T-rex, velociraptor and pterosaur. Her eyes flickered between the mountains, the loch and the great expanse of land, as if she were trying to visualize the sites.

"Are you ready? We should get started."

She held up the map. "How do they know? I mean,

how do they know where the nests are?"

He smiled. She was smarter than she made out. Most people who worked a manual job did so because they hadn't done well at school. He suspected Stormchaser worked a manual job because she chose to.

He wasn't sure why but – out of all of these people – she was the only one he kind of trusted.

The three Nordens seemed fine. But it was clear they'd known each other all their lives and so their first loyalties would be to each other. No one had Lincoln's back, and no one had Storm's.

He shook his head and held his hands out. "You're right, I don't know how on earth they could be sure where the three nesting sites are. The last few expeditions were all about finding alternative food sources. You'd think those guys would have avoided the dinosaurs at all costs." He wrinkled his nose. "In fact, if I'd been them, I'd probably have dug up everything in the forest. It seemed safer there. Why come out here at all?"

"Why indeed?" She let the words hang in the air between them.

"You think there's something about this place they're not telling us?"

She raised her eyebrows. "You mean besides the fact we're stealing from the most dangerous dinosaurs on the planet and probably won't get out alive?"

Storm picked up her backpack and walked over to the transporter, climbing into the front passenger seat.

"I guess I'm driving then," murmured Lincoln as he followed her. The sweat was already beading on his forehead.

First day on Piloria. He couldn't help but wonder if they'd see a second.

TWENTY-THREE

STORMCHASER

After a few false starts the transporter finally began to move. They'd been lucky. A fight had broken out over another transporter just a little way from them. Fists were flying as they headed out of the clearing in theirs.

The vehicle was much faster than they'd expected and it took a few terrifying minutes for Storm's heart to stop thudding in her chest as they bumped and jumped over the uneven ground.

"Where are you headed?" Leif shouted to Lincoln. "Shouldn't you be going that way?" He pointed to the plumes of mud and sand. The other transporters were headed around the side of the loch.

Storm pushed her map into his hands. "Look at the marks. If we go round the loch it will take us two days. If we go across the loch it should take us less than one."

Kronar drew in a sharp breath. "You're joking, right?"

She shook her head. "According to this map, the loch is enormous. But it's much wider than it is long. We can go straight across the middle." She lifted her eyes to the horizon. "We can reach the velociraptor nest a whole day before everyone else. We don't even know how far these transporters can take us. What if the terrain gets too rough for them?"

Rune turned round in his seat. "But how do we know what's in the loch? Wasn't one bad experience on the ship enough for you?"

Stormchaser pointed to the map again. "We don't even know if there will be boats at the loch. There might be nothing. But given someone has obviously put transporters on Piloria and mapped this place, we've got to assume that they've looked at the loch too."

Kronar's voice was cracking. "I don't think we can assume anything. We've no idea what's in that loch."

Lincoln was saying nothing. But it was understandable; his knuckles were white from clenching the wheel as the transporter jumped about. There were no roads here, no level ground. But the distances they needed to cover made some kind of transport essential. They needed to save their energy for the terrain that was only accessible by trekking and climbing.

The sun was baking now, streaming in through the sides of the vehicle. Storm started to finger the water carrier in her lap. "There's no way the water they gave us will last seven days. It's so hot here. I doubt we could even carry enough water to last us seven days."

"All the more reason to go to the loch," Lincoln spoke up. "We've got purification tablets in our packs. We can fill up while we cross over and on the way back. That should give us enough water to see us through."

"Really?" Rune frowned. "I don't remember seeing any." He started to rustle around in his backpack.

Kronar was still white-faced and silent. Storm turned to face him. "What do you want to do? Stay at the side of the loch, and take your chances with the land dinosaurs and anything that comes out of the swamp areas? Or cross the loch with us?" She shrugged her shoulders. "You might not be able to swim, but if something does live in the loch, I don't think swimming will save any of us. I doubt any human can swim faster than a loch creature."

The words sounded braver than she felt. She was going along with the plan for now – it seemed safer to be part of a team on Piloria. But what she'd do once they got there and had to steal eggs? She hadn't quite worked that one out yet.

Kronar's eyes were fixed on his hands in his lap. It was almost as if he didn't want to even look at the loch. There was nothing else she could say. "I bet there's nothing in there." She patted his shoulder and looked back towards the water. The ground seemed to be zooming past and her stomach was turning over and over. Two seconds later Leif put his head out the other side and retched. Thank goodness they were moving at speed and the wind was whistling through the transporter. Sick was the last thing she needed to smell.

The journey to the loch took an hour. In the distance she could still see the snaking curves of the other transporters winding around the side of the water. There were a few dotted along the other side too – as if they'd decided that might be the marginally shorter route.

Lincoln started to drive around the edge of the loch, searching for anything that might resemble a boat. It would be old. It would probably be unusable. But it was worth a try.

Finally Kronar gave a shout. "There!"

Storm was amazed. Not only was it the first word he'd said in ages, he was also pointing to the bushes instead of the loch. Lincoln stopped the transporter and they jumped out.

The smell from the loch was overwhelming. Thick, dank and very rich. Nothing like the loch back home. She stared at the water. It wasn't nearly as clear, and there was a distinct white tinge to it, almost clouding the water over – leaving her wondering what lay beneath the surface. It sent a little chill down her spine.

The boat hidden in the bushes did indeed look ancient. Lincoln ran his hands over it, feeling the texture. "I've felt something like this before. What is it?"

It was dark brown, but covered in a thick green moss. It only took Storm a few seconds to realize. "It's made from trees. It feels the same as the trees in the forest. Most of them were covered in moss too." Inside were three sets of oars, each one looking a little newer than the last.

"Are you sure this thing will float?" Kronar looked distinctly queasy.

"Let's see." Leif started dragging it towards the loch, stepping into the water without a second thought. Rune helped and Storm bent to lend a hand. As soon as the edge of the boat hit the water the weight lessened – one final push was all it needed. It floated easily.

Rune leaped from the edge of the loch straight into the boat. For a few seconds it waivered but it hardly dipped further into the water under his weight.

"You go next." He pointed at Kronar whose feet were edging backwards.

"No." He shook his head.

Lincoln moved towards him. "It will be fine. With us all rowing we'll cross the loch in a few hours. Focus on that. Nothing else."

He held out his hand towards Kronar, whose cheeks filled with colour. Storm could see his whole body trembling and realized exactly how hard this was for him. But, eventually, ignoring Lincoln's hand, he stepped into the water then onto the boat.

It wobbled again, but settled quickly. Storm started passing over the backpacks, climbing on board when the last one was loaded and holding her breath while Leif and Lincoln clambered in.

She shook her head. "Who made this?"

Leif shrugged. "What do you mean?"

"I mean, who can have made this boat?" She could feel

herself starting to get annoyed by their lack of interest. "How did it get here? Have you ever seen anything made from a tree before? Everything's metal on Earthasia."

Leif frowned. "Well, no." He touched the rough bark again.

"This couldn't have been brought here at the same time as the transporters –" she held out her hands – "look at it. Look at the oars. I've been around my loch for years. I've never seen anything like this."

But Leif had obviously heard enough. "Who cares? If it floats, it floats. If getting across this loch more quickly means we'll win, then let's just go for it."

The boat sat much lower in the water with all five and their backpacks on board but the last thing they needed to do was attract Kronar's attention to that.

Storm sighed and handed out the oars. "Who wants to take the first shift?"

They settled themselves on the boat, Lincoln, Leif and Rune falling into a rhythm and matching each other stroke for stroke.

"When did you decide you'd be crossing the loch?" Kronar was clearly annoyed at being left out of this crucial decision.

"From the beginning."

Stormchaser started. She and Lincoln had spoken in perfect unison. They stared at each other, shocked that their thought processes could be so similar.

It was uncomfortable. Stormchaser had never met anyone who was so in tune with her before.

But then Lincoln wasn't, was he? He didn't care about any of the dinosaurs. He was just here to snatch the eggs and run. He didn't have time to notice all the beauty around them.

The strokes increased in pace as the boat cut across the loch. Stormchaser watched the surface. Was this loch as deep as her own? Did it have a link to the ocean?

Her body gave a little tremor. A megalodon wouldn't come to a little loch, would it? Not when it had a whole ocean of prey.

An elegant dark-grey head broke the surface. Kroner stifled a cry but Lincoln slammed his hand over his mouth. Stormchaser stood up, rocking the boat from side to side.

"What are you doing?" hissed Rune. "Sit down, are you crazy?"

She couldn't help but smile. This was something she was used to. It felt good that her first sighting of a creature on Piloria was one that she knew, one that didn't terrify her.

She ignored the sound of Kronar as he retched over the side of the boat, watching the long neck lift above the loch and the body crest along the surface. "It's a plesiosaur." Her heart had finally stilled in her chest with the sight of something familiar. The thick grey skin, the small head and large body and flippers moved elegantly, sending little ripples across the water. The flick of the long tail sent a splutter of droplets across her face.

She laughed and wiped them away, still watching as the dark head cut smoothly across the loch. A few seconds later another little head bobbed alongside the first. "A baby!" Storm held her hand in front of her mouth in surprise.

"So what – it's a baby. Doesn't every animal have babies?" Rune looked irritated.

"You don't get it. You don't get it at all. I've been going to my loch for seven years. I've never seen a baby plesiosaur. I don't even know how often they breed." It was clear no one was feeling the wonder of this like she was. Her heart fluttered at the beauty of it, the way the smaller creature dipped and turned as it followed its mother through the water.

"Who cares?" Kronar was hating every second of being on the loch.

She ignored him, watching in fascination as the adult plesiosaur seemed to guide the baby around the loch. At one point their heads even touched. Were they communicating with each other?

The scar on her back started to itch and she scratched through her tunic as she sat back down. It was an unconscious action, but Lincoln didn't miss a thing. "Are you ever going to tell me about that?" he murmured in her ear.

"No." She smiled. She couldn't look away. She couldn't stop watching the beauty of the mother and child – until, in a split second, they disappeared beneath the waves.

Storm frowned and scanned the surface – what had made them vanish? Her stomach gave a little flip-flop.

There was a flurry at the side of the loch, a squawk, as a large-winged bird emerged from some greenery near the shore and swooped down, plucking up a fleshy-looking fish in its sharp-toothed bill. But its victory was short-lived. A far larger predator erupted from the surface, its skin dark green and scaly; it snapped the bird between its dagger-toothed jaws.

Fear rolled over Storm like a tidal wave. "Row. Row, quickly." Terror was eclipsing everything. Now she understood why the plesiosaurs had disappeared beneath the waves. Kronar's skin was so pale she could practically see the veins on his forehead. There were only three sets of oars but all five pairs of arms were on them, powering the boat through the water as if the creature was already giving chase.

Storm's muscles burned. Rivulets of sweat were running down her back, irritating her scar tissue. The more she tried to breathe deeply, the shallower her breaths became and the more she felt starved of oxygen. Panic was gripping every part of her.

The boat rocked, bumped by a dark green shape moving just underneath the milky surface. "Faster!" she screamed. The edge of the loch was in sight. So close, but not quite close enough. The muscles in her arms were on fire, her stomach clenched in terror.

There was movement again, the noise of some thick skin scraping along the base of the boat and the shingle bottom of the loch – even in shallower water they weren't safe.

The boat approached the shoreline and Kronar stood, leaping across the ankle-deep waters. He hesitated for a second before catching the edge of the boat with his hands to stop it bobbing back into the loch. Storm was next, jumping onto the muddy ground and grabbing the boat – ignoring the burst of pain from her injured hand – to help drag it out of the water.

The creature rose from nowhere, a dark-green flash, jaws wide apart, snarling, fast as lightning. All she could see were the inky fixed eyes and the scaly reptilian skin. There was no time to react – no time to do anything. The scream was lost in her throat as the boat upended, tossing Lincoln, Rune and Leif into the shallow waters.

Leif was luckiest. He landed only a few millisectars from Storm and quickly scrambled ashore. Lincoln was up to his knees in the muddy water and turned to grab at Rune.

But the creature was quicker.

It lunged, jaws gaping.

Rune let out one shriek; the muddy water flashed red. Time froze. None of the others could move. Rune's lower half was subsumed in the creature's mouth – blood staining its teeth; his outstretched fingers brushed against Lincoln's hopelessly reaching hand. A second later he vanished beneath the murky water.

"Get out, Lincoln. Get out!" screamed Storm, reaching over and dragging at his tunic. His hesitation was for the briefest of seconds as the water clouded pink around his knees. It was only two steps to the shore and he flung himself onto the grass.

No one spoke. All eyes were on the dispersing colour in the loch. Kronar retched again, this time into the grass.

Storm couldn't believe it. She couldn't believe what had just happened in only a few seconds. Her brain couldn't make sense of it all.

The boat had been pushed almost completely out of the water by the force of the creature. The spear and battleaxe lay in the bottom – almost mocking them with their uselessness. Their bags were there too. But even though the Stipulators had emphasized the supplies in their packs might be the only thing that helped them survive, Storm couldn't feel lucky about that, only numb.

"Oh no." Lincoln cut through the silence.

"What is it?" Leif's voice was trembling.

"Pull the boat up quick." Lincoln was on his feet, tugging and pushing at the boat to right it again. "Do you think that thing can come out of the water?"

"What do you mean?" The feeling of panic was swamping Storm again, crowding her brain with a jumble of thoughts. She couldn't cope with this. She should never have come here. Dell was right.

This was madness.

"Storm." Lincoln's voice was strong. "Help pull the boat up." It was an order, not a request and she automatically obeyed. She couldn't think straight anyway.

Leif and Kronar got to their feet unsteadily. Leif was shaking his head. "How did it know, how did it know to attack us?"

They pulled the boat away from the edge of the loch, all the while keeping their eyes on the surface. "Who's going to get the oars?" Leif's voice cracked.

Two of the oars were bobbing gently on the water. Stormchaser pointed to the ones that had landed at the side of the loch. "You can forget about the others. We'll make do with what's here."

Kronar shook his head. "Stop it. We won't need oars. We won't need any of this. We'll walk back if we have to. There's no way any of us are going on that loch again."

"Do you think we'll be any safer on land?" Lincoln sounded serious.

All of a sudden Piloria didn't seem beautiful any more. It certainly didn't feel safe. If she was lucky enough to get home, Storm doubted she'd ever swim in her loch again.

"This is your fault. This is all your fault." Kronar's face was red as he pointed at Lincoln. "Why couldn't we just drive round the loch like everyone else? Why did you two have to be so smart? Rune would still be here if it wasn't for you."

Lincoln stepped in front of him. It was the first time she'd ever seen him angry – ever seen a flare of temper. "Quiet," he hissed. "We've no idea what else is around here."

"You think if I stop shouting the dinosaurs won't hear us – won't smell us?"

She saw a wave of realization flash across Lincoln's face. He stepped straight up to Kronar; something flared in his eyes. "I'll tell you what they smelled. Your retching." He pointed to the pool of sick on the grass. "You were sick in the loch, that's what attracted the creature's attention. That's what made it notice us. Up until that point we were just another unknown object crossing the water. Your vomit changed everything."

Kronar's legs crumpled, his face ashen. Leif's eyes widened and he kneeled beside his friend. Mixed emotions played across his face. Storm could sense his confusion. One friend might have inadvertently caused the death of another.

No. Some hideous creature from the loch had caused Rune's death. Not any one of them.

Storm couldn't help but keep her eyes on the water. She'd never once seen a creature crawl out of *her* loch, but then again, she'd never witnessed any attack in a loch before. Piloria was very different from Earthasia. Plesiosaurs were nothing like this.

Lincoln turned and walked away, folding his arms across his chest. Storm was torn. Should she go and speak to him or stay with Kronar?

She took a deep breath. "Guys, let's go. There's no point blaming each other about this. I hate this. I hate what just happened. I can't even think about it. Let's get out of here. Let's get some distance between us and the loch."

It was the one thing she knew no one would argue about.

She picked up her backpack and then stopped. Five backpacks. One of them was Rune's. What on earth were they supposed to do with that?

Her stomach churned. Survival instincts told her she should look through the backpack to see if there was anything in there they might need. Food. Water. Anything that could protect them.

She picked it up, but she couldn't bring herself to open it. It felt wrong. She would stash it somewhere near the loch. If they needed it later for water and food, they could retrieve it then.

But her movements slowed.

A gun. Rune had a gun in his backpack.

It didn't matter how useless a gun seemed right now. Maybe if she'd had a gun in her hands she could have fired off a shot that would have hit or stunned the creature. Maybe it could have given Rune a few seconds of precious time.

She dumped the backpack at her feet. "We need the gun. Where did Rune keep it?" She wasn't going to let anyone argue with her about this.

Leif pointed to the front pocket. "In there." He could hardly look at the backpack. As if even touching it was disrespectful to Rune.

Storm pulled out the gun and shells and put it in the matching pocket of her own backpack. "I'll work out how to use it later." She pushed the backpack into some bushes. "We'll leave it here. If we need supplies on the way back we can collect them."

Out loud it made perfect sense. Out loud it didn't seem quite so heartless as it did in her head.

Lincoln nodded and gestured for them to start moving. He walked at a brisk pace, as if he was trying to get away from everything that had just happened. He pulled out the map again, holding it so everyone could see. "We're going this way. The first nest is the velociraptors'. Anyone know anything about them – apart from what they told us in school?"

"They're vicious, they hunt in packs." Kronar said the words with a blank look on his face as if he wasn't really with them.

Leif was more focused. "They're bigger than us, two heads bigger than the average human. They have razor-sharp teeth, with a killing claw on each foot."

Storm was trying not to focus back on the loch. They were far enough away to be safe now – she hoped. "The tail," she said. "They swipe with it."

As she followed behind Lincoln, the pack weighed heavily on Storm's shoulders. But it wasn't the gun that made the difference. It was that, all of a sudden, she realized the horror of what she'd done.

She should never have come here. The reality of Piloria was nothing like her daydreams. The first few steps off the boat and the short trek through the forest would have been enough. The few seconds of seeing the adult and baby plesiosaur in the loch was the first sense of *normal* she'd had – but it wasn't worth this.

Leif had moved ahead with Lincoln. The two of them were talking in low voices, leaving Kronar trudging along beside her. There was no getting away from the fact he'd switched off. He was in shock.

If she'd had any experience of health care she would have

known what to do. But she didn't have a clue. All she could do was walk alongside him, hoping he'd snap out of it, and trying not to worry about what they were going to face next.

TWENTY-FOUR

LINCOLN

The trek took all day. Lincoln was exhausted. Storm was starting to stumble with every other step, but Kronar was relentless. He only stopped every now and then to take a drink from his water carrier. He didn't respond to any conversation. He didn't seem interested in anything around them.

Leif wasn't much better. Lincoln spent most of his time with his eyes fixed on the surrounding area, scouring for any signs of dinosaurs. There was an occasional flurry of activity in the distance – at one point he was sure he spotted a diplodocus. But the lack of grazing dinosaurs was disturbing. Maybe they all knew that any area around a velociraptor nest was fraught with danger.

When they reached the top of a hill, Lincoln stopped. The sun had almost set. He had no idea what Piloria was like at night, what kind of nocturnal creatures it had. "I think we should camp here."

"Out in the open?" Storm looked horrified.

"I don't think we'd be any safer nearer the swamp. Isn't that nearer the velociraptor nest? I think we should try and get some sleep and start fresh in the morning."

"I won't sleep." Kronar's voice was hoarse.

"We need to try. At least from here we can see anything coming towards us." Leif was trying to sound supportive and failing miserably.

Storm dumped the pack from her shoulders and pushed her hands onto her hips, stretching her back out. "I don't think I could walk another step."

Lincoln rolled out his mat and blanket. After the first night on the boat, the bobbing up and down had lulled him to sleep. Lying on the hard ground tonight would be completely different. The sounds. The smells. The thought that at any moment some kind of creature might decide to turn them into a midnight snack.

The idea set off a little alert in his brain. "We need to make a plan for tomorrow."

"What kind of plan?" Leif rolled out his mat too.

"We don't have enough information about the dinosaurs. We know what the velociraptors look like. We know they hunt in packs. But there's so much more we don't know. We need to be constantly aware that they might see us, hear us, even smell us from a long way off. It's not like we can just march up and steal the eggs from under their noses."

Leif pulled out a foil package from his bag. He wrinkled his nose as he unwrapped the cereal grains. "But if we don't know enough about the velociraptors, how can we plan how to steal their eggs?"

"We could watch them. We know their nest is near the marshland. Once we see it, we could hide and watch for a while," suggested Storm. "Once we watch them, we might know them a little better."

"But what if they smell us and come looking for us?" Leif asked.

Kronar shivered. But Lincoln was determined to keep on track. The last thing he needed was to get into a conversation about how they might die. Once they went down that road they'd all want to head straight back to the beach and wait for the ship to return.

It might be the safest thing to do, but it wouldn't win him health care for his sister.

He took a deep breath. "We make sure we stay downwind. Look, I don't know why the rest of you are here. If you want to go back and wait it out at the beach, that's up to you. But I'm going to stay. I want to be part of the winning team – or to win on my own if need be. I came here for a reason. If I can get those eggs, I will. The rest of you need to decide for yourselves."

Leif and Kronar exchanged glances. Kronar was pale. He shook his head. "I'm not crossing that loch again. No way."

"Well, feel free to walk back, but you'll need to start now. Anyway, surely it's safest for us all to stick together?" Storm had her arms folded across her chest, looking like she meant business. "That's why I'm sticking with you guys."

Leif answered for them all. "So, what next?"

Lincoln gestured for Kronar to sit down next to them. "We need to think about this. We need to plan the best we can." He laid out the map on the ground between them all. The sun was so low in the sky that the details were barely visible.

"Here's what we'll do…" He bent his head and started talking earnestly.

First night on Piloria. Would they even survive it?

DAY TWO

TWENTY-FIVE

STORMCHASER

Storm was exhausted. She'd been hiding behind these trees for hours. Her muscles ached after a hard night on the ground. She'd spent most of it terrified by shrieking creatures that looked like flying rats. One had even swooped down and touched her hair. She'd sat hunched in a ball after that, hands over her head, as if it would make any difference. At least they hadn't seemed to be interested in attacking her.

She rummaged through her backpack, trying to find something to eat. But her chock bars – the things that were guaranteed to give them energy – were gone. They couldn't be. She tipped the contents of her backpack out on the earth.

"What's wrong?" Leif was looking through his backpack too.

"I can't find my chock bars. Did you take them?"

He laughed and shook his head. "Here, have one of mine."

But his head kept on shaking. "I was sure I put the graphite and paper in here. Now I can't find it."

Lincoln smiled. "What were you planning on doing? Writing a letter home? I think we've got more to worry about than chock bars and graphite."

There was a squawk in the distance, causing all their heads to turn, followed by the outline of a velociraptor appearing over the crest of a hill. A few seconds later, five others appeared around him. He was the biggest and clearly the leader.

"They're back," whispered Storm. A bit like mini T-rexes, they stood on their strong thick hind legs capped by fearsome claws, with their smaller arms held in front of them. She'd originally thought they were scaly, but from here it looked as though they might be covered in fine feathers. They'd been prowling around their nesting site for the last few hours. Every time they reappeared it sent a shiver down her spine.

"Aren't they hungry?" asked Leif. "Why aren't they out looking for food?"

"But what if that food is us?" said Kronar, his tone dripping with sarcasm. On the rare occasions when he broke his silence, his comments were edged with cynicism. "We still don't know how good a sense of smell these things have. If the wind changes we might find we're breakfast, lunch and dinner."

He was right. Storm knew he was right, but she couldn't even let her brain go there. Dell's words were echoing in her head again. Why on earth had she come here? Did she really want to come face-to-face with a velociraptor? Of course she didn't. It would be a death sentence. The reality of being on Piloria was sinking in. The first few minutes had been amazing. The colours. The smells. The landscape. But Rune's death had cast a shadow over everything. It was making her stop and think again. "How do we even know if they have any eggs? Okay, so they're prowling around and we think it's a nest, but we can't see anything. We're too far away." Frustration was starting to build.

"You'd think that would be one of the things they gave us for the journey. The captain had a scope on his boat, why couldn't they have given us one too?" Leif snorted.

Lincoln stood up. "It's time for the plan. I'm ready. Are you?"

He fixed his green eyes on her, daring her to say no. Was she ready?

No. She hadn't been ready for any of this. But it was too late now. She sighed. Conversation with Kronar for the next few hours would certainly be fun.

"Go on then," she said. "Go and build us a fire."

Storm looked over towards the hills. "How much longer do you think it will be before they get the fire started?" She was starting to worry about Lincoln and Leif. "I'm not even sure this distraction technique will work."

Kronar sighed. "Everything about this is a bad idea. I vote we hike back to the beach and forget about it all. Maybe the raptors are used to fire. Maybe it won't attract their attention at all."

Stormchaser shifted uncomfortably. "I'm just worried they won't find anywhere to hide. I've no idea what's on the other side of those hills. For all we know it could be a desert or just open fields." She shook her head. "Nowhere to hide then."

In theory, Lincoln and Leif had the most dangerous task. They had to cover the largest area of ground, start a fire, hide and then get back again.

All Kronar and Storm had to do was steal the eggs. That's *all*.

"Look over there." Kronar pointed to a thin reed of pale grey smoke rising up behind the hills. "Have they finally got it started?"

They both caught their breath. The pale grey smoke just disappeared into the sky without a trace. They couldn't even smell it. But after a few minutes it started to thicken and change colour to a darker grey.

"What do you think they're burning?" Kronar whispered.

"I have no idea, but it looks like it's beginning to work."

The velociraptors were turning, starting to pay attention. Their heads were lifted in the air as they stood on their hind legs, using their tails to balance. The red crests rose and they started squawking, getting more agitated by the second.

"Go, please go," whispered Storm, willing them to head off in the direction of the fire.

She watched as the agitation continued. Something about the way they squawked and moved their heads sent a line of prickles down her spine. "Are they communicating?"

Kronar frowned as he continued to watch them. "It looks like that. But they're just dinosaurs with tiny brains. I didn't think they were intelligent enough."

"Me neither." The biggest velociraptor seemed to be the head of the family. It looked almost as if he was issuing instructions. A few minutes later, he and three other velociraptors headed towards the hill.

One of the younger ones seemed to have been left in charge of the nest. The other had wandered off into the distance, towards a watering hole. Storm watched as the four older velociraptors moved quickly up the hill.

"What are we going to do?" She was starting to panic. From this distance, the young velociraptor still at the nest looked tiny, but up close it would be taller than she was. One whip of its tail could knock her clean off her feet, to say nothing of what it would do with its claws.

Kronar was moving from foot to foot, his hands clenched into fists. "We're running out of time. We need to do something now." He made a grab for the spear that was lying at their feet. "Let's go."

"Wait!" Storm pushed her hand against his chest. "Look," she hissed. "It's moving away."

It seemed once the younger velociraptor had watched the rest of them disappearing over the crest of the hill, all responsibilities towards the nest vanished. It looked around, then started meandering over towards the watering hole where the other young velociraptor was drinking.

"Quick, let's go now!" Kronar darted out from the trees, crossing the open land in front of the nest. Storm was running as fast as she could, eyes fixed on the raptors. Kronar easily outpaced her. Leif was telling the truth earlier – speed was clearly Kronar's biggest strength.

One of the raptors raised its head from the watering hole and she instantly dropped to her hands and knees. Kronar did the same, the two of them breathing heavily as the velociraptor glanced in the other direction again and then carried on drinking.

They moved more slowly this time, keeping lower to the ground. Kronar reached the nest first. It wasn't quite what they had expected. It wasn't like the birds' nests back home. It was more like a pit, scraped out of the dark earth and filled with forest debris. But there, nestling in amongst the scraps of leaves and twigs, were two pale-coloured eggs. Kronar didn't hesitate. He reached out and grabbed one. "Hurry."

Storm hesitated for a second, then grabbed the other one. The egg fitted easily into the palm of her hand and she huddled it towards her chest as they took off at a run again. Her heart was thudding in her chest. She couldn't watch the velociraptors, now they were behind her.

There was a screech and squawk. "Move," urged Kronar, who was strides ahead. Storm glanced behind her as she pounded across the open land. It wasn't the velociraptors at the watering hole they had to worry about. It was the ones who had just reappeared over the crest of the hill. They were moving rapidly towards the nest.

Their squawks alerted the younger two, who instantly ran back towards the nest too. "Get into the trees," yelled Kronar, his strides lengthening as they approached the forest.

He was quick, darting through the trees and picking up his backpack on the way past. Storm didn't slow for a second, just grabbing her backpack too, then crashing through the undergrowth with no clue as to what could be on the other side.

The screeches were getting louder, more frantic. It was obvious the raptors had discovered the eggs had been stolen. Kronar looked around anxiously. "Can they climb?"

"I have no idea."

He pushed his egg into his backpack, throwing it over his shoulders, and took a quick look at the trees around them.

There was noise. The sounds of thudding feet. Or thudding claws.

All thoughts of carrying the egg safely were lost – Storm thrust hers into her pack and stuck her arms through the straps.

"Here," shouted Kronar. He was standing beneath the foliage of a thick-trunked tree, with plenty of broad branches. He clasped his hands together and Storm put her foot in automatically to get a thrust up. She hadn't climbed a tree since she was a child. But, if she could climb a cliff, she could climb this.

She moved quickly, hand over hand, from branch to

branch. Kronar was moving so fast he was almost on top of her. Something was crashing through the trees towards them.

Storm panicked and her foot slipped, tangling amongst some vines caught around the tree trunk and sticking fast. Kronar kept moving, climbing over the top of her as if she wasn't even there.

She couldn't speak. She was just too terrified. Every time she tugged at her foot it just seemed to wedge tighter.

There was an almighty squawk as one of the velociraptors launched itself at the base of the tree. Its horrible piercing eyes glared at them both as they clung to the branches. The beast was furious, its screeches piercing their eardrums.

"Can...can they climb?" she breathed.

"It doesn't look like it." Kronar's pale face made him easy to spot in the tree branches. He was visibly shaking but his hands were gripping the tree fiercely.

The rest of the velociraptors appeared. Now they weren't as frantic. Now their style was more predatory. They paced around the base of the tree, eyeing their prey in the branches above.

"We need to get higher," said Kronar.

"I can't." If she hadn't been so petrified she would have been crying. She tugged at her foot again, but it was stuck fast.

Then the largest raptor jumped, landing on one of the branches just beneath her. Thankfully it couldn't balance and instantly fell back to the ground.

"They can jump?" She was horrified.

The creature launched itself at the tree again, squawking and squealing. This time as it attacked, it jumped with its tooth-lined jaws stretched towards them.

Storm screamed. It was only a few millisectars away. Another few and it would reach her foot, be able to clamp its jaws around it and drag her down.

Was that blood on its jaws? What had happened to Lincoln and Leif?

Kronar moved instantly, climbing down and wrapping his feet around the branch she had her hands on, then dangling upside down – putting his head close to where her foot was.

"What are you doing?" she hissed.

"Stay still." He pulled a dagger from the waistband of his trousers and hacked at the vines that held her foot. The pressure tightened for a second then there was instant relief; she pulled her foot up just as Kronar pulled his head away.

In the same moment, the velociraptor launched again, this time reaching further – its bloodied jaws clamped around the loose strap hanging from Kronar's backpack. It fell back – dragging Kronar with it. He yelped as Storm reached across to grab him, holding him with every bit of strength she had. But the full body weight of an adult velociraptor was startling. The strain was too much. Kronar's pale face turned bright red, his eyes were nearly popping out of his head. The velociraptor didn't jump again. Instead, it lowered its head, pulling down. Kronar grabbed Storm around the shoulders, holding on for his life. For a second, her hands were free. She didn't hesitate. "Keep holding," she yelled as she grabbed the knife from her own backpack and cut the straps of his. Kronar's bag fell to the ground, bouncing on impact.

The raptors were on it in an instant, tearing part of it and letting the egg roll out onto the forest floor. The first raptor tapped the shell noisily with its jaw, cracking the already fragile shell. The messy contents spilled out, only to be gobbled up by the squawking raptors.

Kronar righted himself, his breathless face coming level with Storm's. The shrieks beneath them continued, but Storm could only see Kronar's ghost-white face in front of her. Sweat was dripping from his forehead; tiny blue veins stood out beneath his skin. Every part of him was trembling.

She was scared. She was terrified for her life. But Kronar was far beyond that. She reached over and shook his shoulder. "Breathe, Kronar. Breathe."

The shake seemed to give him the start that he needed. He took a long deep breath, filling his lungs slowly.

She hid her face on his shoulder and shuddered. "They just ate their own egg. What kind of creatures are they?"

There was a thud and the tree shook. Another velociraptor was trying to reach them. But every jump was followed by a fall. The tree branches were too precarious for them. Gripping with their claws just seemed to make the raptors see-saw from the branches.

Storm's heart pounded against her chest – she stretched

for a branch above and pulled herself up further. "Move higher," she encouraged. "The branches are thicker. It looks like we might be here for a while."

Kronar pulled himself up next to her, splaying his legs across the thick branch and holding onto the trunk. He rested his head against the rough bark, swaying a little as one of the raptors hit the tree again. They showed no sign of giving up.

After a while Kronar's stomach rumbled loudly and he gave a sigh. His eyes remained closed. "Why didn't we bring food?"

Storm let out a laugh. She couldn't help it. It was so ridiculous. If she ever got off this continent and lived to tell the tale, no one would believe that Kronar had been thinking of his stomach in such a moment. She pointed to her back. "We did." She shrugged the pack off her shoulders and pulled out her water bottle. "Want to settle in for a while?"

It was odd. This was the first time she'd felt a real connection with one of her Norden teammates – but if Kronar hadn't helped her up here, she might not have made it.

He shook his head. "Being chased by raptors definitely plays havoc with the brain." A serious look came over his face. "I don't think my legs will ever stop shaking."

She understood. She understood everything. Kronar had never pretended to be brave. She'd never really found out his motivation for being here. He'd always sort of been in the background to the more vocal Leif and Rune.

She touched his arm. "Thank you. What you did was

amazing." She shook her head. "I don't know if I could have done it. All I could see was the blood on its teeth." She shivered. The words seemed to stick in her throat. "Where do you think that came from?" Her voice was trembling – she was scared of the answer. She didn't even want to think about it.

Kronar's eyes widened. "There was blood? I didn't notice – I mean, I didn't really look that closely. I was focused on other things." He was panicking now and she realized her mistake. Her thoughts had naturally gone to Lincoln, but he was thinking about Leif. He'd already lost one friend. Losing another would probably finish him completely.

"It could be from an animal. Maybe the raptors had been hunting."

Kronar looked upwards, staring at the sky. "The smoke is gone. Did you notice? There's nothing there. What happened to the fire?"

She hadn't even given it a thought. She whipped her head from side to side, looking through the trees and searching the sky for any sign of the plume of smoke. But it was clear. Not even a wisp remained.

Her stomach clenched. Lincoln and Leif. *Please let them be safe.*

"I don't know," she whispered. The tree juddered again and she cringed. The raptors weren't going anywhere.

They sat in silence while the raptors continued to stalk around the base of the trunk. It was going to be a very long day.

TWENTY-SIX

LINCOLN

In theory the plan had seemed so simple.

Light the fire just far enough away from the raptors' nest to attract the creatures' attention – they'd watched them for a few hours and discovered just how inquisitive the raptors really were…enough, they hoped, for their plan to work. Then run to the edge of a nearby rocky chasm and scramble down the ledge they'd found while the other two snatched the eggs.

But things didn't always go to plan.

Lincoln and Leif had barely started stoking the fire, sending the thinnest of grey-green tendrils into the sky, when the raptors had appeared on the crest of the hill.

It was only after Leif had made a kind of strangled sound at the back of his throat, then squeaked "Run!" that Lincoln realized what was happening.

He'd glanced over his shoulder, his heart instantly in

his mouth as he saw how close the raptors were – and getting closer all the time. Watching them from a distance had been intimidating – but being near enough to actually see the tiny feathers on their grey skin, to notice that their claws were much bigger than human hands, and to see the predatory glint in their eyes made the danger all too real.

Leif was already running, but Lincoln caught up fast, adrenaline flowing to his muscles. Their feet threw up little clouds of dust around them.

There was a loud noise behind them – a high-pitched caw. Followed by another, then another. "They can talk?" Lincoln shot at a red-faced Leif as they kept pounding along.

The look in response was one of pure terror. The thudding behind them was impossibly close. In every scenario they'd imagined, they'd started their run long before the velociraptors had even known they were there.

The cliff edge was clearly in sight. They'd tied the two ropes from their packs so they could grab them as they jumped over the edge. Even if they didn't land on the small ledge one sectar down they could still scramble there with the help of the ropes. The hope was that, if the raptors decided to follow them, they would land head-first on the rocks at the bottom of the chasm.

Lincoln's chest was tight, his muscles burning. He'd always imagined he could run faster than Leif, but being chased by dinosaurs was obviously giving Leif the extra burst of energy he needed.

The thundering steps were close – too close; he could

feel the creatures' heat against his back, smell their stink all around him. Then, just as they reached the cliff edge, there was a slash of pain down Lincoln's left shoulder. And from the corner of his eye he glimpsed a flash of white teeth in vicious jaws lunging at Leif's back. One second the pack was there. The next it was ripped away.

Lincoln and Leif dived almost simultaneously, grabbing the ropes just in time. Lincoln swung through the air, the rope burning his hands as it jerked him back sharply towards the jagged face of the cliff. The momentum was too strong, he couldn't act quickly enough and he let out a yelp as his shoulder crashed against the hard rock face.

Leif had been luckier. He'd landed on the ledge, but he still looked shocked and stunned, his breath coming in ragged bursts, as Lincoln scrambled over to join him.

There was noise above them. The raptors had apparently been too clever to career off the edge of the cliff and land on the rocks below. Instead they cawed and scraped at the ground above.

The ledge seemed smaller than Lincoln had first thought. He flattened his back against the rock, sliding down until both he and Leif were sitting precariously on the edge. A few small stones crumbled away. Leif gulped and wrapped the rope around his waist. "Let's take no chances."

Lincoln still hadn't managed to catch his breath. He followed Leif's lead and tied his rope around his waist – at least if the ledge gave way they would still be anchored.

"What happened?" asked Leif.

The adrenaline surge was leaving Lincoln's body. "I have no idea," he sighed. "But that was too close for comfort."

Leif snorted. "You think?"

Lincoln stared out at the mountains before them. Green and grey as far as the eye could see. The cawing and scratching above them continued.

This could be a long wait.

"How long have we been here now?" Lincoln was nursing his injured shoulder – it was stinging more than he cared to admit. It was a pretty deep gash according to Leif, so they'd patched it as best they could with a torn strip of clothing from Lincoln's backpack. He'd no painkillers. Just that weird tub of balm with no instructions on how to use it. It could have been for his mouth or his backside for all he knew. No proper medicines had been included with the supplies. He doubted the Stipulators had even considered wasting such precious commodities on them.

Every part of his body was numb. It felt like they'd been perched on this ledge for hours and darkness was falling. "I have no idea," said Leif, still sitting next to him, looking every bit as uncomfortable as Lincoln was. "Do you think it's safe to climb back up?"

Lincoln was growing frustrated. The plan had gone wrong – they'd never expected the raptors to get that close. He could only hope that Kronar and Storm were safe and had managed to get one of the eggs. "Well, we can't stay here for ever." He winced as he tried to ease the backpack onto his shoulders.

It had been quiet for the last few hours and he was anxious to find out what had happened to Storm and Kronar, so he grabbed hold of the rope and pulled himself up until he could peer over the edge of the cliff.

There was nothing there. The plain in front of them was empty, the remnants of their distant fire a pile of ashes.

"It's clear," he said quickly, glancing from side to side. "Let's go." He groaned as he scrambled back over the edge of the cliff. Leif was right by his side. Lincoln stretched his cramped muscles and arched his aching back. Leif's pack lay abandoned on the ground, torn and dusty, but otherwise intact, and Leif snatched it up. After stowing the ropes away in their bags, they cautiously set off back the way they'd come.

As they trekked, Leif stopped to squint at the remains of the fire. He bent down and let some earth and ashes run between his fingers. "Look, Lincoln. There are piles of earth on the fire. Did the raptors put it out?" His voice was raised in wonder. It did seem beyond belief.

Lincoln took a few steps closer. There were claw marks on the ground, as if the raptors had clawed around the fire to dump earth on it. It sent chills down his spine.

These creatures seemed to show intelligence. Yes, they were predators. Yes, they saw the humans as prey. But the territorial behaviour, the *family-type* behaviour was ringing alarm bells in his head. No one had forewarned them about this. No one had even suggested that the dinosaurs were anything other than mindless creatures. Their behaviour seemed to prove otherwise.

An uncomfortable rivulet of sweat ran between his shoulder blades. He'd assumed their own intelligence was their biggest advantage against the dinosaurs. If that wasn't the case, would they even get off Piloria alive?

He looked around carefully. There was no sign of the raptors anywhere. "Let's go while we've got a chance. Who knows how they'll behave at night. We might be at even more risk now than in the daytime."

The hike to the forest took them more than an hour. There were a few heart-stopping moments when a rustle or noise had them heading for the nearest hiding place, but eventually they made it back. The strange dark trees loomed over them, dense enough to get lost in. There was no sign of Storm or Kronar.

"What do you think?" he asked Leif. Lincoln was scanning the surrounding area, looking for any sign of them. But there was nothing, nothing at all.

Leif pointed forward. "What about there? The ground looks trampled."

Lincoln nodded. He bent down at the entrance to the forest. Leif was right, there were claw marks and a clear path had been trampled through the trees. "Do you hear anything?" he whispered.

Leif shook his head. "Let's go. It's getting late. We need to find somewhere to camp for the night – and find out if they got any eggs."

The boys walked silently through the forest, conscious of every cracking twig beneath their feet. "Storm," Lincoln hissed into the trees. "Kronar?"

They walked further, the already dimming light fading to purple as they disappeared deeper into the trees. They were still following marks on the ground, signs of trampled undergrowth.

Leif let out a gasp. "Look." He pointed to a tree that had claw marks around the lower trunk. Remnants of a backpack were lying on the ground. Both of them looked up.

"Storm? Kronar?"

There was a movement above them, a rustle from the thick branches.

"Lincoln!" Storm's voice cut through the foliage.

Relief flooded through him. "Kronar?"

"Yes," came the reply. "Is it safe down there?" followed the anxious question.

Lincoln looked around. "As far as we can tell."

Storm replied, "Give us a minute to get down." It took more than a minute. Scrambling down the tree was awkward, her backpack getting in the way.

"Just throw it down!"

"We can't. We might break the egg," Storm called back quietly.

Lincoln felt a little surge of adrenaline. Egg. They had an egg.

"If it's not already broken," mumbled Kronar as he finally landed on the earth next to Lincoln.

Lincoln was still watching Storm as she made her way down the tree. He held out his hand towards her as she reached the bottom branches, but she frowned at it and jumped past.

"What happened?"

Storm pushed her hair out of her face and straightened her tunic. "We got chased. The fire worked. The bigger raptors left and the younger ones soon got bored guarding the nest and made their way over to the waterhole. We had time to grab the eggs but before we knew it the rest of the raptors were coming back over the hill. So much for your distraction, what happened?" She sounded annoyed.

Lincoln put his hands on his hips. He was listening to her, but he couldn't concentrate. His brain was fixed on one thing. "Egg. You've got an egg?"

She turned around and Kronar rustled about in her backpack and pulled one out. "We had eggs. Now we just have one. The raptors got the other one." He shuddered. "They ate it."

"They *ate* the other egg?" Lincoln felt sick. Just when he thought he knew something about these creatures, they did something else that horrified him.

He stared at the egg. It filled the palm of Kronar's hand. For Lincoln it was the oddest feeling – almost a disappointment. It was nondescript. It could be an egg of any beast. How would they convince the Stipulators it was a raptor's?

"We lit the fire but the raptors put it out," Leif said absent-mindedly as he gazed at the egg too.

"What?" Storm's voice rose. She looked from one to the other. "What did you say?"

"They kicked the fire out."

Storm glanced towards Kronar then looked back. "How? What do you mean?"

Lincoln was getting annoyed. They had to find somewhere safe for the egg. They couldn't afford to let it get damaged. "The raptors kicked it out with the surrounding sand and earth."

"How would they know how to do that?" Storm demanded. "They chased us, Lincoln. They chased us through the forest. They jumped into the branches. They tried to figure out a way to get to us. They knew we had the eggs. They stayed here for hours – there was no way we could come down from the trees."

It was a horrible sensation. No matter how much Lincoln tried to push it into his subconscious, it kept creeping back up again and again. These creatures were intelligent. They might be predatory. They might be vicious. But they were also intelligent.

"You're hurt." Storm had just noticed his bleeding shoulder. For a few minutes he'd actually managed to forget about the sting. She reached up to touch it and he pulled back.

Her face paled. "That was your blood we saw on the raptor's teeth."

He didn't even want to think about it. Didn't want to consider what might have happened if he'd been even a little slower.

She looked back to Kronar. "That's probably why they were in such a frenzy. The alpha had got the taste of Lincoln's blood." She paused. "That – or the fact we stole their eggs." Storm flinched as she said the words and stared down at the ground.

There was silence for a moment. It was clear she was still uncomfortable with all this. But this wasn't the time and place to talk about it. Storm didn't have the same reasons for being here that he did.

"Let's find somewhere to sleep. We need to hike most of the day tomorrow to reach the pterosaurs' nest." Lincoln was back on task. They had one egg and limited time. They had to move on.

"Any idea where we should camp?" asked Leif.

"We'll find somewhere," said Lincoln as he pushed through the forest. His shoulder was smarting. The sooner they finished the tasks and got off Piloria, the better.

TWENTY-SEVEN

LINCOLN

The second night was worse than the first. Again, there was no shelter. No one wanted to sleep anywhere the raptors had been – which ruled out the cliffs and the forest.

"I hate this place, I hate it," mumbled Kronar as they sat down for the night. They'd settled on the edge of a plain close to some bushes and a few thickets of small trees.

He mixed a little water with some of his ration pack. "What are we going to say to Rune's family? How are we going to tell them what's happened? They counted on him coming back."

Lincoln shifted uncomfortably.

Leif put his head in his hands. "I'm trying not to think about that. The last thing his mother said to me was to look after him. I can't bear the thought of telling her – she'll fall apart."

"What about his little sister? What will happen to her now?"

The stress in Kronar's voice was clear.

The words prickled Lincoln's skin. "What's wrong with his sister?"

Kronar and Leif exchanged a glance. "One of them's got the sickness. The skin disorder. Who knows if the rest of them will get it. It seems to run in families."

Storm leaned forward. "You have that in Norden? I thought it was just Ambulus. The girl behind me at school has it. Her brother and father died last year. From the way her skin was blistering and peeling, I don't imagine she's much behind them."

Lincoln blinked. She said it so matter-of-factly. As if it was inevitable.

And maybe it was. He knew lots of people with the skin disorder. It seemed to work slowly. Peeling at first, then blistering, then redness and infected sores. Draining the life and colour out of the person standing in front of you.

He couldn't watch that last part happen to his sister. He just couldn't.

"We can still help them," Kronar's voice was steady. There was an edge of determination showing.

"How?"

"Easy. There are no real birth records. If we win the reward for ourselves and our family, Leif and I can say the kids are our sisters. We won't be able to get health care for his mother or father, but we should be able to get food and health care for his sisters."

Storm was smiling. She reached out towards Kronar and

put her hand on his arm. "That's so nice. I'm sure that's what Rune would have wanted."

Something twisted inside Lincoln. Uncoiling. He was selfish. Completely and utterly selfish. Since they'd landed on Piloria something had been eating away at him. The last words of the Stipulator on the beach. *May the best candidate win.*

Candidate, singular. Did that mean that the rewards – preferential health care, promoted housing, more food, and access to more energy – would go to only one person? In previous years, when Finalists had been looking for food, whole teams had been rewarded. So it had made sense to assume the same would be true this year. But somehow, Lincoln thought, he wouldn't be surprised to learn that the rules had been secretly changed. The Stipulators weren't exactly known for their openness and honesty.

No one else had seemed to notice the strangeness of the Stipulator's comment. But Lincoln had. And although the Stipulator had mentioned teaming up together, he hadn't actually said a team would win.

Arta was Lincoln's priority. He had to focus on her. And if saving her meant claiming victory above all others – above even his teammates – he would do it.

But the thought that Rune had a sister that he loved every bit as much made Lincoln feel physically sick. Because the others might plan to help Rune's family but the simple truth was – he didn't.

He knew that his mother had registered their births.

He knew that their family was counted in the system somewhere. If he won and the Stipulators found out he was lying and trying to get help for other people – he couldn't even begin to think of the consequences.

He couldn't take that risk. He couldn't jeopardize the help he needed for his sister.

No matter how badly he felt for Rune's family.

A flock of wide-winged black-and-white birds flew over their heads towards the sunset. They moved in perfect synchronization, rising and falling on the wind currents.

Kronar gagged on the thick sludge of rations he was eating, throwing it to the ground. They knew they needed strength. They knew they needed energy. But the ration packs were disgusting.

Storm stood up and stretched her back again – she was always doing that. "You know – I bet there are things here we could eat instead of that stuff."

The others looked around. "Like what?"

She shrugged. "Don't you remember from school? I didn't pay that much attention, but they said that years ago we used to eat things that grew on trees and bushes. Fruits. Is Piloria really that different from Earthasia?"

Lincoln gave a little laugh. "Well, apart from the man-eating dinosaurs and space as far as the eye can see, not much."

She stared at the thicket of trees next to them and reached down into her boot for her knife. "Give me a minute."

Lincoln stood up. "What are you doing?"

She waved her arm. "Relax. Let me see what I can find."

She disappeared into the trees and his heart gave a little lurch. He didn't like it. It was only a small thicket but something could still be lurking inside. There was so much about this continent that they didn't know.

"I'm not sure about her," mumbled Leif, his eyes fixed on the trees.

"Why?" It seemed an odd thing to say.

Leif turned towards him. "It's almost like she's been here before. She's too comfortable. She swims with plesiosaurs back home. Who does that? And what about her eyes? What if she is related to Reban Don? He could've sent her here to spy on us all."

For a reason he couldn't explain, Lincoln was automatically defensive.

"That's ridiculous." He lowered his voice. "Storm doesn't have any relatives. All of her family are dead."

The sun was lowering in the sky, leaving only a few purple rays, but he could still see the two faces next to him. Leif's eyes narrowed. "Are they?"

The implication was there. It could be completely misplaced. But even Lincoln had to agree that there was something odd about Reban Don's interest in Storm. He gave an uneasy shrug. "Maybe he's a long-lost cousin, or an uncle? Or maybe her mother had the same violet eyes."

He could tell from the look on their faces that they didn't believe it.

He shook his head. He couldn't help the strange protective

feeling he had towards Storm. He didn't want anyone to upset her. Beneath the strong exterior he was beginning to see just how fragile she really was. "Don't say anything. Not now."

Kronar's voice cut through the darkness. "She was scared. She was petrified when we were up that tree. I could see it in her eyes – just like she could see it in mine. Believe me – she doesn't love velociraptors. And she was as surprised as I was by their intelligence. She doesn't have any more idea about this place than you or I have."

It was almost a relief. Someone else who seemed to be in her corner.

Storm emerged from the trees. Both hands were full. She kneeled down next to them and let her prizes fall to the ground.

They all leaned forward. Lincoln picked something up. "What is this?"

"I don't know. But it looks like we could eat it." She seemed pleased with herself.

Everything looked odd. Dark, lumpy, clustered little fruits. Large round orange ones. Green things with speckles on them. Red things with tiny hairs.

Leif looked suspicious. "How do we know we won't get poisoned? These things could kill us."

Storm pointed to the bottom of one of the bushes where a small brown creature with long whiskers was snuffling around. "They could. But that little creature seems to have eaten them – and it's not dead. So, why can't we?" She smiled and picked up one of the black lumpy fruits and stuck it in her mouth.

Almost instantly her eyes widened. "Wow, this is so sweet – and tart at the same time. It's great. Like nothing I've ever tasted before."

Kronar looked at his discarded ration pack then back to the pile of fruits. He picked up one of the red ones and nibbled at the side. A tiny bit of juice dribbled down his chin. "Okay, not sure about the hairs, but the rest tastes good." He shoved the whole thing in his mouth.

Lincoln frowned and picked up the largest orange fruit. He smelled it. There was a definite odour, but it was pleasing, almost enticing. He tried to bite into it, but it was hard and the skin difficult to get through. He choked a little. "Give me your knife."

Storm handed it over. She was still eating the black fruits. "These are much better than the ration packs."

Lincoln sliced into the round orange fruit. Juice spurted everywhere. "Wow. Look at this. The outside is hard but the inside is soft. Maybe we can eat that part?" He dug in a little further with the knife, pulling out some flesh. The first taste made his cheeks draw together. The cornup rations back on Earthasia were so bland. This was entirely different. Every mouthful exploded on his tongue. "You need to try this, it's amazing."

Kronar gave a little cough, then a laugh. They all turned towards him. He shook his head. "Okay, so that little bit at the top of the red ones? Yeah, don't eat that."

Leif was still looking suspicious. He took the knife and cut into the green thing. It was odd. "This seems hard in the middle," he said. The green surface split open revealing something brown and shiny. He held it up. "Can we eat this?"

Kronar stared at it. "Who knows? Give it a try."

Leif was cautious. He gave the brown thing a little lick. "It doesn't really taste of anything." He tried to nibble at the edges, then finally popped the full thing into his mouth.

It didn't take him long to change his mind. He spat the chewed thing back out. "Yuck! Give me some water. That's disgusting."

Storm held out some of the black fruits. "Okay, so three out of four isn't bad. Try these instead. I think they're addictive. I might go back and find some more." She glanced towards the bushes and trees. "There was some cornup in there too."

Lincoln was surprised. "There was cornup and you brought us these instead?"

She met his gaze. "We know what cornup tastes like – nothing really. I wanted to try something else."

Leif was smiling now. "So if they have fruits like these on Piloria, how come we ended up with cornup? These are much more delicious."

Storm shook her head. "Who knows? Maybe they take too long to grow. Or maybe they won't grow on Earthasia. It is much warmer here." She paused and stared at the fruits again. "You know what this means, don't you?"

Lincoln had grabbed back the knife and cut the middle out of the orange fruit. "What?"

"That people could live here. People could live off the land. You could walk out every day and find something to eat around you."

Everyone seemed to stop chewing. Leif narrowed his gaze again. "You are joking, right? Who would want to stay here? Some fools might have dreams about living on Piloria – but I know the truth. I've only been here for two days, but I've already seen my friend die a horrible death and had to run for my own life. I'm happy to stay on Earthasia."

The sun had disappeared completely now and the only light was from a few distant stars. Lincoln looked around and felt his breath catch in his throat. Although it was dark, he could see across the landscape for thousands and thousands of sectars. Trees, bushes, hills and mountains in the far distance. This was a terrain he'd never encountered before.

"What happens when we take the dinosaur DNA back?" Storm asked. "What happens if all their plans work? They make something that will kill the dangerous dinosaurs and come back and use it. There's a reason for all this. They're trying to give us somewhere else to live. Can you imagine living in a place like this?" There was wonder in her voice. Amazement. And it made Lincoln cringe. He couldn't even contemplate staying here. Home was a small damp red cave that he hoped to get his sister out of. But he didn't want to get her off the continent.

Lincoln tried to sound reasonable – even though he wasn't feeling it. "I think, ultimately, there will be a choice. Once they know Piloria is safe, people will have the option to choose to stay on Earthasia, or to come and start a new life here." He held out his hands. "It could be that some families will be caught up in the idea of having more space."

Kronar answered quickly. "Fools. What about that thing in the lake? Who's going to deal with that? Why aren't they just killing all of the dinosaurs? Doesn't that make more sense?"

Storm leaned forward. Her eyes were bright. "Maybe they don't know about that yet? Maybe we'll be the people to tell them? But we don't need to kill everything. Some of the dinosaurs eat plants. They won't harm us."

Lincoln rolled his eyes. "Kronar has a point. We thought we saw a diplodocus the other day. We know they won't intentionally do us harm. But do I want to live near a creature that could trample me and my house with one swing of its tail? Of course I don't."

Storm wasn't finished. "But think how big this continent must be. There may be parts of it where there are no dinosaurs at all. Maybe they only live near the ocean or the lakes. It's hot here. They must need water. Maybe there are areas where humans could live safely?"

Kronar made a strangled kind of noise. "I think you're crazy. Wasn't a velociraptor trying to kill you enough? Wasn't seeing Rune die enough?" He held up his water container. "And what about us? Don't we need water too? How could we survive without it?" The more he spoke, the louder his voice became. Lincoln instantly looked around. He hadn't seen a single creature when they'd made camp here apart from the brown whiskery thing, but that didn't mean there weren't any others around.

"Sshh. Keep your voice down."

"In case I attract friendly dinosaurs?" Kronar's voice dripped with sarcasm.

Storm sighed. "I get what you mean. But parts of this place could be good. I love the space. I love how green it is. I love the fact that I can see life here. I love the fact I can pick something off a tree and eat it. Everything back home is just so...so grey."

Lincoln knew exactly what she meant. Although nearly every part of Earthasia was built on, in comparison to Piloria it felt almost flat. Flat from lack of energy, lack of life. The cave he lived in was damp and oppressive. How must it feel to live in a tiny room at a Shelter?

Kronar was looking around too. "But what if they *could* destroy them all?" he persisted. "That could work. Piloria with no dinosaurs at all might be an interesting kind of place." From the tone of his voice it was clear he was really contemplating this now. Thinking it might actually be a good idea.

Storm got there first. "What gives us the right to do that? This is as much their planet as it is ours."

Leif cut in, "But you don't seem to mind the thought of killing the really ferocious ones. That's acceptable. So why not kill them all? That way there'll be lots of space for us."

Silence.

The only noise was the rustling leaves on the trees.

Storm was right – how could they justify wiping out all those species? It really was unthinkable. But maybe that was exactly what the Stipulators were contemplating. The more the thought tumbled around in Lincoln's mind, the more likely it seemed. Why stop at the T-rexes, raptors and pterosaurs? This continent was rich with plant life. Rich with food. It was exactly what they needed.

Storm walked quietly towards her bed mat. "I couldn't be part of that. Not ever." There was a determined edge to her voice.

Another tense silence. Lincoln forced himself to change the subject. He rolled out his mat. "Let's get some sleep. If we start early we can hopefully reach the pterosaur cliffs before anyone else. If we're lucky, we'll get another egg."

"That's if Storm agrees to it. Maybe she'd prefer to be in her own team?" murmured Kronar. The implication was clear.

Storm shot him an angry glance. "I didn't say I wanted to leave the team. I just questioned what we're doing. I don't want to kill *all* the dinosaurs."

"If we're lucky, we'll get off this continent alive and never return," said Leif quickly.

Lincoln didn't reply. There was no point. Every one of them was tired. But at least this time they weren't hungry.

He lay down on his mat and looked up at the stars. Were these the same stars he saw from his home on Earthasia? Was it possible that Arta could be looking up at them too?

He closed his eyes quickly. All he could do was hope.

DAY THREE

TWENTY-EIGHT

STORMCHASER

Storm's night was restless. Her eyes kept flickering open and catching sight of the bright white stars up above.

Dell. When was the last time she'd thought about him? Guilt surrounded her. Was he missing her? Was he thinking about her at all? The truth was, her world was so small that Dell was probably the only person who had noticed she'd even gone.

The ground was uncomfortable beneath her body. She shifted again. How would Dell be with her when she got home? *If* she got home.

It was the strangest noise. And it was invading her dream.

Everything was warm. She wasn't shivering the way she did back in her bed in the Shelter. The ground was a little uncomfortable underneath her, but at least she wasn't cold.

If only that darn snuffling noise would stop. There was another noise and the ground underneath her body gave a tiny shake.

A little warm rush of air hit her cheek.

Her eyelids fluttered open.

And she stopped breathing.

The strangled squeal stuck in her throat.

Something was looking directly at her. Something grey and green.

She could feel its breath on her face. Her eyes struggled to focus. The large duckbill came closer. A tongue came out and it licked her. She winced at the feel and the slurping noise.

"Don't move, Storm," hissed a voice from the trees.

She couldn't reply. This creature was huge. Remnants of last night's conversation filtered through her brain. It could squish her with a foot, or its giant tail. Or it could just eat her.

The creature seemed curious. It nudged her. Then nudged her again with a little more force. She couldn't help it. She moved, rolling sideways and straight onto her feet.

The creature reared up on its hind legs. It was like a giant lizard. A *really* giant lizard. It had a crest on its head and neural spines along its back.

It took another step and this time she really did feel the ground tremble beneath her feet. It was that big. It was that heavy.

Their campsite was deserted. Only the bedrolls were left.

Since she'd got to her feet she felt rooted to the spot. Why hadn't she just kept moving, run into the trees?

The creature looked at her again. But it seemed to have lost interest. It walked over towards the thicket of trees and bushes and she heard a little yelp.

Something flickered in her peripheral vision. Another one. Much smaller – a baby. It followed the first, merely giving her a look of disinterest as it passed. She started to edge sideways, holding her breath, and praying she wouldn't step on a twig.

But the creatures ignored her. They were too busy eating. Eating trees. They were herbivores!

Of course they were. They had duckbills. They had to belong to that family of dinosaurs. The tension sagged out of her body as she continued to shuffle sideways. One breath later someone grabbed her by the arm and dragged her into the bushes.

Kronar was shaking. Leif had his head in his hands. Lincoln was pale but seemed calmer. He gave his head a brief shake. "I'm sorry. It came out of nowhere. I felt the ground shake, I opened my eyes and it was there. I didn't have time to do anything."

Leif looked at her. "It headed right for you. It seemed to like the smell of you."

"Just as well it's not a meat eater then, eh?" She let the words hang in the air. They'd left her. *He'd* left her. It didn't really matter how bad Lincoln felt about it now. It didn't change the action he'd taken. Was that the type of person he really was – one that left a friend behind?

Now she was off the creature's radar she could take another look. She stuck her head out from behind a tree. Her heart rate was only just starting to return to normal.

"It looks like a hadrosaurid."

The creatures were still chomping away at the leaves. The tightness in her chest had started to ease.

Apart from being stood on or swatted with a tail, there should be no real threat from these creatures. But that didn't mean she was happy about finding herself so up close and personal. What if it *had* been a meat eater? The rest of them had managed to reach the trees. Why had no one shouted for her?

Leif's stomach gave a loud grumble and he groaned. "I have belly ache. Those fruits last night made me ill."

Kronar nodded. "Me too. I'm not sure eating them was such a good idea."

Lincoln gave Leif and Kronar a little smile as he patted his belly. "I feel fine. Maybe you Norden boys need to broaden your diets. People in Ambulus City eat anything that's not nailed down." He glanced back over at the dinosaurs. "Anyway, it looks like you're right. They're herbivores. They're not a threat to us. Let's just gather up our things and head to the cliffs. But we need to stay on guard – just because these ones were friendly, doesn't mean any others will be."

They moved out from the trees. It only took a few minutes to stuff things inside the backpacks and roll up the bed mats. The hadrosaurids never even looked in their direction again.

Lincoln kept his eyes firmly on Storm.

She met his gaze. She could sense his anxiety. She blinked. "It's okay, Lincoln. Nothing to worry about." But she knew the words sounded flat. Because she was questioning the loyalties of all those around her.

Right now she was carrying the only egg they had. They were supposed to be friends. Teammates.

But how long was that going to last?

TWENTY-NINE

STORMCHASER

The route to the pterosaur nest was tougher than it looked on the map. They'd planned on a flat plateau. What they found was a deep marshland, filled with nightmarish creatures who only let their noses appear above the surface. The size of the snarling, tooth-lined snouts, and the discovery of the blood-stained remnants of a torn-apart backpack at the edge of the marsh, made them quickly decide that they wouldn't get any closer. That led them to a roundabout route, much longer and much harder.

In the end they rested for a few hours, whilst enduring a torrent of heavy rain that soaked them, and the contents of their backpacks, to the skin. The waterproof covers they had proved useless.

Storm was tired and tetchy. Their water supplies were running low. The only watering hole they'd seen had belonged to the raptors.

Lincoln drained his bottle and then looked at the map again. "We should reach the shoreline by afternoon. We can fill up our bottles there."

"We're going to have to drink seawater? That can't possibly be safe." Leif looked disgusted.

Storm dug around in her pack, tossing some tablets towards him. "Here. You should have some of these. They're supposed to sterilize whatever water you find so it's safe to drink. The guy said it'll deal with salt water too."

Kronar shook his head. "I haven't got any. Where did you get them?"

Storm frowned. "Aren't there any in your backpack?"

"I don't think so." There was an edge to his words. "Did you bring them from home?"

"You think I had anything like that at home?" She shook her head. "Why on earth would I need them, and where would I get them? One of the Stipulators gave them to me when I was packing up. I assumed everyone got them."

Leif upturned his backpack, the contents tumbling out onto the grass. "Food, more food, water bottle, clothes, underwear, knife, compass –" he held up a little tub – "liniment." He tossed it towards Lincoln. "My mother makes it. Heals everything." He held out his hands. "But that's it. No water purification tablets."

Kronar shook his head. He'd picked up what was left of his backpack once the raptors had left. "None here either."

They stared at her. "What?" She held up her hands. "Why would they give them to me, and not to anyone else?"

Lincoln pulled something from his pack, a glistening foil packet just like Storm's. "I've got them too."

"Oh, what a surprise, you got the special treatment too," Kronar snapped. "I've heard Storm call you the poster boy – I guess she's right."

Lincoln shook his head. "I've no idea where they came from. I don't even remember getting them. As for the poster boy –" he let out a wry laugh – "if only."

"Look, it doesn't matter," Storm cut in quickly, anxious to relieve the growing tension in the group, "we can share."

"Right." Leif didn't sound happy but he pushed the tablets Storm had offered into his backpack.

The next hour they tramped on in silence, finally reaching the cliff face where the pterosaur nest was supposed to be. It didn't take them long to notice another group working their way along the coastline. Storm felt her skin prickle once she realized who it was. "Galen. He seems to have added a few members to his team."

"Do you think they came here first?" asked Leif.

Storm was trying to do the calculations in her head. The other group were on foot. They'd obviously had to leave their transporter behind at some point. The terrain they were walking on now was just too rough for any vehicle.

"I thought he only had one person with him? Where did the other two come from?"

Kronar shook his head. "He must have picked them up somewhere along the way. He's obviously decided he needs a few bodies to sacrifice at some point."

Lincoln glared at him and then hissed, "Don't say a word about the egg. Pretend this is the first place we've got to."

They reached the beach at the same time as Galen and his three fellow Finalists.

"Hello, little people," the older man said sarcastically, his eyes never leaving Lincoln's. "I'm surprised you made it this far." He looked again and then laughed. "Wait a minute. There's one missing. Oh no, what happened? Don't tell me, he ended up as lunch for a dinosaur?"

Kronar let out a strangled cry and leaped forward. But Lincoln was quicker. He grabbed Kronar by the shoulders, whispering in his ear the whole time. "Leave it, Kronar. Just leave it. Don't let him bait you."

Galen couldn't care less. He kept laughing as he walked a little further towards the cliff. "Don't worry, it will be the same for the rest of you soon."

Kronar's face was scarlet. "Let me go! Let me go!"

Leif stepped in front of him and put a hand on his shoulder. "Don't. We haven't got time to waste on him. We need to get off this place alive to claim the prize for Rune's family and give them his share."

The words were spat out. But Leif had focus. It was clear he could see the bigger picture. After a few seconds Kronar's shoulders dropped. His eyes were still fixed on Galen. "I hate him. *I hate him.* But you're right. We have a responsibility to Rune. Galen can wait."

Lincoln released his grasp. "Then let's not waste time. We don't want him to get ahead of us." He looked up at the cliff.

It wasn't white like the ones back on Earthasia. This was dark grey. Storm's eyes scanned its surface looking for any sign of the pterosaur nest. It was hard to spot. Finally, she caught sight of a few green leaves, two-thirds of the way up the cliff face. Her vision honed in, adjusting, as she realized the brown twigs forming the nest were virtually invisible next to the dark rocks.

Lincoln must have spotted it too, because he immediately started emptying his backpack out and pulling out his resin-coated socks. He slipped them in his pocket and put the empty backpack over his shoulders. All he needed was his harness and two sets of clips.

"It's obvious. I should do this. Anyone disagree?"

Leif, Kronar and Storm shook their heads. The cliff here was much higher than the ones back home. This time the waters around it seemed deep with only a scattering of rocks down below.

Storm frowned. Her hands rested on her hips as she looked around. "How are you going to get started? Now I can see where the nest is, it looks like we'd have been better off starting at the top of the cliff and climbing down."

Leif butted in. "But it might take hours going round the other way. And what are those?"

Storm looked up to the top of the cliff and flinched as she noticed the outline of some dinosaurs up there.

Lincoln shook his head. "I have no idea, and I don't want to know. They could be fine. They might not be predatory. But we don't have time to find out."

THIRTY

LINCOLN

There was no easy way to reach the pterosaur nest. It was positioned near the end of a cliff jutting into the sea, over a bed of rocks with the waves directly underneath. There was no possibility of climbing sideways along the cliff. It was too far. The only way to reach the bottom of the cliff was through the sea.

Galen was already moving, striding out into the water and diving underneath the waves. There was no hesitation. Lincoln's steps wavered, remembering the creature that had killed Rune. Might it also live in the sea? What if the giant megalodon could come this close to shore?

He pushed those thoughts from his mind. Storm and Kronar had managed to get the first egg. Now, it was his turn.

He fast-crawled across the water, the strokes coming easily to him, until he reached the few rocks at the bottom of the cliff face and scrambled up. He stood for a second as waves crashed over him, trying to map a route up the cliff in his head.

He was in luck. A pterosaur was cawing from its nest above. The cliff face was jagged and worn with lots of jutting rocks and places for hand- and footholds. He scanned it again. There was more than one nest. Galen had already started climbing and Lincoln tried to work out which nest he was heading for. It seemed pointless to race for the same one. He shrugged off his backpack and pulled out the harness, stepping into it and securing his resin-coated socks on his feet. They could be the difference between success in this task, and failure.

He started climbing easily, focusing on the task and pushing everything else from his mind. This time he didn't have to worry about Storm. This time the only person he needed to worry about was himself – and that giant bird now flapping in the sky above him.

The pterosaur swooped towards the ocean and plucked a fish out in its enormous bill, returning quickly to its nest above.

Galen was on his right, moving up the cliff face quickly. He turned to watch Lincoln. "Look out for the little birdies," he mocked. "They could pluck a guy like you right off the cliff."

The pterosaur made a loud cawing noise above. It was almost as if it was agreeing with Galen.

"But look at you, Galen, they would have so much more to eat," Lincoln shot back.

Then he shook his head. He had to focus. Galen was just trying to distract him. Keep his mind from the job.

But as he scaled the cliff, Lincoln's brain started to process what he was doing. They'd taunted each other about being turned into bird food but, as far as he knew, the pterosaur wasn't a predator. They might have attacked Finalists on previous trips who got too close to their nests, but from what he could remember at school they didn't eat human flesh. So, why was he trying to capture their eggs? Why did the officials want to kill the pterosaurs and not the monster in the loch – surely that was more of a threat to humans?

He was climbing the cliff easily, there were plenty of hand- and footholds. There was a half-grown tree just above him and he tugged at it to test its security. He pulled the rope from his waist and wound it around the natural anchor point on the cliff, clipping the rope to his harness. There. Above him was a protrusion in the rock, he could use that as the next anchor point – anything that would stop him smashing into the rocks beneath him.

He could hear the shouts of the others from the shoreline, but he ignored them, focusing only on the climb. This time, his arms and legs weren't burning with the strain. This time, his body welcomed the stress of the exercise. This was almost as good as his practices back home.

Then he felt it. A sharp sting on his good shoulder. More than a sting. He froze for a second just as something else hit his right hip. "Yaow!"

It was impossible to turn right around. He could only

flick his head from side to side. Something hit the side of his face and his hold weakened, his fingers slipping slightly. A trickle of blood ran down his cheek.

The attacks were all on his right-hand side. Galen.

That's what the shouts had been about. They'd been trying to warn him. Lincoln looked up. Galen was perched on a thick outcrop of rock, his line anchored into the cliff face and both feet balanced on the ledge. His hands were free – and he had some kind of weapon aimed directly at Lincoln.

"Give up, poster boy. Go home."

Lincoln's reactions were instinctive. He turned his head the other way just as the next shot hit the back of his neck.

Why? They were stuck on a cliff face on the dinosaur continent. Galen should be worried about his own life – not about the other Finalists. Lincoln could feel the fury building in his chest. The constant jibes. The threats. His ruthlessness. What was Galen even doing here?

Did he have a sister who was dying? Did he need the health care as much as Lincoln did?

He was losing the feeling in his fingers from holding on so tightly. The rage was surging around his body.

He didn't care. He didn't care why Galen was here. He didn't care why anyone else was here.

He had one purpose and one purpose only – to save Arta.

He turned round to face Galen and leaned back from the cliff. "What are you so afraid of, Galen? Can't take a little competition?"

Storm and Kronar were still shouting, but their voices were carried away by the wind.

The first swoop caught him totally unawares. He'd almost forgotten about the pterosaur. The cawing of the bird grew closer and the wind whistled past his ears. The flap of a huge wing caught his back, taking him completely by surprise. His fingers and toes tightened on the rock face as he pressed as close to it as he could.

The sound of laughter carried across in the wind. Galen. He was above Lincoln, but still in his line of vision. He'd unclipped his line and moved from the ledge, heading towards the other nest. The pterosaur was ignoring him, leaving him free to reach it.

Lincoln kept climbing, watching as the pterosaur swooped across the waves again, plucking another fish and heading back to the nest overhead. Lincoln stopped still and pressed against the cliff again. Something about this seemed wrong. The nest was above him. He could hear the loud caws of the pterosaur, but he could also hear something else.

The pterosaur took off again, swooping away. He moved quickly, closing the gap between him and the nest, freezing as soon as he realized the creature was returning.

"Aargh!" The pain shot through him like a thousand thunderbolts, the reptile's beak and teeth coming into contact with his already injured shoulder. His fingers released – it was an instantaneous reaction, leaving him dangling with one hand and foot grasping at the rock.

Pain was sweeping over him in waves and he retched. His

head started to swim, pictures dancing through his mind. Arta. His sister. Her pale face against the dark red walls of their cave. She was fading, disappearing in his hazy vision.

His breathing quickened, panic setting in. "Lincoln!" Storm's voice carried on the wind. "Hold on, Lincoln!"

Her voice brought him back to the here and now. He scrambled to regain a foot- and handhold, clinging on for dear life as he tried to look over his shoulder to spot the pterosaur.

There it was, circling above him. Now or never. He moved quickly, covering the last few sectars in a couple of seconds.

Straight away it was obvious what was wrong. There were no eggs in the pterosaur's nest. Instead, there were hatchlings. Tiny little things with oversized heads and yapping beaks, desperate for food. He moved instinctively sideways. No wonder she was attacking him. She was protecting her chicks.

Galen had reached the other nest already and was climbing back down the cliff. He obviously had eggs in his backpack and was trying to protect them, otherwise he would have dropped straight into the water. The eggs wouldn't survive a fall like that.

Now Galen had what he wanted, Lincoln was no longer of interest to him.

Anger surged through Lincoln. His climb had been a complete waste of time. Pterosaur chicks were no use. How on earth could they transport them back to the ship, and then back to Earthasia? The Stipulators had been clear they wanted eggs, not live young. There was noise again in the air behind him and he flattened himself against the cliff, bracing himself for another attack. But the pterosaur was more interested in her nest and landed inside it noisily.

He kept moving across the cliff face, heading towards the other nest. His rope was starting to strain – it had only been long enough to reach the nest directly above his anchor point. It tugged at his harness as he moved further and further away, eventually impeding his movements.

He hesitated for a second. The other nest was literally in arm's reach. He just didn't have that extra few sectars of rope.

It was instinct. He unclipped the rope from the harness. He didn't think about the consequences. He only thought about the prize.

He crossed the cliff, edging towards the second nest. It didn't take long. It was on an outcrop of rock – not enough for his whole body, but enough for him to lean his elbows on as he searched among the twigs and leaves. There, hidden from view, deep within the interlocking twigs was one more egg. Who knew how many Galen had already stolen? He'd obviously missed this one in his haste.

Something tweaked at his conscience. The other nest was full of hatchlings. This pterosaur would come back to an empty nest. He was taking the final egg. He pushed the thought from his mind and wrestled the egg into his backpack.

It was slower and harder going down. Blood from his

head wound dripped past his eye, landing in the sea below. Fear made his stomach clench as he scanned the water. Would blood attract the megalodon – or something even worse?

Now the fact that he'd dropped his safety anchor started to play on his mind; he gripped every handhold tighter, clung to every toehold with his resin-coated socks. Galen had already finished and reached the shoreline. Lincoln could hear him whooping and laughing with his teammates.

He paused for a few seconds. Would Galen attack Storm or the others? He twisted to watch the beach. But Galen was too exuberant. He had no idea that they'd already got the raptor egg.

Lincoln was almost there. He kept moving sideways, away from the rocks directly underneath. But then as he moved down, the stone crumbled beneath his foot. He had no chance to react – his hand had already left the cliff face to find a new hold and his full weight had just transferred to his foot. For a few seconds he was nowhere, hurtling through the air before his impact on the ocean.

He didn't care about the water flooding over his face. All he cared about was the sickening crunch from his backpack as he hit the water, then the sting from the salt water on his open wounds.

He surfaced quickly, swimming in rapid strokes to the shoreline where Kronar, Storm and Leif were waiting for him.

"Are you okay?" Leif walked quickly round to his shoulder,

wincing at the sight. He handed Lincoln a piece of cloth to press to his face.

Lincoln couldn't speak. He was tugging the backpack from his shoulder. Kronar took it from his hand and opened it, cringing when he looked inside.

He shook his head slowly, barely looking Lincoln in the eye. It was almost as if the others could feel his fury. They all averted their eyes, ignoring the celebrations further down the beach from Galen and his friends.

"Look!" Kronar pointed out towards the ocean. Something was breaking the water. The familiar shape of a monstrous grey megalodon was circling around the base of the cliff.

Every hair on Lincoln's body stood on end. His hand tried to reach around to his shoulder. "Do you think it sensed the blood in the water?" He strained to look at his wound. "But there must hardly be any. How could it have done?"

"Can't they sense even the tiniest drop of blood?" Leif looked shocked. "I mean, I'd heard that. But I'd never actually believed it. Not until now."

They all watched the beast prowling in a circle under the ocean waves. One of the pterosaurs dived down from the cliff face – obviously in search of some fish. As its beak dipped into the ocean's surface, the megalodon rose up.

It would have been majestic, artful – if they hadn't already seen it before. With one snap of its jaws the pterosaur was gone, dragged beneath the waves.

Silence. No one could speak. Lincoln's throat was dry. Kronar's shaking hand passed him a water bottle without a word. Leif was kneeling with his head in his hands. Storm was bent over, facing away as if she was about to be sick.

Moments earlier Lincoln had been in that ocean, swimming across from the base of the cliff with an open wound – a wound that had attracted the megalodon. That could have been him.

Leif picked up the backpack, tipping the sorry contents on to the beach, then he took the backpack and dipped it in the shallows to try and rinse it out.

They still didn't speak as the sun started to drop in the sky. There were no other nests on the cliff face. Other teams might reach here and risk their lives climbing up there for nothing. Lincoln was angry. But he was also concerned. "Let's leave a message for anyone else who gets here. There's no point in other people risking their lives climbing a cliff that has no eggs." He gave a visible shudder. "Or swimming in the sea." No one objected, so he scribbled a note on a tiny piece of paper, leaving it in a circle of rocks on the beach.

"Where's the map?"

Storm pulled it from her tunic pocket, along with her compass. It was crumpled, the markings beginning to fade.

"It's time to plot a route to the T-rex nest," Lincoln said.

"Already?" It was the first time he'd noticed the exhaustion on Leif's face. The strain.

Lincoln pointed to Galen. "Don't you think they'll try and beat us to it? Look at the map, it's going to take another full day to get there, and at least another day to get back to the beach. If we don't start soon they'll reach the nest before us.

And what if we run into trouble on the way? Does anyone want to be stuck on Piloria for the rest of their life?"

"Wait. Chances are they've still got to go to the raptor nest. We might have more time than we think." Storm pointed along the shoreline. "Let's camp here tonight. The megalodon can't walk on land. We should be far enough from the other predators to be safe. We need to rest. We need to sleep. I'm sure I saw some cornup growing on the plain back there. We can gather some of that." She pointed to the ocean. "We can refill our bottles and take the few hours to purify the water. We need to replenish our supplies." She wrinkled her nose. "We need to wash too. If we stay at the very edges, it should be fine."

Kronar was nodding and already unrolling his bed mat. Lincoln's legs gave an uncharacteristic wobble. He understood the sense in her logic. He just didn't like it. He wanted to move on. He wanted to be the first to reach the T-rex nest. But running on adrenaline for the past few days was taking its toll.

Galen and his friends were already leaving the beach. They obviously didn't plan on camping here tonight. Storm touched his arm. "Stop it." She could clearly read the thoughts whirling around in his mind. "It looks as if we were first to the raptor nest. For all we know, that's where they're headed now." She shook her head slowly. "They won't be happy when they get there."

"No. They won't." Lincoln watched as Galen threw back his head and laughed. That wouldn't last long. Once he came across the angry raptors and the empty nest he would be furious.

Lincoln tried to do some calculations in his head. It should take Galen's team at least a day to reach the raptors' nest. They could still reach the T-rex nest first.

Storm was gathering sticks for a fire. She kept glancing over towards the nests on the cliff. A pterosaur swooped down and landed in the nest furthest away. The nest without the chicks.

Storm turned to the others, her tanned skin pale. "The pterosaur – the megalodon ate the mother. What will happen to the chicks?"

Lincoln put his head down and picked up his discarded items, pushing them into his backpack. Leif started building the fire and striking some matches. "Survival of the fittest here – isn't it."

The irony hung in the air between them all.

They had four days left on this continent. Four days to stay alive while waiting for the ship back home. But, more importantly, they only had one egg. One egg between four of them. What would that mean in terms of rewards?

Kronar looked brighter than he had in days. The lack of a pterosaur egg didn't seem to bother him. He constructed some kind of net and caught a few fish to have with the cornup they found.

They settled down for a night under the stars.

Tomorrow was the hike, and the next day the T-rex.

DAY FOUR

THIRTY-ONE

STORMCHASER

Her feet were aching, blistered and bleeding. The boots provided were a disaster. She rinsed out her socks and put them over the straps of her backpack to dry in the sun. Kronar's mood was still brighter. But Leif looked tired and Lincoln had that driven, focused expression on his face again.

She'd slept better on the beach – finally trusting her teammates to keep watch on her behalf – but her imagination had played games with her and she'd thought she could hear the baby pterosaurs squawking for their mother.

The whole "survival of the fittest" concept didn't sit well with her at all. Everything about this place left her torn. Parts of Piloria were beautiful. She'd never seen brightly-coloured flowers like it. She'd never seen trees like it. One tree had almost reptilian foliage – bright green spines that covered the whole branch.

But she was terrified of the ferocious dinosaurs. She

hated not being able to sleep well at night. And yet there were a whole host of other dinosaurs, other creatures that weren't a threat. Living here *could* be beautiful.

As they trudged over the plains they saw herds of duckbills and a few giant apatosauruses. Yes, the apatosaurus could be a threat from its sheer size and weight. But there was no predatory behaviour. No wanting to tear them limb from limb.

She watched for a few minutes. If she'd been closer she was pretty sure she'd feel the ground shake at their steps. With their long necks and tails, four sturdy short legs and huge bulky bodies they moved in a slow, lumbering manner. What amazed her most was the way they watched their young. Actually watched them constantly. Nudging them to move them along and directing them towards the thicker foliage for food.

The thought of stealing the eggs was still playing on her mind. She couldn't possibly feel safe living where there were T-rexes and raptors. But this was *their* place. Not hers.

But what about the pterosaurs? She wasn't sure that they really were predators. Like any creature, they wanted to protect their young. Was that really so different from humans? Why had the Stipulators asked for a pterosaur egg?

She could understand parliament's principles. Trying to eliminate the danger of predatory dinosaurs before they started a settlement here. But should they be living here at all? And what happened if the officials decided that the apatosaurus was too cumbersome? One sweep of its tail could easily kill a human. With a few steps it could crumple a living area and all its inhabitants. What if the government decided to look at its DNA too?

Playing creator or killer didn't feel right to Storm. The humans had evolved on one continent, the dinosaurs on the other. From the look of this place the dinosaurs still had plenty of space. They didn't need to move to another continent, so why should the humans?

"Should we be doing this?" It was out there.

"This again? You should have asked yourself that question before you got on the ship," Kronar answered immediately.

She was taken aback. "Did you?"

"Of course I did. But I have a responsibility. I need to get back off this continent alive. We need the extra rations."

"Who needs them?"

"My family, and now Rune's too. I've got seven brothers and sisters. We're starving. We're freezing. We don't have enough money to pay for both food and power. Our families are barely surviving right now. I had to do this."

"That's why you came?" She was shocked. Lincoln's eyes had widened in acknowledgement but he said nothing, just kept tramping forward.

Leif scowled at her. "Of course that's why we came. Everyone has a reason for coming. What's yours?"

Exactly. What was hers? She still wasn't entirely sure how she'd got here. Her competitive edge had taken over during the Trials. But that seemed like a meaningless and ridiculous thing to say now.

"I'm not sure," she murmured. She kept walking, her head down. Now she felt like an idiot. Lincoln hadn't chimed in to help. What was *his* reason for being here anyway? He'd never said a word about it, but from the fleeting, dark look she occasionally saw in his eyes she knew there was something he wasn't telling her.

She had to be the only person in the group without a real reason to be here. She was risking her life – and for what?

She'd wanted to see Piloria. She'd been curious. And now she'd seen the green vastness filled with life – and horror – it was sparking off a whole host of thoughts in her brain. She'd witnessed first-hand the ferocity of some of the dinosaurs. But she'd also witnessed other things. And it confused her even more.

She felt strangely protective of the gentler dinosaurs. The plesiosaurs like Milo. The apatosauruses. The hadrosaurids. She wanted to protect all of them. But the predatory dinosaurs terrified her. Even the ones she hadn't met yet. She was torn between the fact that there were some dinosaurs she loved and some she didn't. But shouldn't every living creature have the same chance of survival?

From the start, she hadn't been sure about the DNA plan. But the more she saw on Piloria, the more it made her question her own set of ethics and morals. What if Kronar was the person to choose which dinosaurs lived or died? He hated all the lake and sea creatures. He would wipe them all out. Even Milo.

She'd voiced her concern to her teammates and been

instantly dismissed. She'd be too afraid to reveal her jumbled thoughts to anyone else – Piloria was dangerous enough already, and with everyone constantly on edge, she couldn't afford to be seen as a troublemaker. The last thing she needed was to fall out with the members of her team. If she wanted to stay alive, she needed them to be watching her back – just like she was watching theirs. Being left to survive on her own was too big a risk.

The T-rex was a big enough risk already.

They tramped on in silence, passing watering holes and signs of other dinosaur nests. Some of the footprints in the mud were enormous – she could have lain inside the print and still had room above her head and underneath her feet.

Eventually the landscape started to change – the plants were thicker, the surrounding forests denser, the air warmer and more humid.

A rushing river flowed beside them and in front of them was marshland that they'd need to circumvent. Lincoln checked the map again. "It's only another few hours, do you want to go ahead or wait until morning?"

"It depends if they can smell us."

Storm turned to Leif. "How do you mean?"

His eyes fixed on hers. "We thought the raptors couldn't smell us – but after how quickly they reacted, I think they could. What about the T-rex? If they can't smell us, we could watch them overnight and make a plan. But if they *can* smell us, they'll hunt us down. We could be dead in a matter of minutes." He ran his fingers through his hair.

Storm shook her head. "I don't like the thought of being hunted down in the dark." She looked at the surrounding area. Her feet were aching and there was a low watering hole nearby where she could soak them. "Let's spend the night here. Tomorrow is going to be a big day. We can get up early and hike to the nest."

Leif gave a brief nod as Lincoln stood with his hands on his hips looking at the horizon. Storm had already pulled off her boots. He pointed at her bleeding feet and his still-bleeding shoulder. "You're right, we'll stay here for the night. Before we leave tomorrow we need to make sure we can mask the smell of blood on us. Clean up your feet as best as you can."

She nodded in agreement. She could try and make a paste from some of the surrounding plant leaves – anything to stop the smell reaching the T-rex's nose.

Tomorrow would be the biggest day yet.

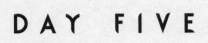

DAY FIVE

THIRTY-TWO

LINCOLN

The T-rex opened its mouth and roared.

The noise was incredible. Lincoln was pretty sure his eardrums just exploded.

Its jaws plunged down towards the poor triceratops who'd clearly stumbled into the wrong place at the wrong time.

Lincoln couldn't move. He was too terrified in his hiding place behind the trees near the top of the hill. They'd finally reached the T-rex's nest late that morning and had been watching it ever since – gradually getting closer. The others were hidden a little further down the slope. But any movement now might attract the T-rex's attention and Lincoln didn't want to take that chance.

The giant jaws snapped at the triceratops' neck; the smaller dinosaur flailed madly. Lincoln winced as he heard the crunch of tooth on bone. But the triceratops wasn't done. Its sharp horns slashed at the skin under the T-rex's throat.

The primeval instinct to survive obviously surged through dinosaurs as well as humans.

The T-rex made an angry grunt, but kept its jaws fastened firmly; it reared back, lifting the triceratops' legs from the ground.

As the creatures continued to fight, Lincoln decided now was as good a time as any. He took off at full speed to a copse of thick bushes closer to the T-rex's nest. He dived straight into the foliage, almost landing on top of Storm. "Yeow!" she hissed angrily, shifting over to make room next to her and Kronar.

"Sorry," he muttered. "I didn't have time to stop and think." He spun around in the bushes, staying hunched down, to keep watching the dinosaurs. The triceratops was feisty. It thrashed its armoured head around and around to cause more damage. This time the T-rex opened its powerful jaws. The triceratops thudded onto the ground. After a few seconds, it seemed to regain its bearings and galloped off into the trees on the other side of the clearing.

"I didn't count on her being so big," he breathed as he watched the T-rex roar after the fleeing dinosaur. "I'm just glad that triceratops isn't us."

"So am I," agreed Storm. "That was more reality than I really need to see."

The stride of the T-rex's footsteps on the ground was at least twice Lincoln's height. Her thick muscular back legs were longer than he was. At full height she must have measured around twenty-five sectars – her eyes would have been able to stare in the second-floor windows of one of the Blocks back in Ambulus City.

Her tail whipped ferociously from side to side, like a separate lethal weapon, as she stalked around the clearing. Her front arms were much smaller, covered in feathers, along with a small straggly crest of feathers across her head and neck.

She walked on her toes. Lincoln had never imagined such a massive creature walking like that. And her head flicked around every few seconds. She lived on her senses – smell, sight, sound. She was the most terrifying predator.

But the worst thing was the smell. She stank of rancid rotting meat, obviously caught between her vicious teeth. The stench alone made him gag.

But it was the discovery of a torn and bloodied strip of tunic – and, even worse, a foot still wearing its shoe – that had left them cowering in the bushes. Chances were they'd actually known the person who was currently wedged between the T-rex's teeth.

So they watched. They watched for a long time, being careful to move position every time the wind changed to try and prevent her picking up their scent.

It was exhausting. Scared to move, scared to speak. Most importantly, she never left the nest. She was the only T-rex around and she guarded her eggs savagely.

"Surely she'll leave soon?" whispered Storm.

Lincoln shook his head. "I have no idea." He straightened his legs out in front of him for a second, cringing at the loud cracks from his joints.

"She doesn't look interested in anything other than the eggs. She's not even gone to look for water. What are we going to do if she doesn't leave the nest at all?"

"Do you think the fire trick will work with her?" Leif burrowed through the bushes behind them, sounding hopeful.

Lincoln considered. "I wouldn't count on it. She seems too clever to fall for that."

Storm straightened up too. Her blue tunic was crumpled and torn and her hair all over the place. "At this rate, we might as well head back to the beach."

"Suits me," said Kronar quickly, staring up at the sky.

It would be easy. It would be so easy to just walk away, go back to the beach and wait it out. The ship would be here in two days. It would take at least a whole day to hike back to the beach anyway – maybe even longer.

But one egg between four people surely wasn't enough to get Lincoln what he needed, given that Galen had at least one pterosaur egg. And the raptor egg wasn't even in Lincoln's backpack. It was in Storm's. He wasn't quite sure how to claim it as his own.

He needed that T-rex egg more than the others. He couldn't leave here without it.

"We need to make a plan. We need to find a way to get her away from the nest. Are you in or are you out?"

THIRTY-THREE

STORMCHASER

Storm put her hands on her hips. "This is your plan? It sucks."

Her hair was matted, her tunic splattered with duckbill blood. Lincoln was holding the knife in his hand and breathing heavily. The carcass beneath them was still warm.

Everything about this repulsed her. She'd only agreed to help drag the carcass into position. She hadn't been involved in the capture or the kill.

Lincoln was in his own little bubble, his own little world. Maybe it was the only way he could do this.

"Are you clear about what you're doing?"

She nodded. "Oh yeah. I'm hiding. I'm dumping the carcass where we agreed and hiding."

He frowned. "Take off your tunic top."

"*Excuse me?*" Had he really just said that?

His face coloured. "I mean swap it for another. We can

use that one. It has blood on it, we can use it as bait to make the T-rex move."

There was method in his madness, so she turned away and pulled the blue tunic over her head and rummaged in her backpack. She spun back round, not bothering to hide her short top. "We have a problem. The only other tunic I have is red. We don't know how good the T-rex's vision is. If they can see colour, I might as well shout, *Here I am*."

Rune rummaged in his backpack then shook his head. "Sorry, I don't have any others left."

Leif did the same, casting an anxious glance at Lincoln. "Me neither, but I'm sure it will be fine. You won't be the one getting close to it anyway."

She turned to face Lincoln. His eyes were stuck on her abdomen, following the scar lines that came from her back and wound around her body like a fine spider's web.

The unspoken questions were written all over his face. But she didn't have to answer them. She pulled the red tunic over her head and handed him the blue one.

"How on earth do you expect to bait a T-rex with this without getting eaten?"

He gave a nervous smile. "Wait and see."

THIRTY-FOUR

LINCOLN

Please let this work. Please let this work. Lincoln repeated the words over and over in his head.

It had taken three hours to catch another duckbill. It had then taken all four of them to hold it down and wrap the tunic around it with rope. Thankfully it was a baby they were dealing with – there was no way they could have persuaded an adult-sized duckbill to do anything it didn't want to.

Nothing about this plan was easy. If a dinosaur could squeal, this one was doing it big style.

"Are we ready?" his voice was hoarse. His muscles were aching and the duckbill was squirming constantly in his arms.

Kronar grunted in response. "Everyone know their safety spot?"

It was a joke really. Was there anywhere on this continent really safe from a T-rex? Climbing trees only worked for the raptors. A T-rex would just trample the trees and knock them to the ground. There was no loch or beach close enough to be of use. Not that many of the creatures in the ocean or in the loch would be any less terrifying or fatal than the T-rex.

They'd found some caves. They'd almost missed them. There was only the thinnest gap in the pile of rocks in front of the entrance that a human could squeeze through.

It was their only chance of safety. Kronar and Stormchaser were going to try and herd the duckbill to run in the direction they wanted – straight past the T-rex nest. How would a T-rex be able to resist an easy dinner – particularly one that was covered in the stench of blood? If it kept going, both dinosaurs would eventually reach the fail-safe, the beast they'd already killed. Hopefully that would keep the T-rex away long enough for them to grab the egg and make a run for the caves.

How they would get out of the caves was anybody's guess. In the meantime, they'd stored all their supplies inside. If they had to wait it out, they could. They just had to hope the boat wouldn't leave without them.

"My arms are breaking here," wheezed Leif.

"Are you ready, Storm?"

She fixed him with her violet eyes and gave a nod. "Ready."

"Then let it go."

THIRTY-FIVE

STORMCHASER

She ran like the wind on one side, with Kronar on the other, keeping pace with the duckbill, which was surprisingly fast. By simply keeping in its line of sight they steered it towards the hill, where the T-rex's nest was. The animal was easily guided, it was used to being part of a herd and taking direction from others around it. Storm slowed as it rounded the crest of the hill. Her part was done. She turned and kept running in the other direction, Kronar keeping pace next to her. By the time they reached the narrow entrance to the cave, Storm was wheezing and even Kronar had broken into a sweat. She leaned over and put her hands on her knees, trying to catch her breath.

A noise bellowed from over the hill. The T-rex. They could only hope it was on the move.

THIRTY-SIX

LINCOLN

Lincoln was crashing through the trees, his legs burning. As soon as they'd let go of the duckbill he'd headed for the forest to camouflage his route to the T-rex nest. The duckbill had already squealed past and the T-rex had snapped its wide jaws.

For a second, he thought she hesitated, before raising her head in the air and thudding after the fleeing duckbill. She must have caught the scent of the blood – that, coupled with the live specimen before her eyes, would be too tempting to ignore.

The whole ground trembled as she thundered past. Every tree, every bush shook, dirt jumping from the earth next to him. His breath caught halfway up his throat, every hair on his arms stood on end and his heart thudded against his chest. It was terrifying. He couldn't let his brain even think about what he was about to do.

He bolted from the trees, hoping his dark green tunic wouldn't attract her attention. The nest. He had to reach the nest. He could hear Leif running behind him.

His eyes scanned the landscape as they ran. There. Something else.

Galen and his team.

They were using *his* plan. *His* distraction.

He pushed his legs harder into the ground, he couldn't even feel the burn any more.

Galen stayed in his peripheral vision, his arms pumping madly as he ran, his face bright red. But they'd started further away.

Lincoln skidded to a halt at the nest, sending dirt flying into the air. It was empty. No egg in sight.

"What?" He couldn't help but cry out in frustration. He spun around to face Leif. "No. No. This can't be right. She was guarding this nest. She was being territorial."

Fury built in his chest. The scant lead they'd had on Galen's team was fading fast.

Leif glanced fearfully at Galen's fast-approaching figure. "Maybe she hasn't had the eggs yet. Maybe she was about to lay them?"

But Lincoln couldn't believe that. He dropped down on to his hands and knees and started pulling all the debris from the nesting area. Leaves, branches and rotten plants all went flying.

"Stop," shouted Leif. He pointed a little way behind them. Sitting beyond what they thought was the nest was another area – the rotting vegetation was thicker, and there, nestled underneath the mess, were two perfect eggs.

They were much bigger than Lincoln had expected, with grey mottled shells. He reached out both hands to grab one – just as Galen knocked him clean off his feet.

"Forget it, poster boy."

The full body weight of Galen was enough to crush the wind from anyone and Lincoln was no match for his muscular build. But Lincoln was too focused to let anyone distract him from his task. He got up even faster than he'd gone down, grabbing an egg with both hands and breaking into a run. The weight and breadth of the egg took him by surprise. That was why they'd been measuring arm spans back at registration, he realized as he ran. Someone on Earthasia knew *exactly* how big a T-rex egg was.

His heart pounded against his chest. He had it. He finally had what he'd come here for. Last time around he hadn't been the one to grab the raptor egg. This really felt like *his*. The egg that could save his sister. Adrenaline surged through his body. "Come on," he yelled at Leif as they sprinted away from the nest.

Leif followed close by. Galen might be stronger and stockier but he didn't have their agility. His curses followed them on the wind.

But within a few seconds Lincoln could hear the man's footsteps thudding behind him again. This was madness. The T-rex could be back any minute. Surely it made more sense for Galen to grab the other egg and go?

But Galen wasn't thinking rationally. That much was clear when Lincoln dared to glance over his shoulder. The older man was bearing down on him again, teeth gritted together and fists clenched. It seemed he'd underestimated Galen's speed.

Lincoln tried to add an extra burst to his pace, but Galen was closing in fast. The air around them was clouding with dust. Lincoln heard the sharp panting of breath behind him and he panicked.

Leif was running parallel to him but about ten sectars away. "Leif!" he yelled. "Catch." He threw the egg. No thought to its fragility. The egg hadn't even reached Leif's outstretched arms before Lincoln's legs were taken out from under him. He landed face first in the grey dust, Galen's full body weight pushing the air from his lungs.

But Galen wasn't finished. He didn't seem to even notice that the egg was gone. He grabbed hold of Lincoln's shoulder and shoved him onto his back.

The first punch was like a thunderbolt. Massive, powerful, leaving Lincoln coughing and writhing in the dirt. As he huddled on the ground he could see Leif running in the distance; it gave him the urge he needed. The T-rex could be on her way back by now. He had to get out of there.

He lashed out with his feet just as Galen pulled back to deliver another punch. The unexpected kick caught the big man in the gut, leaving him doubled over this time. Lincoln sprang to his feet, determined to get away, but Galen lurched and grabbed hold of his tunic.

His grip was like a clamp. Nothing would make him let go.

Except for one thing.

The roar of the T-rex.

From her position on the brow of the hill she could see the activity near her nest. She tipped her head back and roared again. It was pure rage. Pure fury.

The earth shook as she charged at them, heading straight back to protect her nest, while Galen's team scattered in all directions like feathers in the wind. Galen released his grip and started to run. Lincoln broke into a sprint too.

It took him a few seconds to get his bearings and realize the direction he should be following to reach the safety of the caves. Leif was barely a dot on the landscape, well out of the way of the T-rex. At least he should be.

The T-rex's head flicked from side to side. Every sense on alert. Lincoln's whole body was tense with fear.

Then, just short of the caves, Leif fell, the egg rolling from his hands.

There was a noise beside Lincoln. A choked laugh.

Galen was matching him pace for pace. He just couldn't shake this guy. At least he was running for his life just like Lincoln. If they both survived, they could fight about the egg later.

Lincoln raced across the open ground, heart pumping fiercely – he could hardly breathe. *Get up, Leif. Get up.*

Then the T-rex did something unimaginable. She changed direction. She had originally been heading back to the nest, towards Galen and Lincoln; now, it was as if she had sensed Leif had the egg – or maybe it was because he'd fallen and looked the easiest prey – but whatever the reason, she turned and headed directly for Leif and the entrance to the caves. At this rate Lincoln would barely reach Leif before the dinosaur did. Galen peeled off to the side, taking the opportunity of the distraction to head in another direction. He obviously had no clue about the caves they planned to hide in.

"Get up, Leif!" yelled Lincoln, sprinting towards him.

Leif stumbled to his feet. He gave one quick glance towards the egg, then ignored it and dived towards the entrance of the cave.

Lincoln didn't blame him. It was life or death out here. The egg had rolled away in the opposite direction – retrieving it could be fatal.

An extra surge of adrenaline spurted around his body. Breathing was optional now – if he didn't move fast enough he might not need oxygen for much longer.

The T-rex moved her head from one side to the other. Looking first at Lincoln, then at Galen. Leif, her intended victim was gone. Galen and Lincoln were the only prey left. For a moment they were both frozen to the spot, the T-rex an equal distance from each of them. Then she moved. Like lightning. The swish of her tail seeming to drive momentum towards her thundering legs.

Lincoln had had no idea a T-rex could run so quickly. He'd assumed because she was big, she must be a slow, lumbering creature. But she defied every expectation.

Her agility and speed was terrifying. Nobody stood a chance against her.

Not even Galen.

Her head thrust forward. There was a snap. And a blood-curdling scream.

Lincoln was still running but he couldn't help looking round. Blood was spurting from Galen's shoulder. His arm was gone. His face was frozen in shock. His knees buckled beneath him and he tumbled to the ground.

The man Lincoln had thought could wrestle a T-rex with his bare arms was squashed like a bug. Galen's head turned in Lincoln's direction. Fear. Lincoln could see only fear. The pumping blood began to spread across the ground. Galen slumped forward, a plume of dirt rising around him.

But the T-rex wasn't hungry. She didn't want to finish Galen. Her thrill was in the hunt.

She spun around. Fixing her eyes on Lincoln, she roared.

Adrenaline surged. He pushed harder, running for his life. The ground around him started to shake with the sheer weight of his pursuer. He still couldn't believe her speed. And he could smell her now. He could smell the odour of blood dripping from her mouth. Galen's blood.

The next blood in her mouth could be his.

Every rational thought in his brain told him to save himself – to get into the cave.

But that grey egg was a lifeline for his sister. Even though it was a good few steps away it felt like a bright beacon.

A sign.

A sign that it was meant to be his.

The caves were close. Even though it looked like he was running towards a solid wall, he knew the opening was there.

He didn't plan. There wasn't time. His pace never faltered, he just tumbled in a tight ball, rolling sideways at breakneck speed and catching the abandoned egg in two firm hands.

He heard Storm's scream from the cave entrance. He had the merest of seconds. He didn't even stand – didn't even attempt to get up, just tumbled once more back towards the entrance of the cave, reaching it as her arms shot out to grab him.

She pulled him sharply behind the first boulder towards the gap, just as the shadow of the dinosaur loomed over them. Any closer and he could have cleaned the T-rex's teeth.

She tried to squeeze back through into the cave, dragging him behind her. But she got stuck at the second boulder. Or more accurately, the heavy egg got stuck.

They hadn't considered the egg. They hadn't considered its size. It was bigger than expected. Squeezing behind the second boulder, shielding the entrance to the cave, required a flat back against the rock, a sideways movement of the head and a sharp breath in.

No one had thought about the egg.

The teeth of the T-rex snapped at the side of the rocks. They moved. The huge colossal rocks guarding the entrance to the cave *moved*. Moved with the weight of the T-rex.

It gave them the smallest breathing space – just enough

for Storm to thrust the egg through into the cave and land next to it with a thud. But Lincoln was still stuck. He'd forgotten about the backpack. It was wedging him between the rocks.

And the T-rex wasn't finished. She moved faster than Lincoln could ever have imagined, faster than he could push himself through the rest of the gap, her teeth catching the backpack, snagging some of the material from his trousers and slicing through his skin.

Her rancid breath warmed his neck. She jerked her head back with such a fury that Lincoln felt himself being dragged out. Leif and Kronar surged forward and grabbed hold of his arms, weighing him down as the sound of ripping cloth echoed through the cave.

He fell inwards. Inwards to the safety of the cave, landing face first on the damp earth inside.

He'd never felt anything so good.

But it wasn't over.

"Move back," yelled Storm. "It's nudging the rock."

Then came the thing that nobody expected.

A voice from the back of the caves. "You bloody young fools!"

THIRTY-SEVEN

LINCOLN

Lincoln jumped as Storm screamed right next to him. The T-rex was roaring in frustration outside and someone else was in the cave with them.

Kronar said the words that everyone else was thinking. "Who are you?"

A figure emerged from the blackness of the cave depths. He pointed at Storm's red tunic. "How could you be so stupid, wearing bright colours near a T-rex? And you?" He spun around and pointed at Lincoln. "You led her right to the entrance. Are you crazy?"

He didn't look like anyone they'd ever seen before. Wild hair, shaggy with streaks of silver, and a beard that reached halfway down his chest. His clothes were rags. Rags that were clumsily stitched together. And on his feet?

A brand new pair of sneakers.

The T-rex roared again and the whole cave shook. It sounded

as if she was scraping at the ground outside.

"Get to the back," shouted the stranger.

"But what about the stone?" Kronar looked frantic.

"What?" snapped the man. "Do you think you can hold it in place with your bare hands? Get back. If she can move the stone, she'll still be too big to get inside. Just pray she can't reach you with her jaws."

They gathered their belongings and ran to the back of the cave. Lincoln grabbed the egg, holding it between his hands – the cause of all this horror. It had better be worth it.

At the back of the cave he leaned against the damp walls, the cool water penetrating his tunic and nipping his skin. His leg ached. He must be covered in scratches. He hadn't even looked down yet. But the pain was reminding him that she'd managed to graze him with her rancid teeth.

"Did you see?" he hissed.

"See what?" asked Leif.

"Galen," he gasped. "The T-rex ate Galen's arm."

"Galen is dead?" Storm was right in front of him. He could barely even see her. But he could feel the heat from her body. Smell the scent of her skin. He couldn't even begin to explain his relief that she was okay, that she was right there beside him.

"Yes," he whispered. "Galen is dead."

He squeezed his eyes shut for a second as a wave of pain from his leg washed over him. They had next to no medical supplies. Three times his skin had been ripped by a dinosaur. His shoulder twice, and now his leg. He'd probably been exposed to a whole host of infections his body would have no armour against. He'd be dead before he made it home.

Storm reached over and touched his wrist. "Take a deep breath. Your pulse is racing. You need to slow down." She glanced over her shoulder into the darkness. "Let me deal with this."

None of this seemed real. He'd just seen his biggest rival's arm ripped off like a leaf pulled from a tree. A T-rex was waiting outside for him. Furious about her stolen egg.

And in here? In the darkness, was a complete stranger. Lincoln's brain was racing just like his pulse. What on earth was that guy doing here?

Storm pulled her hand away, turned towards the man and asked for the second time: "Who are you?"

"Blaine." A simple answer that told them nothing.

Lincoln sucked in a deep breath. The T-rex had quietened for a second. "Blaine? What does that mean? How did you get here? Do you live here? Were you born here? Are there others here?" One question tumbled out after the other.

Blaine. Something about it rang a bell. From his appearance – and from his smell – he'd been here a long time. But how long?

Someone had actually survived on this continent living with dinosaurs? It seemed incredible. Were there others like him?

Storm scrunched up her face. She reached over and touched Blaine's arm. "How on earth did you get here? Were you a fisherman, did you get shipwrecked?"

Blaine laughed. His laugh was strange – more like a cackle that echoed around the cave. "No, no, I've never been a fisherman." He leaned forward and stared at her. "I was much too intelligent for that."

Lincoln shifted uncomfortably. The name Blaine definitely seemed familiar, but he just couldn't place it. And the way he was looking at Storm was even more unsettling. A tiny hint of arrogance – something that he'd only ever seen before in certain people.

Leif spoke up. "You came with the Finalists, right? And you got left behind. Everyone thought you were dead."

"Not everyone." Kronar's voice startled them. "That's what the extra box was for. The one they left on the beach." He struck a match that set a warm orange glow flickering around them. It showed instantly how pale they all were compared to Blaine and his dark skin.

Lincoln could vaguely remember it. The large wooden crate that was unloaded and left sitting on the yellow sand untouched. He stared at the guy as tiny pieces of the puzzle started to fit together. He opened his mouth to say something else, then stopped.

Blaine shifted.

"It was you," Storm gasped. "The graphite, the paper, the chock bars. The boat! It was you, wasn't it?"

Of course. He hadn't thought much about it at the time – the missing items from everyone's backpacks. He'd just assumed they'd misplaced stuff – not that anyone could actually have stolen it.

But most importantly, the boat. They knew it hadn't come from Earthasia. They just hadn't figured on someone actually managing to survive amongst the dinosaurs.

Blaine shrugged. "I suggest you settle down for the night. We won't be able to leave here till first light. T-rexes hunt mainly at night, and you've annoyed this one too much for her to leave right now."

Lincoln slid down the wall, ignoring the pain in his shoulder. His legs were turning to jelly. They couldn't take his weight any more. The enormity of how close he'd just come to dying was finally hitting home.

Blaine pointed at his leg. "I'll do something about that tomorrow. Open wounds are practically an alert system for dinosaurs. Nothing gets their attention like the smell of blood and flesh."

The match flickered out between them.

It was going to be a long, long night.

DAY SIX

THIRTY-EIGHT

STORMCHASER

They finally crept out of the cave at the first light of dawn. Blaine had pulled some rags from his clothes and wrapped them around her bleeding feet and Lincoln's wounds. He was adamant they had to remain covered.

He led them silently to the forest, weaving his way through the trees. It was strange. He had the calmest air around him. It silenced the questions that were clamouring around her brain.

Storm walked slowly. Her feet were aching. She was aware that her heels and toes were bleeding and was dreading taking her boots back off. Maybe Blaine would have more than one pair of sneakers?

They almost missed it – even though it was right in front of them.

A house – or shack more like – built in the middle of the forest. It was much sturdier than she ever would have

297

imagined, with three separate rooms, all constructed from thick tree branches and an intricate weave of broad, dark green leaves. It was almost invisible. Was there a chance they'd already walked past this in the forest? And the smell… it enveloped them as soon as they walked in. Thick, rich, evergreen – with something else she couldn't quite place.

Blaine pointed to a large basin in the corner. "Everyone, wash up there. I'll take a look at those wounds. We need to disguise the smell before you move again."

Storm walked towards the room next door and let out a little gasp. There was a low-slung bunk on the floor – a bit like the ones they'd had at Camp – but the dark leaf walls were covered in paper. Every scrap of paper had drawings, numbers and graphs. All about the dinosaurs. Notes on how they lived, notes on their anatomy, their hunting skills, their nesting sites. Huge pieced-together maps of the whole area. It was so much more than they'd ever learned in school.

Something else caught her eye. A tiny hand-drawn picture of a woman and two kids. The paper had yellowed slightly and the corners started to turn in.

"How long have you been here?" she gasped.

Blaine walked past her and picked up a pile of fresh green leaves in the corner of the room. "Eight – no, nine years."

She still couldn't believe it. "How come you were left behind?"

He lifted up the bottom of his tunic to reveal a huge scar running across his thigh. "I got injured."

It covered nearly the whole front of his thigh, the skin

thinner and paler than the rest of him. She kneeled down, her hand automatically reaching out to touch it. "What happened?"

"The T-rex." He said it simply – as if it happened every day.

Lincoln moved behind her, bending to look down too. He was horrified. "What did the T-rex do?"

"Snapped my leg in half."

"And you survived? How?"

It seemed incredible. The injury and blood loss should have proved fatal, and even if by some miracle he'd survived that, the infection should surely have killed him.

"She attacked us while we were searching for new food. Her camouflage was much better than we'd been led to believe. If a deinosuchus hadn't come out of the water to fight with her, I would have been dead." He shook his head. "The rest of the Finalists scattered and I managed to drag myself back into the forest."

Kronar swallowed. "Deinosuchus?"

Blaine nodded and fixed him with a hard stare. "Fifty-sectar long crocodilian. Lives in the loch. It will attack anything that comes too close to the lake edge."

For a few seconds no one spoke. The monster that had killed Rune finally had a name.

Kronar's voice couldn't hide the terror. "You know about that m...monster?"

Blaine gave him a wary glance. "I've been here nine years – of course."

Kronar shook his head, his eyes bright with tears. "But

why on earth would you build a boat and go on a loch with that kind of monster living in it?"

"Because I never usually have a problem. I have to fish on the loch to survive. I had to make a boat. I cross the loch quietly, I don't leave any sign that I'm there."

The words hung in the air as Kronar's legs crumpled under him and he put his hands over his face. The guilt of Rune's death was still running deep.

"How did you make it?" Storm was fascinated.

Blaine held up his hands. "With these. And a few tools. It took a long time, months."

Lincoln moved forward. "How on earth did you survive the T-rex bite?"

He held out his hands. "Everything you need to survive is in this forest. My wound was open, but I wrapped it in some of the leaves I found. They must have had medicinal properties." He held one under Lincoln's nose. "Smell. You must have noticed when you stepped inside. That strong evergreen smell – it disguises everything."

He walked over and touched the paper on the wall. "My leg took months to heal. I drank water that collected in the leaves of the forest. I ate food from the forest floor. I started to build a shelter."

Lincoln frowned and kneeled down next to the bunk. "But some of this is manufactured. How did you get it?"

Blaine gave a sly smile. "By the time the ship pulled up the next year, I'd just started to walk again. They told me without question I couldn't go home."

Storm was horrified. "Why on earth not?"

"It's simple. They don't want people on Earthasia to know there's any chance of survival here. They want everyone to think that we need to wipe the dinosaurs out first. Taking me home would have proved that it was possible to stay alive on Earthasia for a year at least. It's not in their plans. Parliament had already decided that colonizing Piloria would be the next step for humans. But they wanted to do it on their terms. Which means destroying the dinosaurs."

His words were clear, but had a twisted edge. In a way, she almost understood why they hadn't told anyone about Blaine. She didn't think for a second that any normal person could survive here. It had been hard enough staying alive for a week.

"You don't want to go home?"

"They won't let me. I'll never see Earthasia again." He stared at one of the walls for a few seconds, then lowered his head. "Or the people on it."

Storm racked her brain. She couldn't remember anything about him. She'd been so young when he'd gone to Piloria and she guessed he was just one of so many Finalists presumed dead. How sad. Did he have family? From the way he'd spoken those last few words, and the picture stuck to the wall, she guessed he did.

From the corner of her eye she could see Lincoln, Leif and Kronar exchange glances. Maybe they remembered more than she did.

Blaine took a deep breath and looked up again. "I've learned to work this to my advantage. Every year they come

I trade with them. I give them information about the dinosaurs and about the land. They give me the things I request." He pointed to the corner of the room. "They won't give me what I really want, so I have to ask for material things. Sometimes it's a bed, sometimes it's clothes or sneakers. Mainly I ask for paper, graphite and matches. Most other things I make myself."

He gave a crazy kind of laugh. "There's no point asking them for weapons. They haven't found anything yet to fend off a dinosaur attack."

It made sense. She'd wondered how the Stipulators and Lorcan Field knew so much about Piloria. They'd always maintained that the only information they had was from the Finalists' brief trips.

"Come here," he said to Storm and gestured for her to sit down. "Let's see to your wounds." She eased her feet out of her boots and peeled her socks off, wincing at the pain. He lifted a blanket that was covering a variety of open clay pots.

"What's in those?"

He smiled and pointed. "The yellow one is a kind of gum, it sticks the papers to the leaves for me. The green is medicinal. It will help your wounds." He lifted up the strong-smelling leaves. "It's made from these." He wrinkled his nose and gave a little smile. "It will disguise the smell of the wounds, and the smell of being human."

Storm shifted self-consciously. It wasn't easy to get washed on Piloria. The splash in the ocean was virtually the only chance they'd had. Blaine worked quickly, cleaning off the blood and smothering her heels and toes in the green mush. She found a clean pair of socks in her backpack and pulled them on.

Lincoln sat precariously on the bunk next to her. As he peeled back the cloth it was clear the wound on his leg was gaping, and the one on his left shoulder was swollen and looked infected. Her abrasions and scrapes were minor in comparison.

Lincoln flinched every time Blaine squeezed cool water over the wounds, then smothered his shoulders and leg with the green ointment. He put some more into a large leaf then tied the edges together to make a pouch. "Put it in your backpack. You'll need it for the journey home."

He handed it to Lincoln, who gave him a rueful smile. "You think we'll get home?"

"Why not?" He gestured towards the T-rex egg, which was sitting in the corner of the room. He hadn't seen the raptor egg – it was still hidden inside one of the backpacks. "What do you need that for? I thought the whole point of visiting Piloria for the last few years was to find new kinds of food."

Storm shifted uncomfortably on the bed. "This year it changed. It's like you said – they want to wipe out the dinosaurs so we can take Piloria for ourselves."

"What new idea do they have this time? Last time they went for electrocution – and failed dismally."

"They what? Why didn't we hear anything about that?" Leif expressed the surprise that filled them all.

"Probably because it was a disaster." Blaine was clearing up around them. He walked over to the doorway and looked outside for a few seconds.

"You're covered now, you should be safe." He glanced at the egg again. "So what was the plan this time?"

"DNA," said Lincoln slowly.

"DN-what?" Blaine's brow wrinkled.

"It's supposed to be one of the building blocks of life. They've found it in humans and they want to find it in dinosaurs."

"But I don't get it. What happens when they do? And why do they need an egg?"

Storm sighed. "Because they think it will be simpler to get dinosaur DNA from an egg. Once they've got it…" She paused for a second. This still didn't sit well with her. It didn't matter how terrified she'd been of the T-rex and the raptors – it still felt fundamentally wrong. "Once they've got it, they think they'll be able to find a way to get rid of the dinosaurs." She held up her hands. "I'm not quite sure how: make a poison that will only affect some dinosaurs and not others, do something to stop them breeding, create a disease that will kill only them. They weren't really specific."

"They don't have a clue. In one hundred years' time they'll still be working on the same useless idea. The Stipulators are fools. The scientists are even worse."

She sucked in a breath. No one ever said those things out loud. No one spoke out against the Stipulators. No one interfered with the scientists' work.

But Blaine could say what he wanted. They'd left him behind on Piloria. They probably came back every year hoping he was dead.

He threw up his hands. "They know nothing. Not all dinosaurs are a danger. Not all dinosaurs will attack humans." He pointed to the egg. "I might like it better if the T-rexes weren't around, but the Stipulators would never stop there. They have delusions of grandeur." He swept his hand in front of his body. "They will wipe out everything. All of Piloria's living creatures. Have they even stopped to think that might be why we have problems growing crops on Earthasia? That we can't survive alone? No. Because they can't see a bigger picture. They don't understand how the world around them fits together." He let out a grunt and walked away. "They only see themselves!"

Blaine started pacing, tension emanating from him. No one spoke for the next few minutes, guessing it was best to let him blow off steam. He was muttering, "This is *my* home, not theirs."

Storm pressed her lips together. Blaine thought the same as she did – that the Stipulators would wipe out all dinosaurs, not just the ones they collected eggs from. But from the looks of the others, it wouldn't be wise to agree. She swallowed and stared at her feet. The doubts and suspicions that had been coiled in her stomach since the beginning had grown exponentially since she'd got here. Should she have trusted her instincts from the start, been brave and refused to help collect the eggs? She'd come to Piloria to discover the truth, and she'd done that – but she'd gone along with the Stipulators' horrible plan not knowing what else to do. Should she have stuck it out, tried to survive alone, until she could go home and tell everyone what she'd found?

But Blaine wasn't finished. "The hadrosaurids are the most nurturing creatures on the continent. The tiny head, tiny brain theory? Rubbish. I've seen them supporting smaller sauropods. I've seen them foraging for food and giving it to the creatures that can't reach."

Storm held her breath. She couldn't speak as she was struggling to process what he was saying.

Leif stood up, visibly uncomfortable and wanting to change the subject. "How long do we have to get back to the beach?"

"Less than twenty-four hours," Blaine answered sharply.

"How do you know that?" Lincoln asked.

"I usually try and stay hidden for the whole time the Finalists are here, so I'm on a countdown from the second you arrive."

"Don't you meet with the Stipulators?"

"Only if I have to. I give them a list of what I want for the following year and hand them the notes and drawings I've made since their last trip. They leave the box for me, and I empty it once all the Finalists have left the beach."

Storm smiled. "Sneakers."

Blaine lifted his eyebrows. "Shoes are a lot more difficult to make than you'd think."

Lincoln shook his head. "Don't you miss company? Don't you want to speak to the others?"

"Not really," he said simply. "Too much noise with you all here. I prefer the peace and quiet."

Storm looked around the humble dwelling. He'd managed to make a sort of home here – even if he did miss his family. And his comments had struck a chord with her. More than she could admit to anyone.

From the second she'd arrived on Piloria, she'd sensed the wonder of the place. But it was clear that Blaine didn't want to share it – he wanted rid of them. How would he feel if the Stipulators' plan worked and people moved to live on Piloria with him?

Blaine was outside foraging for more leaves for their trip home. Lincoln silently waved Storm over to where he, Leif and Kronar were sitting on the floor.

"Do you recognize him?" he whispered.

She frowned. "Blaine? No, why? I mean, he was a Finalist, so I guess I might have heard his name at some point, but there's been so many of them…"

Kronar shook his head. "Think again. Blaine wasn't a traditional kind of Finalist."

"What do you mean?" She had no idea what they were talking about.

Kronar turned towards her. "Blaine. Blaine Thredell. Don't you remember who he was?"

She shook her head. "I guess I was too young when he left to remember anything about him."

Lincoln cut in, "It was him, wasn't it? He was the one?"

Leif glanced towards him and nodded. "It was definitely him. No wonder they won't let him come home. Surviving the dinosaurs is only a tiny part of it."

She looked at the three faces around her. What on earth was going on? She folded her arms across her chest. "Spit it out, guys."

Lincoln pressed his lips together. "Blaine Thredell was the Stipulator they discovered had a family. He wasn't a Finalist in the usual sense. He was more or less flung onto the boat. They sent him here to die."

Storm's heart skipped a beat. "What?" She shook her head. "I thought that was only a rumour. I'd heard people talk about it happening. But I wasn't sure it was really true."

Lincoln pointed outside, where they could see their host still collecting leaves. "Well, it's true. You just met him. That was Blaine."

She stared back in wonder. "Poor, poor guy. Here all alone, for all these years."

Leif frowned. "I wonder why he doesn't even try to get back? He has family – that's why he's here. He must want to see them again."

Something clicked in her brain. "Do you think they won't tell him about his family? He said they wouldn't give him what he really wanted."

Lincoln bristled next to her. "We've no idea what kind of things they've said to him. We don't even know where his family are – or if they're still alive. But we all know the

Stipulators are capable of anything." He looked back over at Blaine. "One guy, alone on a continent of dinosaurs. I wouldn't ever want to be him."

THIRTY-NINE

STORMCHASER

They walked back through the forest. Every footstep hurt. But this time she wasn't scared. This time she could admire its beauty. Blaine was in tune with the dinosaurs, he would know what precautions to take. This was the first time since she'd arrived that she felt at ease.

The journey back was much shorter due to Blaine's familiarity with the terrain. But where it ended shocked them all.

"You can't be serious. Why on earth are we here? I don't think I can do this." Kronar's face paled, his breath quickened.

Storm was surprised too. The last place she'd expected him to take them was to the loch. Blaine was dragging the boat out of the bushes. Even the sight of it made her feel nauseous.

He picked up a set of oars and eyed them with distaste.

"You managed to lose a pair of my oars. Have you any idea how long it took me to make those?"

Lincoln crossed over to him. "There must be another way. A quicker way to get to the beach. We can't go across that loch again. Not now we know what lies beneath."

Blaine smiled. A twisted kind of smile. "There's no other way to get back in time." He pointed across the vast loch. "You can walk if you want, but to cover that distance? It will take you the best part of two days. You won't make it."

Silence.

Everyone was frantically searching their brains for another answer.

"I can't. I just can't," said Kronar.

Blaine was pushing the boat to the edge of the loch. "Well, you can't stay with me. I don't want company." There was no mistaking his tone. "What other option do you have?" It wasn't really a question. There was a sinister edge to his voice. Something they hadn't heard before. She'd thought he was joking before when he said he wanted rid of them – too much noise. Now, it seemed he really meant it.

Leif's reaction was instant. He hauled Kronar by the shoulder. "Get in the boat."

But Lincoln turned back to Blaine. He seemed more cautious. "Tell us how to get across the loch safely." He took both sets of oars from Blaine's hands. The time for niceties had gone.

Blaine tilted his head to one side. "Go slowly, go steadily. No noise. You hardly want to make a ripple on the water.

Your wounds are covered. There shouldn't be any odours to alert him to your presence." He started to walk away. "Pull the boat out of the water on the other side...if you get there."

He gave them one last glance and disappeared into the trees.

"Did that just happen?" Storm was beginning to feel it was all just some bad dream.

Lincoln stood at her shoulder. "I guess being alone for nine years is bound to make anyone strange. Maybe he could only keep it together for so long. We've only been with him since last night. We don't know what's normal for him."

"I just hope normal for him isn't sacrificing Finalists to the dinosaurs." She couldn't stop the words coming out. This felt creepy.

Lincoln seemed more determined. "He had a chance to do that with the T-rex. Let's just get out of here as quickly as we can."

There it was again. Whenever there was the tiniest danger he might reveal any doubts, any vulnerability, Lincoln hid behind practicalities. Maybe that was his coping mechanism.

"Come on, guys." She sighed. "You heard the man, quietly and steadily." She climbed into the boat, reluctant to put her feet anywhere near the water for fear of releasing the scent of blood into the loch. She held out her hand towards Kronar and took his trembling arm as he jumped across.

"Sit at the back of the boat," she whispered. "The rest of us will row. Close your eyes and think of something else."

Kronar nodded and gathered the remaining backpacks around him, clutching them to him as if they had some kind of magical power to save him.

Lincoln and Leif took a place at either side of the boat, dipping their oars gently into the water. Lincoln gave a silent count of *one, two, three* and they stroked out across the loch. Storm was holding her breath, praying that nothing would rise up from the depths.

She could hear a stilling in the air around them. Wasn't that what happened just prior to an attack? She almost didn't want to breathe. Didn't want to disturb the eerie atmosphere.

A giant red dragonfly buzzed past, its wingspan as long as her arm. Her natural reaction was to shush it. But she resisted and watched it fly across the still water.

Was that a ripple? Her throat was instantly dry. But the last thing she was going to do right now was ask Kronar for her backpack to wrestle around for her water bottle.

Lincoln and Leif were powering across the water, their oars so in tune that they made the minimum disturbance on the loch. All they could hear was the strokes on the water. The silence and pace seemed to increase the tension. Every second Storm was just waiting for something to happen.

Kronar had finally managed to open his eyes and was scanning the water frantically.

Lincoln was totally focused, sweat dripping down his face. Storm nudged his leg and pointed to the oars, silently offering to take a turn. But he shook his head. They'd developed their rhythm now and didn't want anything to break the pace.

Time seemed to hang above them. They were crossing the loch much faster than they had the last time. But last time they hadn't been so full of fear. Last time they'd been at the start of their adventure. This was different. This time they were just hoping to reach the other side and get to the beach.

As the pace continued Storm started to feel a little more relaxed. She could see the transporter in the distance. It hadn't been trampled by some dinosaur. It hadn't been stolen by any of the other Finalists. It was there. Waiting to take them back to safety.

Fixating on it seemed like the best idea right now. It gave her focus. Made her feel as if the end was in sight.

She stared at the backpacks Kronar was clutching. Two eggs. That was all they had.

Two eggs and one dead teammate.

She had no idea how the others had got on. The only other team they'd come across was Galen's. There had been a few signs of other teams – but nothing positive.

She stared up at the sun. A few hours must have passed. The edge of the loch was in sight – even if it was still a long way away.

It seemed an age before they neared the shore. Lincoln and Leif were red-faced and sweating. They'd rowed for almost four hours, with only a few short breaks where Storm had taken a turn. Every muscle in their bodies must ache.

There had been no sign of anything in the loch. No fishes swimming close to the surface – no sign of the plesiosaurs. It was almost as if the deinosuchus attack had been a figment of their imagination.

Then it happened. A rustle. A squawk. A whole cluster of giant dragonflies took to the skies above the forest near the loch. Seconds later the rancid stench of the T-rex flooded through the air.

She burst through the trees towards them. Tipping back her head and roaring.

They couldn't speak, silenced by shock.

She was far away from her nest now, far away from the swamp area she favoured. But far too close to them – only two hundred sectars away.

"She's hunting us," breathed Storm. Horror filled her. They'd travelled for a whole day, they'd spent the last few hours crossing the loch. They'd covered their wounds. Disguised the smell of their flesh and blood. She shouldn't have been able to find them. Dinosaurs weren't supposed to be this intelligent.

Yet here she was. Foaming at the mouth, spitting mad, her head and tail thrashing wildly from side to side. One sweep of her powerful tail felled a small tree as her deafening roar echoed around the loch.

She thundered towards the shore. Lincoln and Leif were panicking, scrambling to pull their oars from the water, but unable to stop the momentum of the boat carrying them forward. Kronar was still hunched in the back of the boat.

What little colour he'd had in his face drained away completely.

There was a flash of green. Dark, crocodilian green.

The deinosuchus must have been resting beneath the rippling water at the edge of the loch, waiting for prey. Not caring what the prey was – T-rex or human.

If they'd reached the edge of the loch first, it would have gone for human.

Its jaws were even wider than they remembered, the yellow teeth clamping around the neck of the T-rex with terrifying speed and a sickening crunch. The T-rex thrashed and whipped her tail from side to side. But the jaws held firm. The deinosuchus' short webbed feet didn't slip on the muddy bank – it tightened its grip around the T-rex, then slowly and deliberately dragged her backwards into the water.

"Get ashore, get ashore now. They're too busy fighting to notice us."

The smell was horrific; between the rotting remains in the T-rex's teeth and the septic stench from the deinosuchus, the air around them was poisonous. The boat ground ashore on the shingles of the loch. Lincoln didn't hesitate, he jumped out straight away and made a grab for a backpack. Stormchaser was right behind him, leaping onto the grass and picking up another pack. Leif was next, while Kronar seemed rooted to the floor of the boat, staring at the epic struggle happening right next to them.

"Move!" shouted Lincoln. He was ready to start running towards the transporter. Ready to get away from all this.

Storm was torn. It would only take a few seconds to jump back and pull Kronar from the boat, but all her instincts were telling her to run as far and as fast as she could.

"Kronar!" she hissed.

He jolted, then panicked, his feet tripping over themselves as he tried to leap from the boat. He landed in water that was rapidly changing colour with the blood that oozed from the T-rex's neck.

He struggled upright. But the T-rex was fighting for her life. Trying to free herself from the deadly jaws of the deinosuchus as it pulled harder to drag her underwater, trying to drown her. The T-rex's powerful tail thrashed madly, flailing this way and that – whipping Kronar from his unsteady feet and sending him flying ten sectars through the air.

It happened in the blink of an eye. No time to react. No time to stop it.

He landed with a sickening crunch in a crumpled heap on the ground.

Storm ran to him. She'd heard the bones snap as he landed. One leg was twisted, one arm thrown back; the side of his chest had slammed into the hard ground.

There was the tiniest noise as Kronar rolled onto his back.

Leif ran over and grabbed hold of Kronar's arm. "Come on, let's go." He hadn't heard what Storm had.

But Storm knew instantly that Kronar couldn't get up. His chest crackled, he wheezed. His pale face was turning blue. Lincoln dropped to his knees next to him, grabbing his other arm. "Kronar, can you get up? Can you move?"

But the frail human body was no match for the sheer muscle mass of a powerful T-rex tail. Leif fell down beside him. "No, Kronar. Get up. Get up now. We're nearly there." He pulled at his friend's clothes as his voice started to break.

"I think he's broken his leg." Storm's eyes scanned Kronar's body as she tried to fight back the tears. "Maybe his shoulder and" – she held her hand above his chest, too scared to actually touch – "possibly some of his ribs."

Leif and Lincoln exchanged anxious glances. The blue tinge around Kronar's face was changing again, darkening.

Kronar was struggling to talk. He couldn't catch any air. His breath was stalling, and seconds later, blood-filled bubbles spilled from his mouth. His face contorted. "Family," he wheezed to Leif as the last breath left his body. Then his muscles relaxed and his eyes rolled.

Leif choked, put his head on his friend's chest and let out a wail.

Storm looked away in despair and gazed blankly across the loch. When her eyes refocused she noticed something. The last backpack, trailing in the water next to the boat which, with all the turmoil, had bobbed back out onto the loch. Lincoln must have noticed it too – because suddenly he darted forward with a yell.

The T-rex had stopped thrashing her tail, obviously succumbing to the effects of being held underwater for too long. Lincoln dived onto his belly, straining to reach the strap of the bag, which slipped from his grasp. She could see the fury on his face, the rage at what had just happened.

Nothing about what he was doing was rational. They should be in the transporter right now – getting as far away from this place as possible.

"What are you doing?" yelled Storm. She couldn't help herself. She couldn't leave him in danger. She ran forward too, hoping and praying the deinosuchus would remain distracted by its prize.

Lincoln reached out again, just as the body of the T-rex shuddered. Storm saw the black fathomless eyes of the deinosuchus lock onto Lincoln. She couldn't breathe. Not for a second. She'd just seen one friend die. Was she about to witness another?

The effect was instant. The deinosuchus unlocked its jaws from the torn throat of the T-rex. Lincoln reached just that little bit further, his fingers brushing against the strap and struggling to grasp it.

She'd forgotten. Forgotten how quickly the deinosuchus could move. As Lincoln's fingers grabbed the strap and pulled it sharply back, the creature swept round. It had won its first prey but there was another available. Storm didn't hesitate. She grabbed Lincoln's tunic with both hands and yanked hard.

There was a flicker in the deep water nearby. A head and long thin neck reached upwards, followed by a broad body with thick front flippers. A plesiosaur, soaring out of the water in a way she'd never seen before. The front end of the body landed hard on the deinosuchus's back, one broad flipper slapping it across the eyes.

She darted backwards, amazed by the sight. The deinosuchus was momentarily stunned – stunned enough to allow Lincoln and Storm time to get to their feet and sprint straight towards the transporter. She reached down and dragged Leif away from the body of his friend as they passed.

Storm got to the transporter first. It didn't matter that she hadn't driven before. She gunned the engine, waited ten seconds for the others to scramble in, then floored it. She wasn't about to wait and see if the deinosuchus would pursue them on land.

"You fool, what were you thinking?" she yelled at Lincoln.

"I was thinking about the reason we were here in the first place!"

A bump in the ground sent their heads crashing into the roof before they thumped back down onto the hard seats.

Storm turned to glance back at the loch. She was scared to look. Would the thin neck of the plesiosaur be lodged between the deinosuchus's teeth?

She sucked in a breath and turned round quickly. The deinosuchus was feasting again – on the body of the T-rex. The plesiosaur was nowhere in sight.

When she looked back, Lincoln's green eyes were fixed on her. She couldn't read his expression at all.

"Tell me I didn't just see that. Tell me one dinosaur didn't just rescue us from another... Storm?"

She had no idea what to say. She couldn't even rationalize what had just happened in her head. She grabbed her backpack and thrust it against his chest. "Hold this. I need to concentrate on getting back to the beach. The last thing we need is to miss the ship."

She looked past him. The lush Pilorian vegetation was a blur of green. She picked a spot on the horizon to focus on – trying not to think about the events she'd just witnessed.

Everything they'd been told about dinosaurs was a complete and utter lie.

Unintelligent creatures didn't track you for thousands of sectars across a continent.

Creatures who only acted on instinct didn't know how to put out fires.

Tiny-brained dinosaurs didn't put themselves in harm's way to save a human life.

FORTY

LINCOLN

And then there were three.

The journey over the uneven ground rattled his bones. Rattled what few remaining nerves he had left. He imagined every flicker in his vision was something else that wanted to eat them. Every noise in the background sounded like a predator.

Family. The last word that Kronar had said to his friend.

Lincoln knew exactly what he meant. Kronar expected Leif to look after his family as well as Rune's.

It hurt Lincoln more than he could say – because he knew his actions would affect every one of them.

DAY SEVEN

FORTY-ONE

STORMCHASER

Storm was tired. She was hungry. She wanted to taste fish again but was too scared to go anywhere near the sea. She wanted to do anything that would take her mind off the thoughts currently swirling around her head.

Night-time on the beach had been colder than she'd expected. Between the noises from the jungle, and the noises from the sea they'd hardly had any sleep. Since morning they'd sat in the blistering sun for nearly six hours, watching the horizon anxiously for any sign of the ship.

At first there were only three other people on the beach with them. Added together, it was the highest number of Finalists ever to have returned from an expedition. But none of the Finalists were happy.

For some, Galen had been the ultimate competitor. Getting into a showdown with the T-rex had turned him into a mixture of hero, martyr and legend. A couple of the other survivors were people from his team and they glared at Storm and her friends as if they wanted to kill them.

Frustration was evident. The pterosaur egg in Galen's backpack had been lost when the T-rex got him.

His team had nothing.

None of the others had any spoils.

Gradually a few stragglers appeared. In the end, there were ten survivors in total. One guy admitted he'd spent the whole week on the beach. He hadn't even glimpsed a dinosaur on Piloria.

Most were injured. All were filthy. But at least none were hungry. It seemed they'd all found food on Piloria. Some had even brought plants back with them.

One thing was clear. None of the other Finalists had ever really rated Storm, Lincoln and Leif. It didn't matter what they'd achieved to get here in the first place, no one had ever expected to see the youngest team again.

There were a few whispers. A few calculating glances.

But from the second they reached the beach, Lincoln, Storm and Leif stood guard over their prizes. They hadn't lost two friends to be cheated at the last moment.

Lincoln sat with a knife between his hands. Leif, with the gun. It was a clear message. No one was going to attack them and steal their treasure.

But Storm couldn't get the thought of what would come next out of her head. She didn't trust the Stipulators. She didn't trust them at all. They'd lied about Piloria. They'd left someone here who'd survived for nine years and they'd told no one.

Piloria was terrifying. But wonderful too.

There was a whole host of terrifying dinosaurs.

But there was also beauty. Beauty in the plants – there were new foods, a vast expanse of land and vital supplies here – and beauty in some of the creatures. Whatever they did with this DNA stuff, could she really believe that harmless dinosaurs wouldn't be put at risk? What if the plesiosaurs were affected? A plesiosaur had just saved their lives – of that Storm had no doubt. Surely they owed the plesiosaurs some loyalty? Part of her wanted to grab the eggs and smash them both now. Get it over with and get back home. Leave the dinosaurs with their own continent.

But she'd left it too late. Both Leif and Lincoln were already guarding the eggs with everything they had.

She could be about to make the biggest mistake of her life.

Finally the ship appeared on the horizon. Its familiar grey shape filled them all with relief. They watched nervously as the small boats, each with a Stipulator on board, made their way towards the beach.

Lincoln whispered in her ear. "Funny, isn't it? When we arrived there were ten boats. This time they're sending only two. Did they already know how many would survive?"

She licked her lips, watching the surface of the sea for any sign of disturbance. She wrinkled her brow. "The ship – where does it go? It can't have time to get back to Earthasia. Where does it go while we are here?"

Lincoln frowned as if he'd never given it any thought. "I have no idea."

Storm pressed her lips together. Leif stood up and stretched. "I don't care. Just so long as it takes us straight back home."

The journey over on the boat was quick and uneventful. After their experience on Piloria that was a welcome relief.

Once they were back on board one of the Stipulators wrinkled his nose – probably at the smell – then waved them all towards the servery and the dorms.

Storm found Lincoln sitting in their dark corridor. The ship was being pounded by waves, but it was quieter down here. Less stormy.

"What do you think will happen when we get back?" she asked as she slid down the wall next to him.

He played with the laces on his boots. "What always happens. Celebrations. Parties. Prizes for the Finalists." His voice had a strange, wistful tone.

"We're the only team with eggs."

"I know." Things had been awkward; once they'd cleaned up the Stipulators had asked them to declare any eggs and unpack their goods. Leif, Lincoln and Storm had emptied all the backpacks together, leaving the contents on a large wooden table.

The Stipulator had contained his excitement and just labelled the specimens, taking a note of the members of the team.

After that, they'd been so exhausted they'd gone to the

bunk rooms, ignoring the signs for male and female this time, and all going into one room together. It felt cold and empty with just the three of them in there.

They'd fallen asleep instantly and hadn't woken for two days. No one else had joined them.

Leif had hardly spoken. Grief was etched across his face. They'd taken to escorting him down to the servery and back to make sure he was eating.

"How do you feel about what we're doing?"

Lincoln looked at her. "I feel fine. Why wouldn't I?"

She shook her head. "After everything we've seen, everything we've done... Piloria isn't our continent, Lincoln. We have no right to be there." She started scratching at the skin on her back – it was bothering her again.

He was indignant. "I don't get you, Storm. I really don't. Why did you even go to Piloria if you didn't believe in what we were doing? Capturing the eggs was always the goal. How on earth can you have any sympathy for killer dinosaurs? Wouldn't Piloria be a whole lot better without them? Wouldn't you actually like to live there eventually – if the dinosaurs weren't there?"

"Do you really think that will ever happen? Blaine didn't. He thought they were crazy to try and get rid of the dinosaurs. He should know – after nine years."

"But he's spent nine years *hiding* there. And Blaine's clearly crazy. Did you see that look in his eyes when he told Kronar he couldn't stay? If he hadn't said that, Kronar might still be alive." Lincoln was getting mad. His voice was rising and echoing around their little corridor. If he didn't quieten down he'd attract other people to their hideaway. That was the last thing Storm wanted. This was the only place on the ship where she actually felt she had some privacy.

Her skin was irritating her more than ever. If she scratched again she would break the skin and the scar would bleed. The last thing she needed was more abrasions. Her toes and heels had finally begun to heal with the green gloop Blaine had given them. At least he'd been useful for something.

"Stop that." Lincoln grabbed her arm and pulled it away from under her tunic. He sagged back against the wall. "What is that anyway? What happened?" He was still holding her hand, stopping her from scratching again.

This had been the longest few weeks of her life. In the last few days she'd started to think of these guys as family. She knew they didn't see her that way – they had families of their own.

But Storm didn't. And these guys had broken into the little world that she kept protected around herself.

Lincoln had broken into her world in a whole other way. She didn't feel the same about him as she did about Leif, as she did about Dell. There was something more. Something different. Something she didn't even want to contemplate.

It was hard enough to let people in. Hard enough to talk. These guys had filled a void in her life that they didn't have in their own. But she'd never tell them how she felt. They'd probably think she was being ridiculous.

And to say anything more? She stared at her hand, the one Lincoln was holding. He couldn't possibly understand how much that touch meant to her – the girl who had lost her mother years ago, who had no one. The sensation sent a warm glow through her body that she couldn't even begin to put into words. It made her crave more. And the way he was looking at her pushed her even further. It made her want to trust him. To tell him the story no one but Dell knew.

It was easier in the darkness. Saying the words seemed simpler. She couldn't have said them if she'd had a clear view of his bright green eyes.

"I had an accident."

"Where?"

"At the loch."

He didn't let go. But he moved, he slid his fingers over the top of her hand and intertwined them with hers.

"What kind of accident?"

"I was diving. I hit my head."

"Were you alone?" She could hear the rise in his voice. Hear his concern.

"No. I was on a boat with some other people. But when I dived in I must have knocked myself unconscious. I got dragged underneath, caught in the nets there. That's how I got my scars. The metal underside of the boat."

He flinched. "How did they get you out?"

She sighed. "They didn't." There it was. That horrible feeling that always swamped her when she thought about this. The fact that no one had noticed. The fact that no one had cared.

His voice was quiet. "So, who rescued you?"

"Milo."

"Who?" He was sitting upright now. Probably staring at her through the darkness. His thumb was drawing imaginary circles in the palm of her hand.

"The plesiosaur."

His eyes widened. "You gave it a name?"

This part always seemed hard to believe. "Milo saved me. No one on the boat even noticed I was gone. When I came round I was lying at the side of the loch. I could barely move, the wounds on my back were so painful. Milo's head was resting next to mine. I must have passed out again. But when I woke, Milo was still waiting next to me. He hadn't left me. He hadn't left my side."

"Plesiosaurs – rescuing humans." Lincoln shook his head. "If I hadn't witnessed it with my own eyes I wouldn't believe it. It just seems so unreal. That these creatures can have intelligence, compassion…"

She pulled her hand from his and stood up. "Think about what you've seen over the last few days. Was all of that really just instinct? Can you honestly tell me that some of that behaviour wasn't intelligent? That T-rex tracked us for two days – far away from her nest. Those raptors used earth to put out a fire. Why? And a plesiosaur had the intelligence to get me to shore when I was unconscious."

She kneeled back down in front of him. "Are these really monsters? Or are they just creatures, like us, living their lives? I think what we've done was wrong, Lincoln. We should never have taken those eggs. We should never have stolen those babies from their mothers and I think, as beautiful as Piloria is, it's not our continent. It's theirs." She was back on her feet again. "It's time we took responsibility for our own behaviour. We've caused the problems on our own continent. And it's up to us to solve them."

FORTY-TWO

LINCOLN

Her footsteps echoed down the corridor, fading into the distance until all he could hear was the thudding of his own heart.

He understood everything she was saying. It was an intelligent argument.

But it wasn't his. He couldn't let it be his.

There was a noise from the depths of the ship, voices echoing towards him.

"It's only three days. Reban's anxious for us to make good time. We can't afford for those eggs to hatch."

"They won't. We're keeping them at a low temperature. They should be fine."

"Only one team proved their worth. And it was the team he told us to watch. What was it about them that interested him?"

"Who knows? One thing's for sure – when we reach

Earthasia they won't be a team any more. Only one person can claim the rewards for each egg. Thank goodness they only found two. Resources are so scarce they'll struggle to provide what they promised to more than one Finalist and their family. Three team members, two eggs. It's going to get ugly."

The voices faded again.

Lincoln pressed back against the cool metal wall. He'd hoped his suspicious would be proved wrong. That there might be a way... But there was no room for doubt now. He pushed Storm's words from his mind, all thoughts of her. All thoughts of Leif, Kronar, Rune and their families.

The time was getting closer. He was going to have to betray them all. If resources were already scarce – he couldn't hesitate. He had to claim both eggs, had to claim the only prize, otherwise Arta had little chance of survival.

His stomach twisted. The betrayal would be brutal. Leif had become his friend. And Storm, maybe something more.

It made this even harder.

But he knew exactly what he had to do.

FORTY-THREE

STORMCHASER

Storm was in the servery. She prodded at the fish on the plate in front of her. She'd never seen one like this before and probably never would again. It was good. But eating was difficult.

Since she'd arrived back on the boat she'd been exhausted. Living on adrenaline for seven days had used every tiny bit of energy she'd possessed. And it seemed to have affected them all.

All of the survivors just dragged themselves from their beds, ate on occasion, then went straight back to sleep. The whole ship had a strange aura about it. Maybe it was because it was so quiet. Their first time on the ship there had been a hundred Finalists buzzing with excitement at the thought of what lay ahead. Now, they just seemed to be surrounded by emptiness.

It was the beds that haunted her. Turning over at night

and seeing the raft of empty bunks next to her made her squeeze her eyes closed. Ninety people. Dead – or as good as.

In a way she hoped they *were* dead. Blaine might have survived on Piloria but she doubted any of the other Finalists could manage so well if they were wounded.

Some stories had come out. One Finalist told them about being stuck in a swamp for two days while his teammates were devoured by a creature that lived there. He'd finally realized that the creature detected motion and only escaped being eaten by keeping completely still in the mud while he watched the horror play out around him.

Another Finalist had been attacked by the velociraptors. Her three teammates had died and she had a broken arm and ugly wounds across her face. Those scars would last a lifetime.

But what if they'd left someone behind? Someone like Blaine who would have to learn to survive on the dinosaur continent?

Even the thought of Blaine made Storm wince. How would he react if another person was left on Piloria?

Lincoln and Leif thudded down at the table next to Storm. Both had platefuls of fish. Lincoln nudged it with his cutlery. "We'll probably never get a plateful like this again once we get back to Earthasia. I may as well eat it while I can."

Leif looked up. "You don't know that. I'm sure the Stipulators get fish. Once we get back we won't be on rations any more. Chances are we'll never be hungry again."

A strange expression flitted across Lincoln's face. He fixed his eyes on his plate. Storm's stomach gave a little lurch. In all the time they'd spent together, she still hadn't found out why he was there. He'd never mentioned his family. He'd never revealed much about himself at all. But he'd saved her life, and she'd saved his. Things like that couldn't be forgotten. Couldn't be undone. She'd be connected to him for life. He'd be someone on Earthasia she could rely on. She was starting to believe he felt that way too.

She set down her fork. "Should we tell them?"

Lincoln looked up. "Should we tell them what?"

"The Stipulators. Should we tell them that we met Blaine?"

Leif choked. "Not if you want to stay alive."

She frowned. "What do you mean?"

Lincoln nodded. "I think he's right. I think the less we tell the Stipulators the better. Blaine said himself that he usually hid from the Finalists every year. I doubt anyone else knows that he's there. And if the Stipulators thought you might announce that someone had managed to stay alive on Piloria for nine years, despite the ferocious dinosaurs…" He shook his head. "I don't think that would fit in with their plans."

"But what happens if Reban Don questions us when we get back?"

Leif shot her a suspicious glare. "Why would he question us? What is it with you and that guy?"

"What's that supposed to mean?"

Leif pushed his plate away. "It means that I think you know him. I saw the way he looked at you during the Trials. He was constantly watching you."

She shifted in her seat. "I don't know him. I don't know him at all. I've never even spoken to him." Her voice stopped dead.

Lincoln tipped his head towards her. "What?"

She'd tried to push it out of her mind. But it was still there, lurking away in the back corners. "Before we came here, before the announcement. Dell and I had to deliver something to parliament. He spoke to me then."

Leif raised his eyebrows. "What did he say?"

Her mouth was dry. She reached out for her glass of water. "He asked me what my name was."

"And?" Leif wasn't going to let this go.

"Then he asked me what my mother's name was."

Lincoln took a deep breath and glanced over at Leif. "Did you tell him?"

She shook her head. "No. I just told him my mother was dead."

Leif closed his eyes for a second and then spoke carefully. "How did he seem when you told him that?"

She threw up her hands. "I don't know. Upset. Angry. Surprised. I just wanted to get out of there. My mother never liked me talking to Stipulators. We always avoided them." The questions were making her uncomfortable.

They did it again. Exchanged that look.

"What? What is it?"

Lincoln put his hand on her arm. "Did he ask you anything else?"

She racked her brain. "He asked where I stayed. That was it."

Leif bit his lip. "Storm, have you ever noticed anything unusual about Reban Don?"

She was getting more frustrated by the second. "Unusual? He's a Stipulator. They're all unusual. They wear black cloaks for a start."

Lincoln turned to face her. "The first thing I noticed about you was your eyes. I'd never seen eyes that colour before. They're really striking."

"So?"

Leif leaned forward. "Did your mother have violet eyes?"

She shook her head. "My mother had brown eyes."

"Who else do you know has violet eyes?"

It was like a wave of fear and emotion hitting her all at once. She hadn't seen it. She hadn't seen it at all. But as soon as Leif said the words, she knew exactly who he was talking about.

Everyone said she was the spitting image of her mother. Was that why Reban Don had asked? He'd known her mother? Had he recognized something of her mother in Storm?

Her reaction was instantaneous. Her stomach heaved. She leaped to her feet and dived towards the nearest waste bin, retching up every bite of fish she'd just eaten.

Lincoln appeared at her side, standing for a few moments and rubbing her back.

When the retching finally stopped she straightened up and Leif handed her a glass of water.

All the hairs on her arms stood on end. The ship was warm, but she was freezing. "You can't…you can't think that…"

Lincoln's low voice was calm, reasonable. "Stipulators aren't allowed families. But he could be a relative. An uncle. A cousin. Or…something else. Could that explain the questions he asked you?"

She shivered and wrapped her arms around herself. "I don't know. I just don't know."

Leif led her back over to the table, taking the seat opposite. "Didn't your mother ever tell you anything about your father?"

She shook her head. She'd asked. She'd asked a thousand times. But her mother had been resolute. Her father wasn't up for discussion. "She wouldn't talk about him at all. She just said he was dead. She wouldn't even tell me his name."

Tears sprang to her eyes. She hated this. She hated all the thoughts she was having. She'd been devastated when her mother died. There was no other family to go to. She'd spent the last five years alone, in a Shelter. Learning how to survive on her own. Dell really had been her only friend.

But this? This was bigger than she could ever have imagined.

She'd always known her eye colour was unusual. All her life people had commented on it. She'd never seen anyone else with eyes like hers. Why hadn't she noticed Reban Don's? The others obviously had.

Was there a chance that Reban Don was her father? Why had he never come to find her? Had he even known she existed? And if he did, why on earth had he left her alone? To live in that horrible Shelter.

It was almost as if Lincoln could read her jumbled thoughts. He put his hand on hers. "He's a Stipulator, Storm. If he had family…and they found out…"

"What? He would end up like Blaine? So he sent me to Piloria to die instead? Is that what he wanted? What kind of a person is he?"

She stood up again, her plate crashing to the floor. The tears that had been brimming in her eyes were threatening to spill over.

She would not cry.

She would not cry over someone who'd selected her for a suicide mission.

There was a surge of anger. Reban Don had sent them to Piloria for the eggs. Eggs that had cost two of her teammates their lives. Why should he get what he wanted? He didn't deserve them. He wasn't worthy.

Lincoln stood up next to her. "Storm, wait."

But she couldn't wait. She had to get out of here. "Leave me."

And she rushed out of the door before the tears really fell.

PART FIVE

THE HOMECOMING

FORTY-FOUR

STORMCHASER

The noise was incredible. Music was playing, people lined the streets cheering. Coloured foil streamers flew through the air.

The Stipulators in their ominous black clothes were walking on all sides. Keeping them away from the waving crowds. Stopping them from talking to people they recognized.

The parade finally came to a halt in front of the city auditorium. Lorcan Field was practically bubbling with excitement, presumably at the thought of finally getting his hands on some real dinosaur DNA. It chilled her to the bone.

The two pale eggs were sitting on display on the table at the front of the auditorium. They were surrounded by glass, but that wouldn't be hard to smash.

The eggs wouldn't be hard to smash either. She should have listened to her gut instinct sooner. She should have acted when she had the chance. Instead, she'd allowed herself to be overwhelmed by fear, the judgement of others and her own indecision.

She glanced nervously at Lincoln and Leif, who were next to her. The rest of the surviving Finalists were behind them – they didn't have any bounty to show. They'd all been made to change back into their stained and ripped clothes before they marched from the ship. The Stipulators hadn't wanted them to look primed and polished. They didn't want the people around them to know that they'd eaten more on the journey home in the last week than the rest of the population would eat in a year.

But Storm wasn't interested in the promise of health care, food or energy. She wasn't interested at all.

Leif seemed overwhelmed by the spectacle. Lincoln just had that glassy expression. The one he wore when he wanted to block out everyone and everything around him.

They entered the crammed auditorium, walking along the side and up the steps onto the stage.

Reban Don was staring at her again, muttering to someone under his breath. Adrenaline surged through her. Being in this man's presence made her mad. Was he really a relative who had abandoned her? Could he really be her *father*? Even she was starting to suspect it was true, and the thought made her sick to the pit of her stomach.

How had he felt when he'd seen her? But for her eyes, she was the living image of her mother. If he'd really had a relationship with her mother, it wouldn't have been hard for him to put two and two together.

All she could feel was rage. Rage that he'd abandoned her. Rage that he'd known what she'd face in Piloria. Rage at the death of her teammates for a cause she didn't believe in.

If he'd known she existed, at any point in her life he could have approached her. Could have talked to her.

But he wouldn't have wanted her to get in the way of his role as Chief Stipulator.

So, he'd let her take part in the Trials and sent her to Piloria to die.

Maybe she hadn't even done that well in the Trials. Maybe he'd even fixed it so she'd qualify when she shouldn't have?

Truth was, she wouldn't put anything past this man.

The formal announcements started. "Three weeks ago we bid farewell to one hundred Finalists sent to Piloria on a quest." Reban held out his hand to the small group on the stage. "Ten have returned."

Cheers erupted around them again. It was apparent that the relatives of the ninety Finalists who hadn't returned hadn't been allowed inside the auditorium. Although the anger was burning away inside her, the atmosphere in here was electric. If she wasn't careful she would find herself carried away by it.

"Two eggs were returned with them. The egg of a velociraptor and the egg of a Tyrannosaurus rex. Two of the most deadly creatures on Piloria. From these eggs we will be able to study the dinosaur DNA. We will be able to create a disease to kill these creatures, and free the continent of predators, so that we may spread out across the land."

There was hysteria. The shouts and cheers were reaching a crescendo. Just the thought of "spreading out" was causing mayhem. For families who'd lived in shared accommodation and people who'd spent their whole lives with no space to call their own it was as good as a miracle. The crowds were trampling nearer the stage, more and more people pushing through the glass doors at the back and crushing those at the front.

She had to do this. She had to do this soon.

Reban had stepped over to the exhibit table, lifting the glass covers and leaving the eggs exposed. He shot a glance at the other Stipulators and her stomach rolled over with unease.

His voice carried across the crowd. "Previously, everyone on each team who'd visited Piloria and successfully returned was rewarded. However, our resources are dwindling all the time. Because of this, the government have made the decision that only one Finalist can claim ownership of each egg; only one person can claim the prizes that are granted with each egg. Specialized health care, preferred housing, power privileges and no limit on rations."

What? Since when had they decided that? She looked frantically from Leif to Lincoln. Neither of them seemed to be listening. She hadn't told them what she planned to do, but she'd always assumed that the privileges for finding the eggs would be accorded to all members of the team. She'd hoped her actions wouldn't affect the recognition of the others, and that she'd be the only one to lose her privileges.

For the good of the people. For the good of the planet. For the good of mankind. The crowd started chanting the words around her, filling the room with their fervour.

It was too much. It was too much for her. She had to do this now. She had to show them that this was wrong. The dinosaurs weren't all unintelligent beasts. They deserved to keep their land for themselves.

Reban pointed to the T-rex egg. "Who claims credit for this?"

The egg she'd dived out of the cave for. The egg she'd risked life and all her limbs to help Lincoln grab from under the T-rex's nose. She swayed a little. Remembering the smell of flesh and blood on the T-rex's breath. The odour of death.

She moved in the blink of an eye.

She had to.

She ran at the eggs, raising her fist ready to smash it down on them.

Everything happened in slow motion.

For some reason, Lincoln was right by her side.

She reached the table in a few steps. Reban's eyes – *his violet eyes* – were wide in shock.

She thudded down with her fists.

But the darn T-rex egg didn't smash. Instead, it rolled to the side.

"We have to stop this! This is wrong!" she screamed.

The room erupted. People were shouting. Black cloaks were everywhere. She jumped onto the table. If she couldn't smash the egg with her fists, she could stamp on it with her feet.

But as she lifted her foot, two things happened.

Lincoln moved so fast she couldn't stop the downward stamp she'd already started. He snatched the egg from under her foot just as huge arms grabbed her around the middle and pulled her from the table.

"This is wrong! This is wrong! We shouldn't kill the dinosaurs, Piloria is theirs!"

The crowd surged forward. They were furious. Furious at her. Baying for her blood.

Lincoln threw her a glance then turned towards the crowd and lifted the T-rex egg above his head.

"I claim credit for the T-rex and the raptor egg. I, Lincoln Kreft from Ambulus City."

For a few seconds there was silence.

Then the crowd erupted. The Stipulators at the front of the auditorium seemed to breathe a sigh of relief. Lincoln moved forward, keeping their attention and never looking back.

Never looking back as Storm struggled and shouted in Reban Don's arms.

There was a strangled cry to her left. Leif was trying to battle his way through the Stipulators – trying to make himself heard above the cheering.

But the crowd weren't listening – they had what they wanted. They had a hero.

Now, they could wipe out the dinosaurs. Now, they could claim the continent as their own.

She watched as Lincoln was lifted up on the shoulders of some of the people who'd crowded onto the stage.

It was done.

It was over.

FORTY-FIVE

STORMCHASER

She couldn't breathe. She couldn't think straight. All around her the crowd were celebrating, rejoicing. And no matter how much she wriggled and kicked and screamed, Reban Don's arms held her solidly in place. Away from the eggs. Away from the DNA she should have destroyed.

"I'll kill him! And I'll kill you!" Leif tried to push his way through the crowd but it was useless. His broad shoulders couldn't find a way between the packed bodies. He turned to face Storm, his eyes blazing. "What were you thinking? What were you doing? And did you know? Did you know he would do this?" The blood vessels were pulsing on his face as he pushed it up towards hers, furious.

"I needed this," he shouted. "What about my family? What about Kronar's? Or Rune's? We made a promise to each other. A vow. Whoever survived would feed the other's families. How can I do that now?"

Her gut twisted. Hadn't Kronar told her he had seven brothers and sisters? And what about Rune's and Leif's families? They were starving. What would they do now?

She looked down at her feet. She couldn't even look at Leif. She felt betrayed by Lincoln too but she couldn't keep kidding herself. The decision she'd made would probably have had the same devastating effect, stripped Leif of the rewards. She would have left the Nordens' families with nothing. She was no better than Lincoln.

But the crowd weren't finished with her.

They hadn't forgotten what she'd tried to do.

Chants gradually filled the auditorium. In a few hours they would parade Lincoln through the streets and the celebrations would start again.

But right now, their attention was on her.

"Punish her! Kill her! Send her to the mines!"

The chants grew louder, the momentum in the room was building.

One of the Stipulators started to bang his staff on the floor in time with the chants. All eyes were on her.

Reban Don's arms loosened around her.

Black cloaks surrounded her.

And then, suddenly, Lincoln was in front of her again. He didn't look triumphant. He didn't look as if he was celebrating his success.

Their gazes connected. All the noise faded into the background. She could see two women standing to the side – waiting for Lincoln. The youngest was paler than anyone she'd ever seen and it looked as if the other was propping her up.

Trust. That's what she'd felt for Lincoln. That, and something else she couldn't quite decipher.

This was a betrayal.

A betrayal that hurt more than she could have ever imagined. But the pain cut deeper as she realized that this was exactly how Lincoln and Leif would have felt about her had things gone the other way. She would have been the one taking everything away from them and their families. That felt worse than Dell not being with her. Worse than the suggestions about Reban Don. Worse than being alone. Worse than waking up every day in a place where no one noticed her – no one cared.

But she had never set out to hurt Lincoln or Leif. Her actions had been about something bigger than them all. About something that just felt fundamentally wrong. While Lincoln had knowingly lied and stabbed his friends in the back as if he'd planned it all along. It felt *personal*. She'd been so open with Lincoln, but after everything they'd been through, everything they'd sacrificed, Lincoln had been keeping secrets.

She fixed her gaze on the two women. One of them was clearly sick. But Lincoln hadn't shared that. In all the conversations they'd had together – when she'd told him about her scars, when she'd told him about the Shelter – Lincoln had never mentioned his family. He'd never mentioned his reason for being there. He hadn't trusted her and he hadn't trusted Leif.

This was why. This was what he'd always intended to do. And it cut to the bone.

She'd made a mistake. She'd made the mistake of believing that Lincoln might actually care about her. She'd trusted him. She'd been a fool.

Storm stepped forward. Nothing could make her pull her gaze away from his. "Why, Lincoln? Why?"

She tried to ignore the pain in his eyes. He reached forward and grabbed either side of her face, bending to whisper in her ear. "I'm sorry, Storm. I truly am. But my sister...I had to."

Her hand reached up and coiled around one of his. His sister. His sister was sick.

She peeled his hand away from her face. The rage that was building inside her was threatening to explode. After everything she'd shared with him. After everything they'd seen together, *this* was how he treated her.

He stepped back, as if he was trying to steady himself. But the emotion and regret she'd seen a few seconds ago had vanished from his face. "I'm sorry, Storm. Family comes first. They have to." She could almost see the shutters coming down over his eyes.

She could see how sick his sister clearly was. The girl looked as if she could blow away in a puff of wind. Her mother had her arm tightly around her.

Family. Lincoln had family.

And she?

Anger surged through her. The crowd kept chanting. "Send her to the mines!" It was the equivalent of a death sentence. Everyone knew that. But that's what they wanted for her, that's what they thought she deserved.

The Stipulators seemed to be closing in on her, surrounding her on all sides. She didn't hesitate. She turned and walked a few steps back to Reban Don.

There was no fear. None at all.

She moved closer, thrusting her face up towards his. She heard the Stipulators next to her suck in deep breaths at her brazenness.

She could see the tiny lines around his eyes. The furrows in his forehead. She could see the full violet of his eyes. It was like looking into a mirror.

Her hands clenched into fists.

Her voice was low. "Dalia Knux."

He didn't move. He didn't flinch. Everyone was watching them.

"What?"

He'd heard her. He'd heard exactly what she said, and she knew because his face had paled. "You asked me my mother's name. Dalia Knux. That was her name."

The noise from the crowd was getting louder. She glanced over her shoulder. Lincoln met her gaze. This time he looked panicked.

She moved even closer to Reban Don. Every muscle tensed.

"My mother's eyes were brown. I, apparently, got my eyes from my father."

It was a risk. Of course it was a risk. She had no proof of anything. Only supposition.

This time he blinked. His hand gripped her arm.

She was still looking directly at him. "Get me out of this."

His words were low, so low, at first she barely heard them. "Challenge him."

"What?"

"Challenge him. Claim the eggs as yours."

She spun round and faced the crowd. She scanned the faces, looking for Leif and gave him a little signal.

She pointed at Lincoln and shouted above the crowd. "I challenge him. The eggs aren't his. They're mine. I won them."

Leif elbowed his way through the crowd. He stood side by side with her.

"I challenge him too. Storm won one egg, and I won the other."

For a few seconds the room was silent. Confused faces turned and looked at each other – like Storm, most people didn't even know that a challenge could be submitted.

Then it erupted again.

Lincoln jumped back onto the stage. His eyes were fixed firmly on his sister. "What are you doing?" he hissed.

She wouldn't be bullied. She wouldn't be manipulated. If the girl had been her sister, would she have done the same? She pushed the thought away.

She tilted her chin up towards him. "I'm doing what's right." Her voice was icy cold. "This isn't over."

Reban pushed his way between them. "Silence!" he shouted. "The challenge is made. There will be one last Trial between the remaining three Finalists. There can be only one winner. The Trial will take place tomorrow."

She reached down and squeezed Leif's hand. "I'm sorry," she whispered.

Then she turned and walked away.

FORTY-SIX

LINCOLN

He'd betrayed them. He'd been devious and betrayed his friends. The people he'd trusted with his life for that week on Piloria.

The damp walls of the cave felt as if they were pressing in around him. He'd spent the night cradling Arta in his arms. Her skin was blistering, layer upon layer, and exposed to the elements. In places it looked infected.

The four weeks away had been too long.

Whatever her disease was, it had progressed.

And it hadn't been enough. What he'd put himself through for her hadn't been enough. Now he had to pit himself against his friends – again. He had to be declared the ultimate victor. Nothing else would do.

At least this time it would be upfront. At least this time they would know why he was doing it.

This time it would be final.

FORTY-SEVEN

STORMCHASER

Storm stared at the pale walls. She hadn't been allowed back to the Shelter. In a way, that was a relief. Instead, she'd been ushered to a room in the parliament quarters with a comfortable bed, a change of clothes and a private bathroom.

Only thing was – she couldn't sleep.

After the camp bed on the ship, and the bedroll on the ground on Piloria, the soft comfortable mattress made her back ache.

And every time she closed her eyes she was haunted by thoughts of the mines.

She was relieved when the dawn light began breaking through her shutters. At least now she could wash and get changed. The clothes they'd left for her made her laugh. Black fitted trousers and a violet tunic. It made her eyes stand out. Who on earth had chosen that? She felt her skin crawl

– did someone else have suspicions about her connection to Reban Don?

A Stipulator had brought her dinner and breakfast and been posted outside her door all night. There had been no sign of Reban Don. She didn't want to see him anyway. What did you say to someone who could be your father, but wouldn't think twice about feeding you to the dinosaurs? If she hadn't whispered her mother's name in his ear, right now she'd be on her way to the mines.

The door opened. "Time to go."

She climbed in the back of the transporter. There were five Stipulators with her. Could she outrun them all? It didn't matter. She wasn't going to try.

This was a matter of pride.

Reban Don had ignored her – his own flesh and blood – for her entire life. Lincoln had betrayed her. She didn't need either one of them. She was her mother's daughter. Strong. Independent. She could survive on her own. She didn't care what the Trial was. But she wasn't going to let anyone beat her.

She knew that, even if she won, they would never let her destroy the eggs. They'd probably already extracted their precious DNA. But if she could just survive – stay alive, stay out of the mines – maybe there'd be a chance she could find another way to stop them destroying the dinosaurs.

A Trial had never been carried out in public before. This could actually work in her favour. The crowd had been enraged when they'd seen her trying to smash the eggs, but people were fickle, she'd watched the Stipulators manipulate them on multiple occasions. If she could get the crowd onside by performing well, by becoming the victor, surely Reban Don would have to pardon her. So to have a chance at saving her own life, and the dinosaurs', she needed to win.

She stared out of the window. The route seemed familiar. They were heading to the cliffs. The cliffs that she'd seen Lincoln scale as if he did it every day.

Her stomach turned over. She didn't want him to have any kind of advantage. Defeat wasn't an option. She wanted to beat Lincoln above everything else. The person who she'd thought was a friend.

She cracked the knuckles in her injured hand. It still ached but she wouldn't let it hold her back.

The transporter finally came to a halt and she climbed out. Leif arrived at the same time. He gave her a little nod.

There were crowds – everywhere. On the beach, on top of the cliffs and near the hastily constructed stage.

Lincoln was already up there waiting. Reban Don stood next to him.

They walked up the stairs. "You know I need to win this," said Leif quietly. "I owe it to Kronar and Rune."

"And I can't let Lincoln win," she said simply and looked straight ahead. Her head was spinning. It was clear she could never trust Lincoln again. But Leif? He had responsibilities. He'd told her straight. He was the only Norden left – he owed Kronar and Rune's families.

Maybe if they'd had time to talk, time to plan, they could

have worked something out. But the opportunity was lost. She pushed the guilt away. There was no room for it. She had to focus on the Trial ahead. The only person she could trust was herself. And she needed to win this for her own survival.

There was a flicker in front of the stage. A voice. Someone jumping from the back of the crowd. She squinted, trying to see.

Dell! It was Dell. Her breath caught in her throat. And she lifted her hand to wave frantically. Finally someone out there who was on her side.

She could pick out his voice amongst the rumble of the crowd. "You can do this, Storm. You can do it. You know you can. This is yours."

He sounded so sure. So confident in her it gave her a surge of pride.

Reban Don walked to the front of the stage. "The Trial is in three parts," he announced. "The first part is in the sea."

Storm felt a chill go through her body. The loch was fine. She was familiar with the loch. She knew the creatures in there. But the sea? There could be anything out there. Including a megalodon. The sea was the last place she wanted to go.

"There are boxes buried in the sand. Each Finalist must dig up a box, bring it back to shore and open it. The contents are important."

The crowd started whispering to each other. Staring out at the dark, rolling waves.

"The next part is the cliff climb. Which you'll do carrying

the contents of the box. When you reach the top, the third part of the task will be obvious. The person who arrives back at the stage first will be declared the winner."

She gulped. For swimming and diving she probably had the advantage. For cliff climbing, Lincoln would have the advantage. For the third part? Who knew? It could be anybody's game.

Reban Don walked in front of the three of them, his eyes glancing from one to the other. "Ready?"

"No."

Leif and Lincoln turned in surprise. Storm stepped forward. "Take out your gloves and socks, Lincoln. This has to be fair."

He flinched, then pulled them out of his pocket, tossing them onto the stage. She couldn't even look at him.

She gave a nod of acknowledgement and turned back to Reban Don. "Now I'm ready."

His eyes drifted over her violet tunic and she noticed a little tic in his jaw as he pressed his lips together.

He turned back towards the crowd.

Lincoln dipped his head. "I'm sorry," he said in a low voice, "but my sister is worse. If I don't get her this health care, she'll die. I have to win." His fingers brushed against hers. She wanted to grab them. She wanted to intertwine hers with his.

Because she believed him. He was sorry. His body language told her so. But that didn't change her mind.

Lincoln pulled his hand back and looked forward.

"We all have to win, Lincoln," said Leif. He had his eyes fixed on the horizon too. He was focusing. Getting ready to give his everything to the Trial ahead.

There could be no trust here. No friendship. No loyalty.

Reban held up his hand. "Ready; three, two, one, go!"

Storm jumped clear of the stage and sprinted towards the beach. Now there was nothing else on her mind. Nothing but winning.

Her feet thudded on the ground. Lincoln was first to pass her, closely followed by Leif. Their pace was quicker and it made her mad. Both of them hit the water before her, Leif discarding his shoes but Lincoln not. Her dive was cleaner, smoother. She'd had more practice and she started swimming straight away. Leif was still wading even though he was up to his chest in water.

The cold hit her straight away. Now she was underwater she kicked off her shoes. Her eyes were open. The seawater stung a little. The loch water never did that. And this water was murky. Sediment and sand made it difficult to see where she was going. How far out should she swim?

She wasn't sure. But someone must have put the boxes out here and she could only guess that they wouldn't have wanted to go too far out. No one wanted to be dinner for the megalodon.

There was a movement to her left. Leif. He was right alongside her. She dived further down to the seabed. Trouble was, as soon as she touched it, sediment lifted and blurred her vision. She stopped swimming for a second and looked around.

There were no markers. No clues in sight as to where the boxes were buried.

She let out a tiny bit of air. This could be like looking for a needle in a haystack – a near impossible task.

She swam out further and stopped again, waiting until the sand settled around her. The further she swam, the deeper she got, with less light reaching the seabed. How on earth was she supposed to find anything?

She pushed herself to the surface to get some air and try again. Leif burst from the water at the same time. "Where are the markers?" he spluttered.

"I don't think there are any," she said, pushing her hair back from her face.

"Then how on earth are we supposed to find them?" he asked.

She shook her head and filled her lungs again. This time she planned to stay down for longer. This time it would be like diving at the loch.

As she pushed towards the bottom there was a movement to her right. But it wasn't human-shaped.

Her heart missed a beat.

It only took that beat to recognize the colour and shape. A plesiosaur.

It settled on the seabed just a little ahead of her. Her instincts kicked in and she swam towards it. Could it be Milo?

There was another movement in the water. Lincoln. Treading water halfway down. He was staring at Milo.

She swam closer. As she neared, she noticed some bumps on the seabed. Her heart rate surged. Surely not?

Something floated past in her in the undercurrents – catching in her hair. An ancient fishing net. She shook it off and pushed it behind her.

Last time she'd been this close to Milo had been just before the Trials were announced. She'd missed him. She didn't hesitate. She swam straight up with her arms outstretched, capturing Milo's head with her hands and pressing her forehead against it. This was exactly what she'd seen the plesiosaurs do in the lake in Piloria.

Milo stayed there for a few seconds, then his whole body moved. Silt and sand dislodged, clouding the water around her. He swam off, his tail churning the sea around them.

His movement had helped. It had revealed the top of the boxes buried in the seabed.

She swam to the nearest. But Lincoln surprised her. He got there first, cutting through the cloudy water and reaching another box easily. He pulled it from the sand with one hand and immediately kicked towards the surface.

She couldn't let him beat her. She couldn't. But something was wrong. Just a little to her left the water was churning. Fear swept over her. Was there something else in the water? Another creature?

She tried to adjust her eyes. It only took a few seconds to realize. It was Leif. Trapped in the fishing net. His face was set in a panic, his arms and legs thrashing furiously.

She looked up. Her only view was Lincoln's disappearing

feet. She couldn't leave Leif. She just couldn't. The more he struggled, the more the fishing net seemed to wrap around him. Leif couldn't hold his breath as long as she could. Any second now he would panic and suck in water. After that?

She pulled her knife from her waistband and kicked her legs furiously. She grabbed part of the billowing net and started cutting, slashing at it with all her might. After a few seconds Leif stilled. She grabbed for his hand and gave it a squeeze. Had he even registered?

She didn't stop. She kept slashing away. Freeing the net from around his arms, shoulders and head. Her actions seemed to rouse Leif and he pushed at the nets around his legs and feet, finally kicking them free.

Storm looked up. There was no sign of Lincoln. That couldn't be good.

Her lungs were starting to protest. She swam back down to the seabed and made a grab for one of the boxes. It surprised her. There was no weight to it at all. She pushed up to the surface.

As she burst out of the water she sucked in a breath, inhaling some of the water that was running down her face. It made her choke and splutter. The shoreline was directly ahead and Lincoln was standing in the surf, opening his box.

The muscles in her legs ached as she kicked forward. She had to focus. She had to find the energy and strength for the next part of the Trial.

The box floated easily in the water as she pushed it to shore. A noise behind her let her know that Leif was following.

She'd done what she could to help him but it had cost her precious time. Time she couldn't get back.

As soon as she felt the seabed under her feet, she tried to stride out of the water quickly, throwing the box onto the beach in front of her.

She dropped to her knees. The catch on the box seemed stuck and her fingers were so cold she could barely make them function. The breeze swept around her, chilling her even more.

Leif thudded down next to her. "Thank you," he muttered as he tried to prise his box open.

It opened easily, he grabbed the contents and stood up as Storm still struggled with hers. Before she had time to think, Leif jabbed the box with a sharp kick, tipping it over and unjamming the lid.

The contents fell out onto the shoreline.

And she froze.

Knives. Throwing knives.

She looked around. Hundreds of faces were staring at her. The crowd were held back from the beach but they could see her clearly. But she couldn't find the face she was looking for. Reban Don was nowhere in sight.

Leif was already running towards the base of the cliff, and Lincoln had started to climb. But she was frozen to the spot.

No one knew. No one knew that her mother was a master of the ancient sport. The skill of knife-throwing had long since vanished. When the last few forests had still existed Storm's mother used to practise her talent there. It was something that had been passed down through her family – Storm's grandfather had taught her mother, and his father had taught him.

But no one had taught Stormchaser. There hadn't been time. She'd watched her mother practise sometimes along the trees. And she'd held a knife before – of course she had. There had always been a set in their home.

But once her mother had died, the throwing knives had vanished.

There was only one person who could have chosen this task.

Reban Don.

Perhaps he thought he was doing her a favour – giving her an advantage. If he knew her mother, he would have known her special skill. Maybe he thought she'd passed it on to her daughter.

The shouts of the crowd broke her concentration. "Come on!" they goaded. They weren't really supporting her – they just wanted to see a decent race.

She tucked the sheathed knives in her waistband and started running towards the cliff. She was already behind. She'd lost her focus. Would there be a traditional target at the top they had to hit?

She snapped on the safety harness at the bottom of the cliff. She could see Lincoln's blue tunic – more than a third of the way up. Leif was climbing fast.

She started to climb. The ache in her muscles was intense. But she ignored it. What was harder to ignore was the wind, cutting through her wet tunic and freezing her to the bone.

She was trying to move quickly. But her left hand objected. She hadn't climbed a cliff since she'd broken it on the first Trial. She gritted her teeth. Lincoln. It was all his fault. His fault she was here. His fault she was doing this again.

She focused on the cliff. On the handholds. On the outcrops of rock. On the white crumbling cliff that was turning to powder around her as she tried to catch the two people climbing above her. They were all more or less following the same path up the cliff. The most straightforward. The easiest climb to the top.

She ignored every ache. She ignored every twinge of pain. All her anger, all her rage was focused on the here and now. On reaching the top of this cliff.

She hated that she was here. She hated that she was doing this.

As the palms of her hand scraped on the crumbling rock she winced.

One set of shouts from the crowd was getting quieter, while another set grew louder. They must have allowed some people to watch from the top of the cliff.

Her stomach churned a little, wondering what was waiting for her.

There was a cheer. Lincoln must have reached the top. It spurred her on, making her drive harder and faster up the cliff.

Within moments the cliff edge was there, and she hauled herself up and over onto the thin grass above.

The crowd was huge. A Stipulator stood nearby with his arm raised, pointing in one direction.

As soon as she'd pushed herself upright she started running.

Lincoln and Leif were directly ahead but she couldn't see exactly what they were doing.

As she ran, she grabbed for the knives tucked into her waistband. The crowd was shouting.

Leif turned back towards her. The expression on his face was pure panic. Her eyes fixed ahead, looking for the target. And her running slowed.

There were no traditional targets. Just the other seven Finalists, standing in a row, with a variety of items balanced on their heads.

Two were crying. Three were shaking. The other two had their eyes closed.

No.

They were expected to aim at the top of the Finalists' heads? With a weapon she'd only handled as a child?

Lincoln raised one hand, lifting the knife to his eyeline. But his arms were shaking so badly he couldn't even try to take aim.

"I can't do this." The voice came from the other side of her. Leif. "I can't kill someone to get more food for our families."

The crowd was still shouting. Jeering now. They were getting impatient.

Storm glanced to where some of the Stipulators stood.

One of them glared at her. "Complete the Trial," he snarled. "Knock one of the targets from your fellow Finalist's head. First to get back to the starting point will be declared the winner." His eyes narrowed as he continued to hold her gaze. "For the others, there might be a different end."

The mines. He was talking about the mines. If she didn't do this that's where they'd send her.

The wind was whipping her hair around her face. Her stomach was in knots. She looked at the face of the woman directly opposite her. She was trying to stand still and failing miserably; her feet shuffling, tears streaming down her face. It was the blonde Finalist who'd broken her arm and had a wound on her face courtesy of the velociraptors. She'd been through enough. They'd all been through enough. They'd survived an attack by a megalodon and seven days on the dinosaur continent. Why put them through any more?

She took a deep breath as she pulled the knife from its sheath with her shaking hands. It was smaller than the traditional one that her mother had used, but there was an aching familiarity about it. Now she could see it up close and feel the weight in her hand something washed over her. The glinting edge of the blade, the weight of the soft grey handle. It could have been one of her mother's knives.

Something twisted inside. Did Reban Don think he'd given her an advantage picking throwing knives? Why would he do that? He'd sent her to Piloria, probably hoping she would die. But maybe she'd been wrong about that. After all, he hadn't known her identity for certain then. She hadn't told him who her mother was. And since she didn't have a birth record, he couldn't find out for himself.

If she didn't win he'd have to send her to the mines – anything else could put his own position at risk. But if she was being given a death sentence, she'd have nothing to lose in revealing his secret to the world – a secret that could destroy him. So maybe he was simply trying to keep her quiet, trying to keep her onside. If he helped her, and she won, he might think his secret was safe.

So much was tumbling through her mind she could hardly think straight. But the crowd were restless. They wanted to see a winner.

She looked up at the blonde Finalist again. The woman looked as if she could collapse at any minute. She had cornup balanced on her head. How ironic. The food that had been discovered on the dinosaur continent could now cause her death.

Leif and Lincoln kept raising their knives, trying to find an aim, and then dropping their arms again without taking a shot. Neither of them would look a fellow Finalist in the eye and risk killing them. No matter what was at stake. It was a step too far. Even for a desperate guy.

The top of a cliff was the worst place for this task to be set. The wind was fierce, whipping around and changing direction. That, along with a trembling target and shaking hands, made this task near impossible.

Leif gave a little sob next to her. This was too much. Too much for them all.

The blonde Finalist met Storm's gaze again and blinked. "Hurry," she mouthed. She wanted this over with too. She wanted to know if she would live or die.

A wave of quiet seemed to come over Storm. She wasn't on the cliff any more. She was in the forest with her mother. Her mother was wearing a long black dress with a tie at the middle. She was laughing. Her brown shiny hair was swinging from side to side as she walked, the knives held easily in one hand. The sun was shining brightly in the sky and she could hear the birds in the trees above.

They reached a clearing. There was a large traditional canvas target pinned to a tree. "Here we are," her mother's voice lilted towards her.

It was the ease. The surety. Her mother spun around, lifted her hands and let the knives take flight – one after the other. They whipped through the air landing squarely in the middle of the red target before her mother's dress and hair had stopped swinging.

She could do this. She was her mother's daughter. She was meant to do this.

She lifted the knife with a steady hand, swiftly took aim at the wobbling cornup and let the knife fly.

Now, she held her breath. Now, she wanted to squeeze her eyes shut.

The target hit slightly off-centre, the cornup flying from the woman's head and landing on the ground below.

The crowd erupted.

Storm looked around her. Leif and Lincoln were open-mouthed. "Aim slightly to the right," she murmured as she dropped the rest of the knives and started running.

She'd done it. *She'd done it.*

Now the crowd screamed at her as she ran past. She still had to make it down the crumbling cliff path, then back along the beach to the stage.

It should be simple. But her competitive edge and drive pushed her on. She had to keep moving. It didn't matter that every bone in her body ached. Her feet thudded on the ground. Her hands and arms were outstretched to keep her balance as she tried to stop herself from tumbling down the cliff path.

There was a loud cheer behind her. Had someone else hit their target? She grabbed onto the rope that was supposed to stop anyone falling from the precarious path. It slid through her hand as she kept running, chaffing at the already worn skin on her palm.

Beneath her was the beach and the stretch of ground she had to run along. Crowds lined the way. They were all watching. All eyes were on her. Some had their hands in the air cheering. Others were pointing. Gravity and the momentum of her feet on the steep slope kept her focus. She slid, the ground coming away beneath her feet. She stuck out her hands to break her fall as she heard the thudding behind her. The thudding of another pair of feet.

She rolled down the slope, tucking in her head and letting her shoulders take the impact. It knocked the wind from her, but the downward slope of the ground was almost an advantage. She virtually landed on her feet again as she swayed and tried to steady herself.

"Move!" came the yell from behind. Dust flew up around her as someone tried to stop himself crashing into her. The voice was instantly recognizable. Lincoln. He was right on her heels.

She didn't even give herself a second. She just started running again, brushing the grit and dirt from her skinned elbows. She couldn't even think about the pain. There was no time.

The faces of the crowd blurred as she ran. She didn't want to look. Didn't want to be distracted. Reban Don stood on the stage ahead, his arms folded across his chest, his black cloak billowing in the wind.

She heard a voice again, screaming above everyone else in the crowd. "Go, Storm. Go!"

Dell. He was still there. Still in her corner. Would he still be there when he saw what she might do next?

As the ground flattened beneath her feet she could sense Lincoln. He was right at her shoulder.

She tried to suck air into her lungs to give herself more power. More energy to fire her tired muscles. All she could hear was the thudding ground next to her.

She didn't let herself look sideways. She didn't need to. On a flat run, Lincoln would always beat her. He had longer limbs and more power. She just had to keep the pace, keep the momentum of her stride going as she ate up the ground underneath her.

"Go, Storm!" chanted the crowd. It was compelling, almost addictive. It drove her on, gave her that one final burst of strength and speed that she desperately needed to reach her goal.

The finishing line was ahead. Closer and closer.

But not quite close enough. She could sense him. Sense him right there beside her.

She gave one final push, one final leap as she reached her arms out ahead and put all her power, every tiny scrap of energy left into that final jump, as her feet left the ground and she surged through the air.

This time when she hit the ground all she heard was noise.

This time when she hit the ground she didn't jump back up. She lay on the ground and looked up at the sky.

The sky that looked exactly the same on Earthasia as it did on Piloria.

Two continents. One planet. How had it come to this?

Lincoln was on the ground next to her. His head was in his hands. He was sobbing. He knew he'd lost and he knew what it meant. She'd never seen him cry. He'd barely shown any emotion the whole time she'd known him.

Something in her heart wrenched. Finally, he was showing vulnerability. The side of himself he'd kept locked up tight. It made him seem more human.

And it made her *feel* more human. If she had a sister, what would she do to save her?

A figure in black appeared above her. Reban Don. "Get up," he said.

She raised her eyebrows at him and held out her hand. The challenge was there.

Everyone in the crowd was watching. He could hardly refuse. And she could tell that he knew it was deliberate. Good.

He reached down and grabbed her, pulling her with more strength that she would have expected. She practically flew off the ground.

His face was unreadable. Was he relieved or mad?

She didn't know and she wouldn't let herself care.

He spun round, his cloak swirling out behind him as he headed back up the steps of the stage. She touched Lincoln's shoulder and followed.

Reban Don stood in front of the crowd. "We have a winner." He grabbed her hand and lifted it. "Stormchaser Knux."

The crowd erupted. It was as if her earlier actions had been forgotten. All they knew now was that they'd watched the final Trial and found a victor.

She looked across the sea of faces, searching for any she might recognize. Searching frantically. This time it wasn't Dell.

As the crowd quietened she found who she was looking for.

She threw a glance at Reban Don and addressed the crowd. "I, Stormchaser Knux, claim the rights to the rewards. I claim the unlimited food rations, the promoted housing, the health care, the extra power. I claim it for me..." She glanced at Reban Don, keeping her voice rock steady as she walked down from the stage towards her target. It was easy.

The frail little girl, who could blow away in a gust of wind, didn't expect it. Storm grabbed her hand and raised it high. "For me, and for my family," she finished determinedly.

The crowd automatically cheered.

Lincoln's head shot up. His eyes widened. Storm put her arm around Arta's back and steered her towards the stage. "Play along," she whispered.

She walked back up on the stage holding her head high.

Reban stepped in front of her, blocking her view of the crowd. "You don't have family," he hissed.

"Prove it," she dared.

But she didn't wait for him to answer. "I also have family in Norden," she shouted, pointing at Kronar's and Rune's siblings, who were crowded near the front. "Brothers and sisters who will join me."

Leif had appeared next to Lincoln and Storm, his eyes wide as the crowd swarmed around her and Arta, lifting them above their heads.

Lincoln looked stunned. His mother rushed over and flung her arms around his neck. His gaze was fixed firmly on Storm's. "Thank you," he mouthed.

She nodded. The crowd were jubilant, the energy electric and as they spun her and Arta around she caught sight of Reban Don, still on the stage.

He looked at her directly with his furious violet eyes. "This isn't over."

She smiled. "I know."

And as the crowd carried her away she saw a head and slim neck appear above the waves.

ACKNOWLEDGEMENTS

There's so much fun in writing about dinosaurs. The whole world seems fascinated by them – everyone seems to love them, even though some were pretty terrifying!

This is a work of fiction, and as such, with some dinosaurs I've been quite creative about what we know about them. I know that we don't "think" pterosaurs would attack people. I know that velociraptors were actually the size of chickens. But this is fiction, and this is my world. So, humans exist at the same time as dinosaurs, and as a result, things might be a little different from what you find in the dinosaur encyclopaedias.

Huge thanks to my agent Sarah Manning from The Bent Agency, who believed in this story and helped me shape it into something submissable. I will always be proud to be her first sale and hope we have many more together!

Also huge thanks to Sarah Stewart at Usborne Publishing who loved this story from the start. I'll never forget the day she phoned me and spoke to me about Storm and Lincoln as if they were real people, and Piloria and Earthasia as if the continents really existed. To the rest of the lovely team at Usborne, Stephanie King, Stevie Hopwood and Amy Dobson, thank you for helping get *The Extinction Trials* out there in the world.

I also have to mention my cheerleading team, Heidi Rice, Fiona Loakes, Iona Garrett, Daisy Cummins and Sally Bowden. Although we generally write adult fiction they've been hugely supportive of my desire to write YA fiction.

And finally, to my friend Rachael Blair's son, all the way over in Australia. Thank you, Hamish, for being my first dinosaur fan!

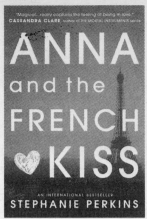

Love this book? Love Usborne YA

Follow us online and sign up to the Usborne YA
newsletter for the latest YA books,
news and competitions:

usborne.com/yanewsletter

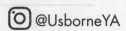 @UsborneYA